The Shakespeare Wallah

Born Geoffrey Bragg in the Cumbrian town of
Kendal, Geoffrey Kendal was to become the
Shakespeare Wallah – the Indian chap who
plays Shakespeare. His career began with
small parts in repertory and he toured the
length and breadth of Britain treading the
boards. In 1944, he and his wife Laura travelled to India as members of an ENSA unit
under the guidance of Jack Hawkins. They
played Shakespeare in every part of the subcontinent, in palaces and village halls. In time,
their troupe was joined by their two daughters, Jennifer and Felicity, and the experiences
of the group were the inspiration for the
Merchant–Ivory film *Shakespeare Wallah*.

Clare Colvin is a journalist and writer who has
written about theatre and the arts for many
major newspapers, including *The Times* and
the *Sunday Times*, *Observer*, *Daily Telegraph*
and *Standard*. She has spent much of her
life travelling and studied drama and literature at the American University of Beirut.
She has lived in India and the Middle East.
She met the Kendals during a visit to India,
when she was on a journalistic assignment,
and was immediately fascinated by their life.
She is at present working on a collection of
short stories.

The Shakespeare Wallah

The autobiography of

GEOFFREY KENDAL

with Clare Colvin

❊ ❊

Introduction by

FELICITY KENDAL

PENGUIN BOOKS

For Laura

Penguin Books Ltd, Harmondsworth, Middlesex, England
Viking Penguin Inc., 40 West 23rd Street, New York, New York 10010, U.S.A.
Penguin Books Australia Ltd, Ringwood, Victoria, Australia
Penguin Books Canada Ltd, 2801 John Street, Markham, Ontario, Canada L3R 1B4
Penguin Books (N.Z.) Ltd, 182–190 Wairau Road, Auckland 10, New Zealand

First published by Sidgwick and Jackson Ltd 1986
Published in Penguin Books 1987

Made and printed in Great Britain by
Richard Clay Ltd, Bungay, Suffolk
Typeset in Sabon

Preface
to the Penguin Edition

I am amazed at my presumption in writing this book. Re-reading it after nearly a year, I wonder at my being so egotistical as to presume that anyone should be interested in the doings and feelings of a poor player who does not aspire to be a great figure theatrically, yet has the cheek to aspire to the greatest hurdles in the theatre and, not only that, keeps on trying to jump them and, what is probably worse and most surprising, is obviously enjoying it.

Only recently we put on a show in a plain panelled room holding about two hundred people. There was no stage, no lighting, no scenery, absolutely nothing theatrical about the place, not a thing that one would have expected an artist to need to put on a show – all we had was our Savonarola chair and two borrowed school desks. We did a programme consisting of part of *A Midsummer Night's Dream*, part of *Macbeth* and part of *Twelfth Night*. I may add that we are quite old (in years at least) and our audience was young – teenagers mainly, and a few schoolmasters and invitees. The power that is generated by being privileged to speak these wonderful words is so strong that it fuses actor and audience into a magical one-ness – and that is why we enjoy it.

Acknowledgments

I would like to give my heartfelt thanks to all those who helped with the writing of this book – to former Shakespeareana actors, John Day, Brian Kellett, Wendy Beavis, Eileen Garner, Richard Gordon, Coral de Rosario, Oliver Cox and Ralph Pixton, who jogged my memory and gave me access to letters and diaries; and apologies to Ronnie Mee and John Holliday and thanks for their letters pointing out some of the best bits that I had missed; and thanks to the numerous actors and actresses who toured with us in England and Ireland and who missed this grand adventure, and particularly to Conor Farrington, who generously allowed me to draw on his manuscript, *A Strolling Player*. My gratitude, too, to Ismail Merchant and James Ivory, producer and director of *Shakespeare Wallah* for their advice and support, and to Nicolaus Mackie, who directed and produced *Shakespearistan – East of Suez*. I would also like to thank Muriel Stannage (who first saw our shows fifty years ago as a schoolgirl in Colwyn Bay) for her help and encouragement with an earlier version of my autobiography. Finally, my warmest thanks to my family for their love and enthusiasm at all times. Without them this book would not have been written.

Geoffrey Kendal

Contents

Introduction
by Felicity Kendal

This book is the story of a remarkable life in the theatre of two continents. Yet it is not, as is more usual when actors turn to the typewriter, a story of the pursuit of fame and fortune – rather, the reverse. My father's passion was more to do with giving than gaining, and what he wanted to give was Shakespeare – Shakespeare presented with a minimum amount of fuss to the maximum number of people – to hundreds of thousands of people, in fact, who would meet the plays often for the first time, and remember them for ever. In this he succeeded, and that is his achievement.

There is, of course, a special emotion in reading about events in which one played a small part (how naturally the phrase doubles between theatre and life!), but I find myself more moved and fascinated by my father's recollections of earlier scenes, long before I was written in, when he helped to keep alive a tradition which took the English theatre back to its beginnings. This was the tradition of the actor-manager. Many actors of my father's generation, including some of the most famous in the land, learned their craft in a theatre which in my generation is barely remembered and will be forgotten in the next, a theatre of 'fit-ups' and 'portables', of weekly and twice-weekly rep; a theatre which cast its spell on young hopefuls not by the lure of names in lights but by the life itself, a theatre in which the actor-manager stood in a direct line from forebears immortalized by Dickens when he created Mr Crummles in *Nicholas Nickleby*, and by Shakespeare himself in creating the Player King in *Hamlet*. In their own way, these

actor-managers were heroic figures, and this book is an affection-
ate and I think valuable picture of a vanished world.

Not that my father thought of himself as a hero when as a young
actor-manager he toured the country with his wife and baby
daughter, my sister Jennifer, and his company of players. The war
and ENSA took him to India – and the subcontinent becomes the
other hero of this book. He fell in love with it, and returned there
after the war – a touring actor still, but this time under his own
command, travelling from fit-up to fit-up with my mother, my
sister and four-month-old me. There aren't enough pages here,
there never could be enough, to describe it all, but the magic and
wonder of those touring years in India are between these covers.

And what an exotic adventure it was. I can see that more clearly
now than I did then. At the time, it was simply our life. I remember
the hard slog and the fun, the constant laughter and jokes that
helped to keep us going when the adventure got a bit uphill, and I
remember my parents' *determination* to keep going; never to give
up or settle down or – heaven forbid – buy a house, but to
continue – to the next town, the next season, the next generation
and the next. And now they have two grandsons who are actors.

I remember it all with a deep nostalgia for a wonderful
childhood, and with gratitude, for it prepared me for a career I
have come to cherish. And this is the most lasting gift of my
parents. Their respect for good work and good words shines
through these pages – and these pages would not exist, I'm sure,
but for the equal courage of my mother who through all these
adventures was wife, colleague, sympathetic critic and provider of
unwavering support; in sum, the perfect 'good companion'.
Together my parents touched me with their love of the theatre; I
was blessed from then on.

When I was nine my father gave me my first copy of *The
Complete Works of Shakespeare*. I think we were in Bangalore. I
was attending the local convent school for the few weeks we were
there, and playing a pageboy in *The Merchant of Venice* as
required. On the flyleaf he copied out two lines from one of
Shakespeare's sonnets: 'So long as men can breathe or eyes can
see/So long lives this and this gives life to thee.' And so it does.

'The theatre,' my father writes, quoting Chekhov, 'is female. If
you embrace her and hold her she will give you the world, but if
you trifle with her she will bite and the bite will never heal.' Well,

he did embrace her and she gave him the world, more than India — in a sense she gave him his life.

He seized this life, the life of the actor-manager, because he recognized that only in this way — by taking responsibility for his own company — could he achieve what he wanted, the freedom he needed, and the standards he demanded. It has been an extraordinary life, lived by an extraordinary man, a much braver man than he would bother to admit, more stubborn too, inflexible, tirelessly energetic, a dedicated artist and a frightfully undedicated businessman giving Shakespare penny-plain in a tuppence-coloured world — and proud of it.

So here it is, the life and the book. It is not easy to be objective about one's parents or one's childhood memories; it is all the less easy to be objective about a book which speaks of both, written by my father, who was also my teacher, with whom I spent the first seventeen years of my life. But what is an Introduction without a good quote? So here's my considered opinion of my father's autobiography, offered with daughterly pride and prejudice: I think it's wonderful!

Prologue

It is strange, my affinity with India. I was thirty before I set eyes on the subcontinent, yet it is the only place where I feel I really belong. Strange, because I went there purely by chance. India has that quality for some people, and whenever I think about it, vivid pictures come to my mind of the simple and beautiful things that are part of everyday life, things that have always been there, like the bullock cart and the dhow. When I see the lantine sails of a fleet of dhows putting out to sea at Bombay, sailing into the wind like a primitive armada, I realize that part of their beauty is that they have never changed. For hundreds of years fleets have set out in such a way – the great dhows that sail like Elizabethan barquentines across to Arabia, and the lovely little catamarans for offshore fishing at Goa and Mangalore.

Other things have changed, though, since those days in the forties and the fifties when our Shakespeareana Company first travelled around India. Now the world is full of people travelling, and the traveller is just another cog in a great machine of unending airport queues, dull hotels, and plastic meals. Were I young today, I would not become a traveller. The journey has lost its thrill and importance. I remember how it used to be. The anticipation, the train, the packing of different clothes for different climes, the embarkation, the leisurely life on an ocean liner, the friends we made there, the gradual change of temperature: these were not only fun but health-giving, and they prepared one for the difference in everything that awaited at the journey's end. There was romance, excitement, and adventure – and those qualities are essential for me.

It was the need for romance and adventure that made us choose this precarious way of life, that gave us, as travelling actors, our affinity with 'rogues and vagabonds'. We must still need this excitement, or why would Laura and I be travelling today through the heat and dust of India, the founders and only remaining members of the Shakespeareana Company, our props and costumes packed away into two suitcases?

We have spent so long travelling there that occasionally, even at the most tense and unlikely moments, there is a sense of *déjà vu*. I remember one incident, three years ago, when Laura and I were touring North India and our journey took us into the Punjab at the time of the storming of the Golden Temple at Amritsar, which brought so much tragedy in its wake. As I looked down the barrel of a rifle pointed at me by a soldier on the state border, for an instant I thought of the days of the Partition, and the fear and violence in the air then.

I suppose it was unwise not to have paid more attention to the latest disturbances. I had read in the newspaper on the morning we left the hill station of Simla that there was a full twenty-four-hour curfew in Chandigarh, and the whole of Punjab State was sealed off; no one could enter or leave, and there was not even any telephone communication. Yet here we were, packed and ready to go to Chandigarh and from there to fly on to our engagements at Delhi and Madras. The representative of the firm that was sponsoring our tour was in Chandigarh, with all our air tickets and most of our money. I decided we would have to get as near as we could and explain to the military at the border that we needed our tickets from the travel agent to carry on our tour.

It was an optimistic plan, but we could not think what else to do. We left early from Simla and drove down the winding hill-roads to the plain. After a week in the hills, the heat was terrific, and the sun-bleached landscape was harsh on the eyes. As we approached the barrier of Punjab State all hell broke loose. Soldiers with fixed bayonets aimed their rifles at us, and we were ordered through loudspeakers in English, Punjabi, and Hindi to halt and retreat, on pain of death. Our idea of negotiating with the captain to send someone into Chandigarh for our tickets dissolved into air. We fled!

There was a way, we found on the map, to skirt the Punjab and get to Delhi. It was long and circuitous. The driver of our taxi refused to go unless we paid a thousand rupees on top of the taxi fair. There was no getting round this, particularly as we were at the taxi rank, and all the other drivers were listening to the hard bargaining. Finally, we left for Delhi, bumping along on the awful roads that seemed to be full of refugees with bicycles and carts and oxen. We arrived in Delhi after an all-night journey and saw the glorious sight of the Taj Mahal Hotel, lit up and welcoming – shining away in the distance like the Winter Palace, I thought, feeling the hint of revolution in the air. It had not been the worst scrape of our lives, but we were perhaps past the age when we liked such hair-raising adventures!

To give up acting is something I have found hard to contemplate. Our family is totally committed to theatre. For years the family and theatre were one; then Jennifer and Felicity moved away to other lives, other spheres of activity. I can understand why our daughters became actresses because, after all, their parents lived and breathed theatre; but why did theatre claim me, with such insistence? Why did I not follow the search for security and a steady income like the friends I grew up with in the north-west of England?

As we flew more than a thousand miles across the subcontinent for our next engagement, travelling, wandering as always, I thought back to how it all began so many years ago.

1
'I'm Only Pretending'

I must have been very small. I remember my father, the smell of his tweed suit, and the cloth cap he wore. I remember the sunlight and the sea through the boards of the pier deck. I do not remember where it was, but it could only have been some popular resort in the northern part of the British Isles, and the year must have been 1914, just before the Great War.

I remember, too, the funny man that I was told would come on soon, and he proved anything but funny to me. He had a gun; and as I had already fallen to worshipping the line of lovely ladies who had disappeared into the wings, a mystery that baffled me beyond all possible explanation, I could think only that the man with the gun had done something awful. So I yelled and wept and had to be removed from my first theatre in disgrace.

The pleasures of seaside resorts in those days were unsophisticated. Holiday-makers would sit in rows on chairs facing the sea. It was probably the day after being to the theatre that I remember marching up and down those rows of sitting figures, under my arm the daily paper carefully torn into small pieces, uttering the cry: 'Programmes, a penny each!' This was my first speaking part. A gentleman offered me a penny for a programme, which brought my second line and the final curtain to my first play, with the tag: 'I'm only pretending!'

I was born in the year 1909 in the town of Kendal in the north of England, the town that gave me my name when I became an actor. It was in September, the month of the Virgin, and I can see in my mind's eye my mother's bedroom with the large standing shaving-mirror that had belonged to William Wordsworth, the patchwork quilts, and my father leaning over the bed-foot. Yellow sunlight streamed through the window. Although this is a clear early memory, I am prepared to concede that its date is uncertain.

My father, Richard Bragg, was a clerk in a woollen mill, wool being the staple trade of the town. Because of this I thought him a man of importance and I am sure he thought so, too. My mother had been a schoolteacher, and so had all her sisters. The only member of their family not to have been a teacher was their brother, who early in life had taken the Queen's Shilling and gone to India. I thought my mother beautiful and with what could be described as a mind above her station. Like her father, she was slim and very erect, and walked with a purpose. She had lovely brown eyes, straight brown hair, and strongly defined eyebrows. I have photographs of her when she was eighteen, with a bicycle, a leg-o'-mutton blouse, a high collar, and a straw boater, looking absolutely modern; then at twenty in a lace dress, with her hair tied back, but now there could be detected a slight churlishness, a little disillusion, as though she knew then — as we all find out sooner or later — that her dreams would never really come true. Her dreams of travel, and many more that I knew nothing of, were doomed to be only dreams; this was why she spent so much time with books, as a movement by proxy for one who found herself tied to her little Earth.

My first real memories come at about the age of two. The date is definite, as the new Parish Hall was being built for the occasion of the coronation of King George V. The entrance gate was supported by two columns that were exactly like the bricks in my new box of bricks, and I could build a replica of them when I went home from my outings. Opposite the new hall was Mr Blair's smithy, our daily stopping place. We would go into the smithy and watch him with his bellows and his hammer and tongs fashion horseshoes. At the age of four, things became a little clearer: my mother's long skirts being held up from behind as she crossed the dusty and muddy roads; my father's suit with the long vent in the back; a coloured wheel with bells I used to take for walks; my grandfather's whiskers, and my grandmother's black silk coat and bonnet.

My father by this time, being a man of substance, was building a new house. That summer we took regular evening walks to inspect the walls as they grew higher and higher. The house was about a mile from Kendal, near the village of Natland. All sorts of exciting people crowded round, aunts and uncles, and, most exciting of all, a cousin of the female variety a year older than myself. She was Joan, my first love, mainly because she was the only young girl I had ever been near. Another grandmother appeared and gave me biscuits. She lived in what seemed to be a dark cavern that she shared with two aunts with enormous ear-rings, both a little frightening as they had very loud and harsh voices. They were not at all like my mother, who spoke softly, but more like my father, who used to shout. This grandmother, I later learnt, was my father's mother. Her husband had died years before at the age of eighty-one, of drink apparently, and his sickness had started when he was quite young, at the age of eighteen. It never occurred to me to question this information. Our house was always one of great prohibitive tendencies; no liquor except on festive occasions, and then only a glass of port. A bottle of whisky was kept for emergencies and as medicine, and that was all.

My grandfather had been a dealer in cattle, and his drinking excesses were excused to a certain extent because all his business took place in public houses. My father used to recount stories of his bad drinking habits; how he would drink all the money he made (which must have been difficult, with beer about a penny a pint), and how as a boy my father would be sent to find him. In order to do so he would have to visit all the public houses in the town, of which there was a vast number. When at last the old man was located, my father had to sit beside him until he would come home. Later he used to rail at his sons and daughters for not producing a grandson for him! He was an amateur wrestler, and must have been a fine figure of a man and vastly handsome. He was called 'Bonny Bragg', and many times had won Bell's Sporting Life Belt, so I was told. He was over forty when he married, telling his future bride – who was only eighteen – that he was thirty. Apparently she believed him.

I never met him. He died before his first grandchild was born, but we have a pencil sketch of him as a young man, drawn by his cousin John Dawson Watson. In side-whiskers and cravat, he looks like a good make-up for a Victorian juvenile lead, and incidentally very like my own grandson, Karan, the second son of my daughter Jennifer. He was my only connection with my future profession as far as I know, inasmuch as when the players came to town they had to have a surety for their good behaviour. He had to be a well known local man, and I am told my grandfather was always approached in the matter. This may well be because he was always to be located in a pub – the usual place of meeting for the players. His daughter, my aunt Fanny, used to repair and make some of the players' costumes. My father's mother was called Granny to differentiate between her and my mother's mother, who was Grandma. Granny was tall and stern, with black ringlets and man's hands. Grandma was small and soft, totally deaf; she had white hair in a bun and always wore a lace cap in the house. Both dressed in black as was then the custom in emulation of the late Queen mourning for her Albert.

My father's side was not a beautiful family, which is surprising when one considers that their parents were such a handsome couple. They were all fairly small, and had such swarthy skins – really dark, almost gypsy-like, without the usual ruddy cheeks of the northern latitudes. They had long noses and narrow skulls. The family was supposed to have come to England in the reign of Charles II as part of the retinue and followers of Catherine of Braganza, and their appearance seems to confirm this story. They also had particularly hard voices, not so much the harshness of the Westmorland dialect, which they all spoke, but more the rattle of the Spanish and Portuguese. They were all blue-eyed – very bright blue, laughing eyes, which made their frequent and prolonged verbal fights and their high-spirited invective the more amusing, and in many ways more theatrical than real.

My father had two brothers, 'Our John Willie' and Ernest. Both died young. There were also four sisters. Fanny was the eldest. She fell from grace because she married a Campbell – 'Trust no Campbell.' She and the mistrusted Campbell, my uncle Bob, had a grocery store, and Aunt Fanny used to help in the shop. I was allowed to 'help' too sometimes, and had a little green apron with pockets in, just like Uncle Bob's. I still remember the smells of the casks of vinegar, and the hams, and all the spices of the Orient, and now in the bazaars of India the tamarind and masala smells remind me of that space behind the counter in the Lake District.

The next sisters, Aunt Maggie and Aunt Mary, had a business too, a dressmaking establishment in a great room over Grannie's house. There I used to play with the button boxes and pin boxes and was fascinated by the magic of the magnets used for picking up the hundreds of pins that were scattered about after a fitting. Black-and-white fashion drawings adorned the walls of the work-room. Later on Auntie Mary, though still helping in the work-room, opened a shop of her own that seemed to specialize in mourning orders. Almost as soon as I began to understand speech, death and its trappings seemed to be a very important part of our lives. The youngest sister, Eunice, the only one to 'leave home', betook herself to India to marry an engine driver on the Indian Railways. She had met Harry, who was Anglo-Indian, in Black-pool and followed him back to his home in the Punjab. I had to add to my prayers each night, 'Please, God, look after Auntie Eunice in the big ship and do not let it be torpedoed.'

My father had the same swarthy skin as his sisters, the same curly hair, the same small frame. His blue eyes laughed most of the time, though he was supposed to be completely lacking in a sense of humour. When I saw a photograph of him aged twenty, I was surprised how dashing he looked, with a great cavalry moustache with waxed points. When the fashion changed and whiskers and moustaches became obsolete, he shaved the moustache off; ever afterwards his top lip seemed to be too large. He spoke with the same hard accent as his sisters and never bothered to try to improve his speech, even when he left the North and went travelling, which showed a great deal of common sense. He didn't drink except in later years when he was known to take half a pint of beer with his drunken sons. This was pretty sporting, I think, for one who did not in the least like a strong drink. Two cups of tea was all he took, one cup at breakfast and one at tea-time. He smoked cigarettes continually, to my mother's disgust, and used to go to all lengths to indulge, sitting on the lavatory for hours, taking the dog for a walk, anything to get away so that he could have another one without feeling guilty. He was vain to a degree and had a vast wardrobe of all sorts of clothes, plus-four suits to wear at weekends, dark suits to wear when he went travelling, and pyjamas by the drawerful. He had over fifty shirts and suits of pyjamas when he died; as he had obviously worn out many during his three-year illness, he must have had quite a stock to draw on.

My father loved military bands, and would sit for hours listening to them; he liked revues with long lines of chorus girls and rude comics. He liked theatre shows too, provided the leading actors had what he called 'go' in them, and he became a great follower of the 'pictures' after they learnt to talk. My mother said he was a good man, and I suppose he was, though he had a few enemies, people he liked to 'show up' with his terrible honesty. He paid his income tax in advance to annoy those who tried to get out of it, and his greatest tribute to anyone seemed to be to end his tales with the words, 'They don't like me.'

By this time the family had split up into a sort of group of clans, each one vying with the other. There always seemed to be a great deal of tension; one section would not speak to members of the other section, and they would pass each other in the street without any acknowledgement. This phenomenon was only on my father's side, however. The other side, my mother's, were much more scattered and were always very fraternal. This tension lasted for years, and I found it hard to remember who was friend and who was foe. I would sometimes greet a relative, only to be cold-shouldered; whilst another time I would be scolded for not being duly polite to some cousin who I imagined to be on the other side of the fence. These feuds were stimulated by the silliest things; my mother getting a ribbon at the wrong shop, or our grocery bill being enlarged by a halfpenny or so, could cause months of strife and backbiting.

Since there was a war on, these family arguments usually ended in mutual accusations of cowardice among the men, none of whom was in the army because they all considered themselves to be doing vital war-work. One of these rows – when my father and my uncle Bob got completely carried away insulting each other, so much nearer the knuckle than usual – culminated with them both agreeing to volunteer for the army the following day. It was summer-time, and my father was suffering from hay fever to such an extent that he was sure of being turned down. In order to make certain, Dad sniffed new hay all night, with the unexpected result that he could not summon up a sneeze when the time came, and they were both classed as A1. Only the Armistice saved them from donning the King's Colours. Perhaps they were a little more tolerant and not quite so brave after that.

We had two 'skeletons in the cupboard', both in my father's family. We were very proud of these, but both were kept strictly to ourselves; in fact I do not think anyone ever heard of them outside our family circle. One was that we were descended from Oliver

Cromwell. There did not seem to be any proof of this fact extant, but there had been some discreet enquiries made way back in the nineteenth century, and there was, so I gathered, a vast sum of money involved somewhere, which could have come to us if only further proof could be found. The other skeleton was that Granny was a gypsy. She certainly looked like one, and she had lived in a caravan in her youth. Her family had come north with the railroads, running a sort of cafeteria for the workmen, a sort of Mother Courage; but whether she was a real gypsy was again either not proven or kept a deadly secret.

Auntie Mary had a habit of talking in a loud voice, and she prided herself on saying what she meant and what she thought, regardless of the company. She had extraordinary eyesight and would espy one of the tribe or one of her friends far off, and begin her discourse from the moment she saw her quarry in the distance, oblivious of passers-by. To me this was most embarrassing, as besides being horribly shy I had a feeling that this sort of behaviour was rather common and not at all ladylike! I had a great desire to be a gentleman, and this sort of thing let me down. Mary had a friend of uncertain age, also a spinster. One day these two were yelling at each other in polite conversation in the middle of the street, when the local doctor, a man of bibulous habits and also outspoken, shouted across the road:

'What are you two old wallflowers talking about now?'

At which insult Auntie Mary drew herself up to her full five-feet-one-inch and retorted, in an even louder tone, 'Wallflowers you call us – you mean unplucked lilies. Such cheek!'

As time went on she built a house for herself. Although persistently quarrelling with each other, our family always wanted to be together – which does seem to point to some sort of gypsy strain in our blood. Auntie Mary built her house next to Auntie Fanny's, and Auntie Fanny's was next to ours. The aunts started to die off, first 'Our Maggie', and then 'Our Fanny'. In each case the family doctor was blamed, and a new one promptly engaged. Then each old house was sold. I remember going with my mother on the viewing day and very much resenting the viewers handling all the things that I had seen in use and that now seemed as dead as their former owners.

Auntie Mary was now the only one left, 'Our Ernest' being dead and 'Our Eunice' being away in Ambala with her engine driver.

And so the house in which they had all grown up was sold. I did not know at the time, but it must have been a lovely place, overlooking the river, a few doors from the painter George Romney's house and probably of the same period. There was a vast garden at the back with little white-washed lavatories at the end farthest from the house. I can still recall the rather pleasant smell of lime and newspaper and earth. They were shaded from view by an orchard through which a little trout-stream meandered down to the river, the whole place surrounded by a high wall that made it look and feel almost monastic. The place is no longer there. The garden was made into a parking area for municipal vehicles and machines, and the house was pulled down brick by brick and replaced with a modern office block. It was called Bark House, I have no idea why. From the lovely porch was visible the swift River Kent, and across the other side, the old 'K' boot-works factory. To the left was Netherfield Bridge, which was very narrow and had little alcoves for the populace to enter when carriages went past. It was supposed to be in one of these that Henry VIII first saw Catherine Parr. She lived in Kendal castle on the hill to the left, and there too one can see the church and the school where my mother taught before she was married.

My mother's family, the Durhams, were so different. While father's mother seemed to live in darkness surrounded by rusty paraphernalia, Grandma — my mother's mother — lived by the sea in the sunshine of Cumberland. We always visited Cumberland in the summer and spent the winters in the gloom of our old grey town. My mother's father, Granda, was tall, stately, and totally deaf like his wife. He had a stern, beaked nose, like the Duke of Wellington's, a trimmed white beard, and long fingernails that he used for graining. It was the fashion to mark the paint on woodwork with marks of the grain of the wood, which could be imitated with a comb and cloth; but the better tradesmen used their nails, and the longer the nails the better. Although Granda had not worked for years, he still wore his nails like a mandarin as a badge of rank. He was, I suppose, a bit potty by the time I knew him. Although taking meals with his family, and always having just the same as everyone else, he would insist upon cooking his own food in his own pots, and would watch it all the time it was cooking. He wore what was a cross between a topper and a bowler, rather smart, with straight sides.

Granda was supposed not to be of such good family as Grandma, who was the daughter of a Scottish laird. Her family had migrated to England, where they had a house in Liverpool. While their house was being painted by the firm that employed Granda, the scandal occurred of the young girl climbing down a painter's ladder (left there on purpose) and eloping with the painter, whom she married. For this sin she was cut off for ever, and the young couple had to live as best they could on Granda's pay. They proceeded to produce a family, just to make things more difficult for themselves. I loved them all: Auntie Isa, who was the headmistress of the infants' school and had a bad heart; Auntie Nell, who was courting a miner who became, in due course, Uncle Tom; and Uncle Jack, who at first I knew only as a faded picture against bamboo furniture, the fellow in the uniform of the Royal Horse Artillery in India. But he did come home, complete with uniform and spurs and lovely Indian sunburn. He had two good-conduct stripes and a whip – a most romantic figure. He used to ride the lead horses in the gun-team; no commission for him, he liked enjoying himself. They called him Lucky Durham, after the family name and because *Lucky Durham* was the title of a popular play of that time. He was always lucky. His only mishap led him to miss an ambush in which his pals and his horse were killed; he had the good fortune of being put out of action the day before by a bottle of beer that exploded and cut his arm.

When I was five it seemed that my mother had grown enormous. I was sent to stay with Auntie Fanny, who had three bulldogs, of which I was secretly terrified. One day she told me that I had two little brothers brought to me in a basket by the doctor. This exciting event made no impression on me whatever – even when these two creatures had their nappies changed by my father. A nursemaid called Annie arrived, and a great pram was obtained to move the unusual phenomenon of twins about the countryside, and more importantly about the town for all the world to see on Saturday mornings. Their names were Roger and Philip.

Now I had to go to school, the same school where my mother had been a teacher before marriage. The children were putting on a concert, but only those who had fathers in the army were allowed to act, and the 'lucky' boy whose father had been killed was allowed to play the drum and wear the only uniform available. I had a big Union Jack, but because my father was not in the army I was not allowed to carry the flag. I even asked father to join the army; I felt hurt beyond all thought, not being able to march up and down carrying that flag or beating a drum to the stirring wartime songs – 'Keep the Home Fires Burning' and 'Pack Up your Troubles in your Old Kitbag'. But I was not one of them, I was an outsider. Many years were to pass before I found that this was a foretaste of not being of those who conform, and of being an actor as well.

At seven I was moved to grammar school amid great sarcasm from the aunts, who put it all down to Mother having ideas above her station, and the prophesy that such schooling would make me too proud to work. I was taken to the tailors; not a real tailor, but a shop that supplied ready-made suits. After trying one on for size, my father selected two, a green Norfolk suit with belt, for 19s. 6d., and a clerical grey for Sundays complete with waistcoat, 18s.; also a school cap, a ready-made bow-tie with the colours red and green, and six Eton collars. For my first day of school, I was up and dressed early and can well remember the reflection in the mirror, hair too short, ears too large, holding up the cap (also too large), knobbly knees over grey stockings over spindly legs, and the high collar and ready-made bow-tie! My uncle Bob came to see the vision and said that I resembled a monkey looking over a white-washed wall, a remark that suffused the family with uncontrollable laughter and was retold at intervals for many years.

Schools are cruel places. The fact that I was so young, and that I had a collar with rounded points instead of pointed, and that it was made of celluloid and not linen (these celluloid collars were a new invention, and my mother thought what a good idea, he will keep his linen ones for Sundays) – these things caused my class-mates and the big boys of Form 2 to hate me and want to annihilate me completely. All this became plain during my first break, with promises of dire punishment after school, as I was no doubt cheeky, a thing these great men could not tolerate in one so young.

I was called to the headmaster's office, a sumptuous room with a lovely fire. He said he had to write me in a great big book, which he showed me. When asked what was my father's profession I said that he was 'the boss of an office', to which the headmaster replied that he must be a clerk. A clerk! My father a clerk! This depressed me more than the threats of my schoolfellows. After school they were all there, the little cads, with some dreadful creature whom for reasons unknown to me I had to fight or be bumped behind the gym. I had never fought with anyone, so I chose the latter. Four boys grabbed a leg and an arm each and proceeded to bump, lift, and bump me in the muddiest and stoniest part of the ground they could find. This went on for what seemed like an eternity, and then I had to swear not to tell anyone; the punishment for that could not even be spoken of, but it would surely happen if I breathed a word to a soul. I could not even tell my mother. My collar was all torn, and my nice new suit filthy. I told her I had fallen into the river trying to rescue a little dog! I am sure she did not believe it.

About this time we started going to church, the Church of the Holy Trinity of the Anglican (very low) persuasion. We used to go every Sunday morning to the Matins at ten-thirty. We must not be late or we would not get our seat, which was the fourth row from the front on the right-hand side, just behind the special pew with the Mayor's Chair. My brothers and I hated this Sunday church-going. We had to wear our 'Eton suits' and wash behind our ears and the back of our necks even more than usual. It was on one of these occasions that we had a real adventure. A hundred yards from our house was a road junction presided over by an ancient toll-house, now of course out of use. On this occasion there was a drover with cows moving townwards in the same direction as ourselves towards this junction. Coming down the other road there was part of a circus *en route* for Kendal, where it was billed to perform the following day. The circus elephants were walking, and the herd of kine and the elephants met at the road junction. The cattle, never having seen anything like these enormous quadrupeds, panicked, turned, and stampeded down our road towards our house.

Although we were bound for church, this was altogether too exciting. My brothers and I charged after the fleeing cows. One of the cattle was particularly affected and took a wild leap into the river. Now this river was a tributary that passed close to our house on its way to work the water-power wheels of the woollen mill further down the road; so it was fairly deep in the middle. There were trees on either side, and the cow got into this mill race and swam away as fast as it could with us in full chase regardless of our Eton suits and black straw bashers. The drover, meanwhile, was rushing about madly trying to gather the remainder of his herd. By this time a crowd had gathered who helped to get the cows into a nearby field. The errant cow was now well nigh exhausted, and we managed to get a rope round its horns; but pull as we might we could not get it to help. There was this cow, up to its neck in water, and about twenty of us tugging on the rope, and the drover swearing he would lose his job as the cow was sure to get pneumonia and die. At this point my father and mother joined us. The farmworker said the only thing was to goad the beast from the back, which was impossible with it up to its neck in water, or to give it some drink, alcohol. My father went and fetched the bottle of whisky that we kept in the house for medicinal purposes. The spout of the bottle was applied to the cow's mouth, and she swallowed the lot with obvious enjoyment. There was a pause and then she sort of yelped; we gave a heave on the rope, and the cow just seemed to float out of the water and waltz drunkenly up the road. We never got to church that day. Father never got his whisky back either.

The Lake District is a cold, damp place. Our house was by the river, and I seemed always to have colds, or sore throats, or mumps, or other distressing and painful things wrong with me, for which I was continually missing school and being confined to the house or to bed. The two worst afflictions were bronchitis and pneumonia. During the first, I had a vision. An angel was standing beside my bed; she wore a nighty and had lovely long black hair. I don't know how I knew it was an angel, but it was, a female angel, and I was sure she was my guardian angel watching over her poor little weak suffering charge. There she stood beside my bed. It was very cold, and I remember asking her to come into bed to keep warm. It was warm between the blankets, and I was so sorry for this lovely angel standing out in the cold. I can't recall if the angel took advantage of my kindness, but the memory is vivid to this day. The second illness, pneumonia, was worse. I was very ill indeed and had a 'crisis'. I was fed on alum, white of egg, and whisky and soda. I was discovered out of my bed, standing at the top of the stairs, with both arms raised and reciting the only lines of Shakespeare I knew: 'Friends, Romans, countrymen'. I was not acting; it was real. As far as I was concerned I was Marcus Antonius, in the Forum at Rome. My mother found me in this glorious posture, and I was hurried back to bed. It was thought I would die, and on recovery I was assured that I could not live more than another twenty years, since no one had ever lived more than twenty years after double pneumonia. I was doomed and enjoyed it. The fact that I knew I was doomed made me feel superior. This world did not matter, and I was dedicated to the next one.

It was about this time that my father left his desk for the road. He became a commercial traveller, and for the greater part of the time we three boys were left at home with Mother, who had grown deaf like her parents. So there was no check on our language, which grew fouler and fouler. Even at table we would swear and curse in the most manly manner, and always with nice kind expressions on our horrid little faces so that we looked nice but sounded awful.

Now, in Form 3b, my one and only love was made manifest. I went to the theatre. To our local theatre came Sir Frank Benson and his touring company. Announcements were posted on the school notice-board that there would be concessions for parties of schoolchildren. I went home with this news. I had to go to all these shows; there would be a different one every night for a whole week. Mother was on my side and she persuaded my father to agree. I was allowed to get tickets with the school party to the first show, *The Merchant of Venice*, and for *Julius Caesar*, on the Saturday afternoon. The latter would be paid for by the school, as we were to 'do' the play. My mother recited what seemed yards of *The Merchant*, not a word of which I had ever heard before. Her cleverness astonished me. She opened my eyes to a wonder that day in the kitchen when she recited from the court scene in *The Merchant*. To her ever-blessed memory I am still doing the very same thing myself and after all these years.

Never will I forget the first night in St George's Hall, an old horseshoe-like theatre with an antiquated roller curtain with advertisements painted on it. Behind that curtain there was a new world born to me that night, a world of romance, of wonderful people who seemed like gods. The Actors: such handsome, defiant men and such lovely ladies. I think I grew up that night. Walking home, I felt tall. From then on and until today the theatre has been real for me, and the world has been somehow make-believe. I determined then and there that I would somehow, someday, be in that real world. I thought of nothing else, had a terrible feeling that I could never do it, yet all the time knew I would. I was shy, especially with females, and I could not memorize even a couple of stanzas of 'I go by haunts of coot and hern'. In fact I seemed to have none of the things necessary for an actor – neither looks, nor voice, nor brain.

My ramblings and ecstasy about *The Merchant* made my mother give me the money for the two comedies, *Twelfth Night* and *As You Like It*. I had cheap seats in the gods – even more wonderful. I was enthralled. The details of those performances have never left me, and I have been able to recognize costumes I saw in those productions years afterwards in various wardrobes. We went to *Julius Caesar* with the school, and I was very superior to my classmates as by now I felt I knew all the actors personally and what they would do.

After the matinée it was all over. The following day the company were to leave Kendal for some glamorous theatre in Preston, Accrington, or somewhere. If only I could be with them always! There was to be *The Taming of the Shrew* that night, the last night. I had no ticket and no money and was told the house was booked out anyway. I sneaked out my football boots and violin bow, sold them for the price of a ticket, and queued up for the early doors of the gallery. But, alas, I could not get a seat and when I got home I was in serious trouble for selling my football boots, for which my father had paid 4s. 6d. I was no good at football, but the point was I had sold them without permission. He did not realize that one must sacrifice everything for the theatre. What do worldly morals have to do with Olympian heights? Cast out of heaven that night, as I could not go to the theatre, I knew the depths of hell.

When we did plays at school, I was never cast in them. I once played the piano in the school concert in the orchestra and was so nervous that I forgot a repeat and finished with a flourish fifteen bars before the other instruments. We also played a scene from *Peter Pan* in the school gymnasium. I was Wendy tied to a mast. At least I was at rehearsal, but I had to be taken out of the part as I could not remember the words, my voice was breaking, and I stuttered. But all this time, and in spite of these setbacks, I knew that I would one day be an actor. I longed to grow up, to stop being a boy, to be manly, handsome, and attractive. I tried to grow sideburns to look continental. I oiled my hair, tried to look as though I was a devil with women, and tried to smoke cigarettes.

My father's cigarettes were bought in bulk, part of Mother's grocery order delivered every Friday. They were Gold Flake in lovely golden packets, and the price was threepence for ten. Dad took one packet in his pocket, and the rest were stored in his collar-box, which reposed on the kitchen mantelpiece between the clock and the tea caddy. Sometimes when I was alone, I would get down the box and scrape up the crumbs of tobacco that were always at the bottom. These, wrapped in brown paper, made me feel wonderful at being able to smoke, although I hated the burning tongue and acrid taste. When I had twopence collected I went to Bewsher's, the general store nearby, and after plucking up enough courage bought a packet of five Wild Woodbines. With these and a box of matches I had stolen from our store at home, I went on the canal banks. Under a bridge I lit one of the cigarettes. What a lovely smell! But the wind was howling through the bridge and I could not get it alight properly; eventually the cigarette was all burned away, the paper blackened, and the tobacco wet with spit, so this was not so good either. Actually I did not like it at all and cannot remember what I did with the rest of the packet.

Our year was enlivened by the holidays. Everything was packed in the trunk, a great black contraption with leather straps. The 'bus' called for us and took us to the station. This bus was one of the joys of my life. It was wonderful to be seen in it because everyone knew that we were off somewhere. It was horse-drawn, a sort of cube with seats running down either side. There was the usual box for the driver in front – he had a brake that he used to put on before descending the hill outside the station – and there was a rack on the top for the luggage. It was painted green and emblazoned with the legend 'King's Arms Hotel'. Then we would entrain for Morecambe or Blackpool, and once we went to Southport. However, the highlight was to go to Millom, to Grandma's house, and go for picnics on the sandhills at Haverigg and have lovely ham sandwiches, crunchy with sand, and sweetened tea from a flask, also full of sand. Once, to save money, we travelled by horse-drawn carriers all the way to Lancaster, sitting in the back amongst all the trunks and parcels. Dad accompanied us on his sit-up-and-beg bicycle.

Then we would have visits from the aunts and Grandma and

Granda, who was terrified of going over the viaduct at Arnside, sure it would give way one day like the Tay Bridge had done. The bus was ordered to meet them at the station. No one thought of going to the station to meet them; we awaited the bus to round the corner and met them at the door. Once Uncle Jack came home for good all the way from India in his gorgeous uniform complete with spurs, and with wonderful stories and pictures of Agra and Fatepur Sikri. After Granda died, Grandma would come alone and stay with us for a long time. She was very religious in a prayer-book sort of way, and was fond of whispering to me that the devil had me in chains and was pulling the chains tighter and tighter, aided by my repeated and constant sins. By the time I approached the altar-rail to be confirmed by the mitred Bishop I was fully prepared to be struck dead.

School years went swiftly by until at last I reached my zenith. I was in Form 5. Still shy, still a lazy, hopeless scholar, by now I had begun to take an interest in literature and words. My literature was romantic novels, Jeffrey Farnol, Rafael Sabatini. I was never very well read. All I really knew were all the stories from Shakespeare's plays. I found it difficult to read any play that I had not seen, but those I had seen I could remember very well. I began to learn comic songs gleaned from my visits to concert parties while on holiday, visits that caused me secretly to fall in love with all the soubrettes from every show. I remember the Naval Cadets on the sands, playing in what I much later found out was a real booth, just as players had used all over the world for centuries. Very fine they were in their natty midshipman uniforms, looking like pre-war Wrens. Then there were the Pals at Southport; they performed a pantomime –

> *I am the comic sailorman,*
> *To help the hero is my plan ...*
> *I am the villain of the piece,*
> *Of villainies I never cease.*

But the best to my mind was Jack Audley's Varieties on the West End Pier at Morecambe. I knew the whole repertoire, opening chorus and all:

> *So now we take our parts,*
> *Each out to win your hearts.*

For our friends old and new,
There's no better rendezvous,
Than the West End Pier with the Varieties.

I spent all my holiday savings on these entertainments, and at the end of the holiday would know almost the whole of their repertoire. These I would rehearse in the privacy of my attic bedroom; they never got beyond rehearsals except for the repartee that I loved bringing out as though it was my own particular brand of humour. My experience of shows was surprisingly small. Besides the Benson Company and Hamilton Deane's Repertory Company I did not see another play till I saw Inez Howard's touring company in *White Cargo* by Ida Simonton – which I did not really understand, although I felt that these people were really what they were pretending. The rest of my theatre-viewing consisted of the amateur opera's over-costumed *Mikado* and *Gondoliers* and some not quite so good light operas such as *Highwayman Love*. Like John Gielgud as a boy, I saw *Chu Chin Chow* as often as I could. The scene in the slave market I thought the greatest piece of stage management ever. This gave me desires to go East. I bought the music and practised hard until I knew nearly all the script, the first thing I ever really knew of any length. I saw pantomime but was unimpressed apart from falling madly in love with the Babes in the Wood – both of them. I saw modern plays but hated the humdrum scenery and dresses.

One day there was an article in the local newspaper written by a lady from Lancaster who was going to start acting classes and put on plays at our local theatre. Our hairdresser was in this class. He was already an amateur actor of note, and both he and his opposite number in the ladies' hairdresser's were involved. To my surprise, as I was wondering how on earth I was going to get into these classes, my mother on her return from getting a new hairdo, asked me if I would like to join – out of the blue. I am always so lucky and yet I worry how things are going to work out, forgetting that they do tend to work out. I found out afterwards that my mother thought a little hard work on the subject of the theatre might cure what they called being 'stage-struck', and also that if I were forced into some female company it might stop me from being such a mess socially. I was enrolled in the public classes, which cost only 5s. a term, and with a trembling heart I went down to Lowther Street and up to the little room, gas-lit and tawdry, where these weekly classes were held.

The term had started two weeks before, and when at last I plucked up courage and knocked on the door I found myself amidst what appeared to me to be the cream of the bohemian society of Kendal: the hairdressers, the reporter, the artist from the paper, the preacher from the chapel, and all sorts of unknown ladies of various ages and varying beauty. The lady from Lancaster, Mrs Lee, was there in a high-backed chair, looking very handsome with a mass of flaming red hair. She was dressed in black satin with green beads and a cloak of black lined with scarlet. I was awed and speechless (my voice had broken not long before and was in its most dismal state of non-control); I made dreadful noises or just whispered feebly. Breathing exercise and poetry reading were in progress. Then we started rehearsing the play, *The Merchant of Venice*, which was to be produced in the autumn. After a little while I was asked to read the part of the Duke of Venice. Now, although I wanted above all things to be an actor, I never thought of myself as anything but the juvenile lead. The leading parts and the juveniles I had read over and over again, but it had never occurred to me to be bothered with the ordinary small parts in the plays, with the result that I was not very familiar with the part of the Duke of Venice. What with that and my uncontrollable voice-box, the result sounded like a cacophonous horror and not at all grand like I wanted it to sound. Mrs Lee was very kind, and no one laughed. She asked me to come half an hour earlier than usual to rehearsal next week and she would help by giving me one lesson, a private one, for free. I was there next week, and that was the start – the real start – of my being an actor, in an upper room in Lowther Street, Kendal, lit by gaslight.

In one short hour I was taught how to stand still, how to stand on my feet, how not to use my hands, and how and when to move. The result of my lesson must have been pretty crude but it gave me so much confidence that I memorized the part by the time the next rehearsal came round. Then came the verdict, the first word of praise in all my career as a student:

'How and what they teach you in your school I do not know. But one thing is certain, they teach you to remember. You have remembered and done everything I have told you. It must be a very good school,' Mrs Lee said.

I got the part, the Duke in *The Merchant of Venice*. It was to be put on in a few months' time, this first production of the Amateur Shakespeareans. I was to play in the same theatre where I had had my first glimpse of what would become my own world.

Rehearsals were my supreme delight. Our cast was perfect; there could be no better actors anywhere in the world. This is important, this loyalty within a company. It is sort of inbred, and without this feeling of mutual encouragement a theatre company does not work. Certainly Portia was rather large: 'My little body is aweary of this great world' was not quite the thing the author would have put into the mouth of our Portia, who was about sixteen stone, though of course she could have thought of a way to say it. Lorenzo was played by a woman. One actor had to double as Antonio, the Prince of Morocco, and Tubal.

In spite of my loyalty, I had a depressed feeling when I saw the costumes. Mine was a sort of monk's red dolman and a black cap with grey crêpe hair sewn in instead of a wig; and we had only one sword, which was given to Bassanio so that he could draw it in the court scene. Shylock had a cap and wig all in one, just like mine, his wig being made of painted rope. Our settings were local stock, dreadful faded painted cloths and cut-outs that all the town had seen in every music-hall show and every turn that had visited our theatre. Our stage-manager and prompter was the local bank manager, and prior to our opening at the theatre he had to go and discuss our requirements with the theatre's professional stage-manager. We had no scenery and were going to use whatever the local stage could provide. I was asked to accompany him on this visit, and for the first time in my life I trod upon a real stage. It was dark and there was some sort of set held up with braces. I was so thrilled at being at the working end of a theatre, and so enchanted with the smell of paint, dirt, and size, rats, canvas, and dust, and all the wonderful things that go to make a theatre so exciting, that I did not look very carefully where I was going. I fell over a brace, and in my anxiety not to fall further caught hold of it to steady myself.

By then we had been joined by the theatre's stage-manager. Of all those who passed through the magic stage door, he was the only one I had seen outside. He was, therefore, a very romantic figure to me. He had been a soldier, had been to India, had a wooden leg and an enormous moustache, and he lived just beside the magic portal, the stage door. He had an enormous family and, to add to all these exciting things, was a Roman Catholic. He also had a lovely smell that seemed to follow him about. It was whispered in my ear that it was beer. No matter, this was the first time I had ever been in his company and the first thing I did was fall over a brace.

'Steady on, you young bugger,' this servant of the gods said to me. 'Steady. You are like all bloody amachoors. You can always tell amachoors from pros – amachoors are always in t' bloody way.'

But I knew this did not apply to me at all. I was not an amateur; the theatre was my life; and if other people, even important ones like the local stage-manager, did not see this obvious fact, what did I care?

At last the great day of the first night dawned on 5 November 1926. On the 6th there was to be a matinée in the afternoon and a show at night; three performances in all. I was in the theatre three hours before we were due to start. Of course I was only a schoolboy and therefore free from four o'clock, whereas the rest of the cast had jobs and could not get away so early. Although the Duke does not appear till the play is three-quarters finished, I was fully dressed and made up by six-thirty. The show was to start at a quarter to eight. I had on everything including a ring that my mother had given me, my hat with the hair stitched inside, and my whiskers, which tickled my mouth horribly. Of the performance I remember little, except the interval before the court scene, when I got in the way of the stage-hands in my eagerness to climb on to my throne. The old-fashioned roller curtain at St George's Hall had advertisements painted on it informing the awaiting audience where to buy pianos, port wine, pork pies, etc. At the bottom it had a huge roller about a foot in diameter; as it came down this roller hit the stage with a great thud. It was pulled up and let down from the flies on a winch, and the signal for the flymen was a ring on the bell from the prompt corner: one for stand-by, two for go. This bell could be heard all over the theatre, so we were always forewarned when the end of a scene was approaching.

Seated on my throne, hearing my music – the Doge's March – being played on our five-piece orchestra, and watching my friend the stage-manager unconcernedly push the bell-button and then toddle out for refreshment, I saw the curtain ropes taughten and jerk, and the roller started to roll, showing me for the first time in my life the great black hole of the auditorium.

I had been petrified with fright and excitement all day, and felt as if I would run from the theatre, even in my make-up, but now it all vanished. The only thing to do was to breathe deeply and deliver my first line with the gesture I had copied from the poster and in a voice that thrilled me, and that I thought would surely thrill everyone fortunate enough to witness such a début: 'What, is Antonio here?'

The Duke is a good part for a beginner. He can't do much damage. If he dries on every word the scene can well be played without him; and as he is sitting all the while, he cannot get into the wrong position – at least not until the end when he gets up off his throne and exits. My exit was, I thought, masterly. I came down in majesty, bowed to all the court, right and left with great superiority, wheeled round to the right, and marched off walking toes first as I had been told actors always walked.

The next day we had the glory of a matinée, and between the shows we had tea arranged at the café next door, a real North-country tea with ham and plenty of cakes, custards, and tarts. For this event I kept my costume on, whiskers, hat, and all; although it was difficult to consume the lemon tarts with a badly put on crêpe-hair beard, and although the smell of the spirit gum did not really go with boiled ham and tongue, it all seemed part of the grandeur of being an actor. Another wait through the first three acts, and then we had a party on the stage after the show, which I thought sacrilegious. I still hate such things and hate to see people eating on the stage. The local paper gave us a notice, and I was mentioned by name. It said I was 'adequate'.

There lived in Kendal at that time a number of eccentrics. They were called 'characters', and we seemed to be surrounded by one 'character' or another; in fact anyone who did not conform was a 'character'. There was Kelly, who was a great fell-runner and made his living by collecting rags, bones, and rabbit-skins; the Terribul family, who bred prolifically and sold ice-cream from gaily painted carts pulled by ponies; Auntie Raspberry, who dressed one day like Nell Gwyn and another in military uniforms of incredible design; Peter Speight, who attired himself like a music-hall comic and went to all the church services, which he interrupted by the rustling of his bag of mints that he consumed incessantly. Last but not least of these eccentrics was Mr Walker, who was reputed to be a soothsayer. He had forecast my mother's twins years before she had married when she was a young schoolmistress newly arrived in the town. This prophecy had given him the aura of a prophet in my mother's eyes, and to his small dirty room I secretly went one day with a packet of Woodbines and a bottle of jam from Mother's larder as an offering to have my fortune told.

Mr Walker received me with great ceremony, after which he went into a sort of trance, shook himself, and held his head in his hands for what seemed a prodigiously long time. I was terribly frightened and thought perhaps he had been taken ill and would die in my presence. At last he arose, went over to a table covered with books and old papers, and from the pile drew a copy of *The Complete Works of Shakespeare*.

'These are yours,' he said. 'But you will never play the role of Hamlet. Macbeth and Othello yes, but never Hamlet.'

In fact, I did play Hamlet eventually, but was never comfortable in the part. I always tried to emulate the actors I had seen in it, lacking the courage to play it as I would have liked. By the time I had the courage, I was too old.

The years following our *Merchant* saw me in an ever increasing number of roles, and I became an important member of the players. School came to an end, and my poor parents were at a loss to think of any future for an eldest son who would not do anything but play at theatres. I would have wanted to go to a drama school had I known such things existed; but even if I had, the idea would have been promptly vetoed. We could not have afforded such a luxury, and anyway I would have been bound to get into trouble. The whole idea would have been too fanciful for words.

I had to get a job. I had been a complete wash-out at school, not a prize, absolutely nothing. I toyed with the idea of running away to sea. Then I was made to sit for various exams and tests to get a job in a bank or in the borough treasurer's office. I dreaded passing, though I did try, but failed in each case. In desperation my father persuaded a friend of his to try me as an office-boy, with the proviso that I would have to learn about the work of the engineering firm if I was kept on. I was accepted at the salary of five shillings a week; the adult world of work loomed unpromisingly ahead.

2

Good Companions

The day arrived when, on my father's ancient cycle, I reported for work, my school cap discarded for ever and in its place a cap of cloth, the badge of servitude. I had to report at eight-thirty and be shown by my immediate superior how to collect the mail from the post office, slit open the envelopes, and place them on the managing director's table in the boardroom.

From the very start, I hated it. The process of making and marketing laundry machinery seemed infantile. After the lovely romantic smells of the theatre, I found the smell of the new office nauseating. My fellow clerks and typists seemed to attach such an importance to trivialities that it was obvious to me that I was not going to be a great business tycoon. Of course there were compensations; I fell deeply in love with the girl in the telephone room and also with the girl in the strong-room. I liked going into the engine room, the carpenters' shop, and the blacksmith's. I liked the engineers, the carpenters, and all the workmen much better than the clerks and the drawing-office staff, who prided themselves on being so very much more important than the ordinary workmen. The apprentices I thought a bit like their namesakes in old London, and I found the foremen for the most part bossy, like sergeant-majors. I had some very responsible jobs. I had to stick on stamps, and I learnt how to fiddle a little for myself by selling stamps to my colleagues and faking the daily return. This was not dishonest: I needed the money to buy some grease-paint. I had to wind up the clocks (things that a good clerk never looks at during working hours) and go for the mail.

The latter got me out of the prison for a couple of hours, which I was grateful for. I had to answer the telephone and, when asked who I was, answer, 'One of the clerks.' I hated the dreadful instrument. I still don't like telephones and would rather see anyone than speak through this dead implement!

I lived in this den for over two years, making the two-mile journey by cycle in fair weather and foul, and lightening my darkness with my amateur theatricals, which were my real life. Eventually I took over the stage-management and started making all sorts of props – spears, crowns, swords. My parts were arduous and many. In two years, besides my daily work, I learnt and played Lorenzo, Lucentio, Master Ford, Claude Melnotte, Brabantio, Florizel, Frank Freeheart – these in full; and then in short scene performances Othello, Fagin, Sydney Carton, Jean Valjean, and a host of others I cannot remember any more. We started putting on shows in the surrounding villages, which was great fun, and I took my holidays on odd days when we had shows booked, so that on those days I was a real actor. If the shows were near enough, I used to cycle out early on the day and get the stage set ready; we sent the props in advance by bus or carrier's cart, and the artists arrived later just before the performance, not being able or willing to give up their annual holiday to play at being actors. In these shows in the village halls we got a little nearer the truth theatrically, though I was not aware of it at the time. We had no scenery except for some old curtains my mother had given, which I had fixed to a portable frame made from dry-room rods.

Amongst our players was the artist from the local paper. He hailed from Yorkshire, and I thought him the best-dressed and most elegant character I had seen so far. Everyone in the male line seemed to wear drab clothes, but Alec the artist wore russet suitings, yellow shirts, and a pork-pie hat. He seemed to possess all the allure of the big cities compared with my rustic neighbours. It is strange that from this denizen of what I imagined were the great cities I learnt more about my heritage than from my own people. He introduced me to the wonders of Lakeland, our countryside, which I had always taken absolutely for granted. We climbed mountains together, and I got to love wandering over them, now that my eyes were opened. Alec introduced me to modern poets of whom I had never heard, and also to modern trends in the theatre. On one occasion he took me to his old home in a village smaller than mine, and from there we went to the theatre in Middlesbrough to see *Saint Joan* played by the Macdona Players touring company. This is a vivid memory; so much so that when I came to do the play forty years later I remembered it all. I was enchanted with Shaw, intrigued and awed by his magic. His wisdom completely evaded me – I was only eighteen – but I had to admit that perhaps the modern theatre had something after all. No doubt the Macdona Players were just as good as my old friends the Bensonians.

The following day was Sunday. We went for a walk, I in my best Sunday rig, my best Burton, a stiff collar, a natty shirt, and my newly acquired bowler. As we walked, my head was full of the wonders of the play I had seen the night before. I confided to my friend my decision to be an actor, to leave my home, and seek my fortune in the theatre. I said I was going to London, that I knew this was the proper thing to do. His advice was very simple, and good advice too:

'You know, you are an ass. Here you are, born and living in the most lovely part of the world; you are interested in good things that you can enjoy so long as you don't try to sell them to live. If you go you are a fool. Go to London and be buried in your bowler!'

Good advice no doubt, but whoever took good advice with the spring in the air, interminable years ahead, and not knowing what adventure there was waiting round the corner? I did not take his advice, and I think it was fear that drove me on. That is perhaps what drives everyone on in their early years – a delightful fear, a desire to challenge, a sort of mental masochism.

The visit of the Benson Company took place in the autumn of 1927, my first experience of professional actors at close quarters in a real theatre. We had a letter from Sir Frank's manager asking if our actors would care to help by being 'supers' in *Julius Caesar*, helping to swell the Roman mobs, and as soldiers and attendants in *Richard II*. Who could refuse? I was both mobster and soldier, wearing ill-fitting sandals and a sack-like costume, I yelled 'Ave, Caesar!' and 'Ave, Brutus!' and 'Ave, Antony!' deliriously. It was 5 November; and after the curtain descended on the Forum scene as Caesar went up in flames on his funeral pyre, Sir Frank, who was Antony, smiled at the mob and said, 'The fifth of November, gentlemen.' I thought it the height of wit.

The following day was a matinée, and the play was *Richard II*. I was no longer one of the crowd but a guard in the court of the King of England, dressed in a helmet and tabard and carrying the inevitable spear. Sir Frank, in a brown velvet houpalande – a gown-like medieval coat – was reclining on a Victorian sofa smelling a rose; at his feet two of the undertaker's greyhounds and at his side his confidant, the Lord Aumerle. At the King's exit we had to follow him off left. When the cue was given I wheeled around and was the last of the four to march off-stage. I was probably crawling gingerly off as amateurs do when a voice behind me, the grating voice of Lloyd Pearson, said not so very *sotto voce*, 'Can't you buggers run?' I felt awful, sure the audience had heard. But in spite of the rebuke I was allowed to follow the King right through the play, still walking in my best toe-and-heel manner.

How the company managed the following week without me I could not imagine, but I went to see. They were at the Grand Theatre, Blackpool, and that Saturday there was a cheap excursion to Blackpool, to see some football match. I took advantage of this and went to the theatre instead. There had been a lot of publicity in the national press about Sir Frank's feats of walking from one town to the next, and this he had done the Sunday after my *Julius Caesar* performance. I had written a letter to remind Sir Frank of the super who had been such a success the week before and asking if he would see me to advise me how to proceed with my chosen career. I sent the letter round and after a short wait was escorted to his dressing room. He remembered me, gave me a free seat for the evening show, which was *The Merchant*, and told me to come round after the 'cursing scene' when Shylock tells Tubal to meet him at his synagogue.

In the circle of this lovely theatre in Blackpool I felt very grand watching the show that I now knew word for word right through, and knowing that I would be backstage at the end of the act, I already felt like one of the elect. I was called to the front by the house manager and escorted for the first time in my life through the forbidden door. Not even actors are allowed to use it, the pass door leading from auditorium to stage. The first man I saw was Robert Donat, at the time playing Gratiano; Sir Frank was chatting to him on the stairs, and I followed him up to his dressing room.

Benson removed his wig and sat down to tea and toast, saying to me: 'Well, young man, and did you walk all the way to Blackpool?' Then he added, 'Fire away', which meant I had to recite.

Off I went reciting *The Merchant* from the beginning, prepared to go on as long as needed. I spoke all the parts, cues and all, and would have gone to the end, but he stopped me before I got to my favourite bit when Bassanio describes Portia at Belmont.

'Do you play hockey?' he asked.

Now this could have meant anything, as hockey at our school had been looked upon as a girls' game, but he seemed satisfied when I said I could play football and rugby.

Then he said a very wise thing: 'Could your father give you two pounds a week?' Such a sum was quite enough to live on in those days. 'If he can do that for you there is a lovely life ahead as an actor, but if you have to depend on what you earn to live on, it is better not to try.'

I asked him if he could give me a job, but he said I was too young at the moment, and if I still wanted to be an actor next year I should see him again. In the meantime I should see every possible actor and every possible show, be it classical or modern, revue or music hall, and learn as much of Shakespeare's plays as I could. Also, he said, go for long walks and count your breaths as you walk to give rhythm, simple yoga breathing really; play games and keep very fit because an actor's job is tough and hard work, and one must be strong in mind and body. I went home elated. I had not got a job, but I was surely on the way; the door of the sacred temple was opening.

Another year passed while I continued at the office with the mail, dockets, and other dreary things – all except the girl in the strong-room. I was by now quite bold. My fear of the fair sex had turned to reverence, and I felt such a great chap. This particular young lady was a terrible flirt and intrigued me no end. I was in the strong-room with her when I was asked to go and see the manager, not in his office as usual when he wanted something, but in the boardroom. These calls had been going out to various members of the staff at intervals during the last fortnight: the delinquents were given lectures on their shortcomings, others got praises for their good points; either you came out with a rise in salary or you were demoted and threatened with ruin. Now it was my turn. I was anxious, as my conscience was not altogether clear on many points. I was asked to sit down and whether I liked my work, if I was happy, whether I intended to stay with them for all my life, and why I did not go to night-school. Night-school, forsooth! When I had to go to rehearsals! Then the manager suggested that perhaps it would be better if I wasted all my time with my theatricals, as in two more weeks I would not be wanted with the firm whether I liked the job or not. I was sacked: just like that. Looking back I cannot help thinking that the firm was very long-suffering as far as I was concerned.

I dared not tell my parents of this calamity, but went to see Mrs Lee. She was not a bit perturbed, and said that she might be able to get me a job. Twenty miles away by the sea at Morecambe there flourished the Royalty Theatre, which had one of the first weekly repertory companies in England at the time. They put on a different play each week during the winter season, from October to Whitsuntide, during which time they had a permanent company. Mrs Lee's husband helped them when they wanted to augment the cast, and at the moment they wanted a beginner at a low salary to help with the stage-management. She knew the manager and would recommend me, and suggested that I went myself as soon as possible. It was then Friday night, so I took a train after the office the following day.

This was the theatre in which I had first seen *Chu Chin Chow*, a lovely small theatre, with gallery and balcony and bars. There were very few resident companies in those days. There were stock companies run by actor-managers, but the resident reps had not yet started. The Royalty company aspired to be a little better than the old stock companies. To me the task seemed impossible; to put a different play on every Monday, week after week, seemed super-human, but apparently they did it and were attracting great crowds in the process. I saw the manager, a little man in a wing collar who smoked cigarettes all the time. He asked me if I thought I could do the work. I would have only small parts and help with the stage-management, which would be the most important part, I felt. My title would be A.S.M. (assistant stage-manager). The job would begin at rehearsals the following Tuesday at a salary of £2 per week.

I had done it – I was to be a paid actor and to start in just one week! In my excitement I had forgotten to tell him that I would be employed for another fortnight. I did not realize this dreadful mistake till I was half-way home. Now what to do? If I tried to put off my opening perhaps I would lose the job, as there was to be a large-cast play starting rehearsal. Perhaps if I could not be in it I would not be wanted after all, but then the office might insist on my staying with them till I had worked out my notice.

In desperation I told my father the whole thing. I think he was impressed by the fact that I had had so much initiative, and he went to see the manager of our firm. He came back saying they did not care when I left. This was hardly flattering, but it served my purpose. Only a week to go before I was to have £2 a week, enough to be independent, (my office-boy's salary with the firm had been raised only once to the princely sum of 7s. 6d.). In the space of a weekend I had got the sack and a 500-per-cent pay rise and was an actor at last. I was nineteen.

My last day in business was singularly undramatic. There were no farewell speeches or formal gifts except for the lady in the cashiers' office who gave me a beautiful leather-bound volume of the plays of William Shakespeare. My immediate superior in the cost office gave me a fountain-pen and a little lecture that I must beware of wine, women, and song – the very things that I was after, did he but know it (perhaps he did)! Wine at the time did not interest me; women I was still afraid of, but I had a secret ambition to be a great lover, if not in real life, at least in the minds of my audience in the theatre.

Mother was not very pleased. She called on Mrs Lee, whom she accused of engineering the whole thing. But Dad was delighted. Since going 'on the road' he had become a frequenter of theatres. He perhaps believed that his son being an actor would enable him to gain access to an otherwise forbidden world. Anyway, I always had a feeling he was on my side. My poor mother, in tears on the day of my departure, confessed that perhaps it was all her fault, since before I was born she hoped her child would like all lovely things, and during her pregnancy made a point of reading the plays of Shakespeare and masses of poetry. She had overdone it, and this was the result! She gave me as a present *The Imitation of Christ* by Thomas à Kempis, and on the flyleaf she wrote in her bold hand the poem about the passage of time. I still have the book, though the writing is now brown and faded. Auntie Mary gave me an alarm clock so that I should not be late for the show. Thus with my trunk packed with two suits, my father's cut-down evening dress, my Shakespeare, and whatever else I possessed, accompanied to the railway station by my father, I left home for ever to be an actor. As the train pulled out, he gave me a ten shilling note and a packet of ten Players cigarettes, and that did it. As the engine gathered speed, I just blubbered. I had not even done so when bumped on my first day at school, but this time I had to let go, and I had not even a match to light a cigarette.

Later that day, in my new hat and sporting a folding mackintosh, I sauntered through Morecambe to the theatre. Outside the Royalty Theatre the bills announced *The Joan Danvers* by E. Stayton. There was a sweet-shop on the corner. I strolled in and nonchalantly enquired if they knew where I could get lodgings, hinting that I had come to join the theatre and giving the impression that I was quite at home looking for 'digs' in a strange town. I even affected what I thought was a foreign accent. I did not know that the shop belonged to the theatre, and was soon deflated when I found that I was addressing the Royalty's assistant manager, that he knew all about me, and that as far as he was concerned, I was only the new boy. He sent me to an address not too far away, where I engaged a bedroom and sitting room in a cottage for the sum of 28s. a week. This was very extravagant. I could have had what we called a combined room, a bedsitting room, for much less; but I had never heard of anyone eating in a bedroom. For all my pretended intimate knowledge of the inside of an actor's life, I knew nothing of how actors in a small provincial town lived.

I unpacked my case, put out my Shakespeare and Auntie Mary's alarm clock next to my bed, and hung up my wardrobe (the rep actor's name for his clothing). Then I found the best café in town, had a glass of Horlicks malted milk, and went on to see the show in my theatre. A beautiful little theatre was the Royalty, Morecambe, old fashioned in design, the usual circular shape but without the gods, just a circle and a balcony. The decorations were in Wedgwood blue and white; it was not as gaudy as most theatres of the period, but with the house lights on it looked majestic.

This was Monday night, the opening of *The Joan Danvers*. I had a whole row of stalls to myself, there was a smattering in the pit, and the balcony was about half full. The upper circle I could not see. Most of the audience were 'dead heads', people who had free seats for putting out posters in their shops or lending some props to the company, and a few landladies given seats by the cast. There was a small orchestra, a trio led by a violinist who looked like Punch. They played what I supposed was appropriate music, and the curtain went up. A modern set, a room in a house near Bristol, the house of Mr Danvers, a shipowner. Like all houses in rep plays it had a large French window at the back. The actors seemed nervous, and some of the make-up looked wet. They had had only four rehearsals, and these whilst they were playing another play. The leading lady came on. She was lovely, with red golden hair and a saucy turned-up nose. It appeared that in the play she was going to have a baby. My God! A sex play – I had been warned! What would my boss at the old firm think if he knew? Come to that, what would my family think?

During the second interval I was taken backstage and introduced to the stage-manager, who seemed a nice fellow, quite young. He was in the prompt corner and holding the book, not actually a prompter, but to keep the cast straight if they went seriously wrong. Rep actors usually gag when they forget their lines, and someone can invariably keep going till the scene gets straight again; but it is possible on a first night to go so far wrong that one finds oneself in the wrong act or even the wrong play. In such cases, on the first night at least, it is important that there is someone with the book who can pull them together. Otherwise, I found that a prompter is not used at all.

When the play finished, the actors stood in line, and the leading lady thanked the meagre audience. She told them that the next week the company would perform a new play called *The Green Cord* by M. Bower and A. Ellis. I was to be in that play – oh Lord!

The auditorium died, the house lights dimmed, covers were put on the stalls and circle seats, the attendants left, and all was still as a grave; but not so in the working end of the theatre. After the anxiety, great gaiety broke out in the dressing room below the stage. Few actors dare drink during the show on a first night, but now that it was over they made up for lost time. There was a bar adjoining the dressing rooms, used mainly by stage-hands, the cast, and a few favoured members of the audience. Now with the great load off their shoulders, the actors relaxed; even the air seemed lighter.

In this atmosphere of a great party I was introduced to my new comrades: Phyllis Claude, the leading lady; Arthur her husband, tall and saturnine, just as I thought an actor ought to look. Against his appearance I felt a little hopeless. I am only five feet eight inches, and have been since I was an overgrown schoolboy of twelve. In those days to be an actor of note called for a 'tall presence' unless one was a comic, and it was to be another ten years before I began to suspect that I could make people laugh. Anyway, here was an actor who looked like one, and I began to feel like an impostor. Any minute I might be thrown back where I belonged. Then I was introduced to the juvenile leading man, Philip. He looked handsome in his sea captain's uniform, his hair painted grey at the temples. I had admired him tremendously from the front, yet he was not as tall as I was! How did he manage to cut such a grand figure? I learnt the secret in time, simple if one knows how. I felt better now and was introduced to Maureen (the Irish juvenile), Derek (the heavy), Molly (the *ingénue*), Peter (the scenic artist), Scotty (the character juvenile), and Maudie (the aristocratic lead).

I was given my part: Captain Ffolliott in the play to be rehearsed tomorrow, *The Green Cord*. I was to be in the theatre by ten a.m. the next day to help to 'set for rehearsals'. I left by the stage door, not as a visitor, an amateur, or a seeker after employment, but as an actor, an acolyte in my new-found temple. In my pocket was my talisman, my part in *The Green Cord*. I hurried home to read it.

Auntie Mary's alarm clock went off at eight o'clock the following morning, but even before that I was dressed and ready. I breakfasted alone in my sitting room, then went out for a walk along the sea front. After a Horlicks to give me strength, I was at the theatre fifteen minutes before my 'call'. Not a soul was there; the stage was in darkness. I waited about, and then Jack arrived. He went up into the light-loft and switched on. We called it a 'bomb', one solitary naked bulb hanging from the flies, casting ghostly shadows around the cold, darkened stage. The sides of the *Joan Danvers* setting had been struck and stacked so that we could have plenty of room for the rehearsal, and all the furniture was piled under dust-sheets. All this had been done whilst we were carousing after the show the previous night. From the paint dock at the rear of the stage we carried a table and two chairs, placing these against the safety curtain facing up-stage.

Jack had the script of the new play and had already made out plots for the settings and furniture, and a rough measurement of all sets. We 'set' the first act; that is, we chalked the shape on the stage and placed furniture in approximate positions. The two chairs on either side of the prompt table were for the director and the stage-manager. As A.S.M. I had a chair alongside the S.M.'s. I had a notebook and pencil and was told to jot down every prop that was mentioned as the rehearsal progressed.

Now it was almost eleven, and the actors began to arrive. I had met them all the night before, but how different they appeared now, all muffled up against the cold. Theatres are very cold places in the winter. The heating was turned down during the daytime and stoked up only in the afternoon so that it would be cosy for the show. Even with the heat on, the stage was always colder than the auditorium. The actors seemed shabbily dressed, all except Philip, the juvenile lead, who had a natty overcoat. Rep actors keep their best clothes for the plays; and although the adverts in *The Stage*, the weekly theatre paper, ask for actors who 'dress well on and off' this lot seemed to me to be particularly scruffy. I could not have told they were actors if I had not known. Maudie had a great shopping-bag with groceries peeping out. Phyllis and her husband arrived last, just on time. No one was late – actors never are. Phyllis looked very grand with her two fox terriers and wearing a fur coat; the dogs climbed on her chair and went to sleep. Her husband Arthur was not quite so impressively dressed as his wife. His coat was a little frayed, but he wore a most unproletarian type of cap and smoked a romantic-looking Sherlock Holmes pipe. There were two members of the company I had not met the night before, another married couple, Teddy and Winnie Ashworth. They were not in *The Joan Danvers* and had not come to the theatre the previous night. 'Reptiles' do not see shows they are not in on a first night.

I was shivering with cold and nerves, fearful of my rehearsal performance. Phyllis started the proceedings by describing the setting of the play, all very casually and in a most matter-of-fact way, and then we took up our positions and started to run through Act 1. I had the first word. We were supposed to be in a hotel in Egypt, on the terrace. Teddy was my superior officer. My first words were, 'Whisky soda, *lao*.' No one knew that the last word was Hindi, and no one knew or asked why we should be using Hindi in Egypt. What 'Shlon jepek djinebek' means I have not the foggiest notion either, and it was no use asking, as obviously neither did anyone else; but I suppose it sounded romantic and foreign, and I said it with gusto. No one told me how to say anything, no one made any comment whatever. Phyllis just told us when to move and where to stand. The whole thing was casual and easy, and there were only three more rehearsals.

Tomorrow we would go through Act 1 twice and be d.l.p; 'dead letter perfect'. This appeared to me to be impossible, but no one turned a hair; they had been doing this rep business for years. Most of the company went to the pub on the corner, but I went home to my cottage for a lunch of herrings and chipped potatoes, and to my part to be d.l.p. by the next day. Somehow I managed it, the words of Act 1. I had only a page and a half in the act, and by walking up and down the sea front all afternoon saying my lines aloud I managed to get some sort of order into my head. However, I was terribly worried about how I was going to learn all the rest of my seven pages to be able to say them next Monday. I could not remember after just the one rehearsal who on earth gave me the cues; no one had told me to write down these important facts in my part in the first rehearsal.

Nor did I know how to cue myself by covering up the lines and seeing only the cues; also the art of forgetting was quite foreign to me. The trick is to mark all the lines you remember automatically – in everything you read there is quite a lot that you always remember – and concentrate on those lines that do not impress themselves and on those speeches that have to be learnt parrot-wise. Then you go through them again and mark what you know and worry only about what you don't. In other words, the art of quick memorizing is really the art of forgetting and not burdening the mind with what is obvious, so that you can concentrate only on what has to be assimilated. Without this simple system, memorizing is a most exhausting task.

The following morning we stumbled through Act 1. We did it twice and the second time got quite a pace on. Then we did Act 2 and part of Act 3. This took us to nearly two o'clock. In the evening I had to go backstage again to see the prop man, who was not there in the daytime, and he would tell me what the theatre could supply out of stock and what I should have to beg, borrow, or steal from outside. Rep theatres keep all essentials like writing materials, bottles, syphons, ornaments, and pictures; these are used again and again, some disguised of course to look different each time, but there are also special props, which various shops and houses would lend.

I found I had other duties as well as looking after the props. I was a sort of 'go-for-when-wanted barman'. I had to help in the 'stalls bar', which was the name we gave our snug. People from the stalls could use this bar, but they all preferred the pit bar at the back of the stalls, which was much better furnished. The stalls bar was really for the stage-hands and the actors. Here we had beer from the wood, great hogsheads of Worthington, and the price to us was twopence per half-pint. I had to help to check the sales and learnt how to set up the barrels and how to lift their seemingly immovable weight.

By Saturday rehearsal the play came to life. I don't think I had improved much, being still uncertain of my lines. When not sure, I am always inclined to gabble, my mind racing ahead in its anxiety. Now we came to the last night of *The Joan Danvers*. The houses after Monday had improved each night, and by the end of the week the theatre was full. When the show was over, the set was 'struck', all curtains and props were folded and stored away, lights dismantled, and the old set placed in the scene dock ready to be repainted for some future production. The new scenery for *The Green Cord* was by now ready. There were three sets: our hotel veranda, a house in London, and a desert set with a tent.

We then had to fix the 'deading off' and lighting. Deading off, or masking, means seeing that all the lights are masked off from the front row of the stalls, that all borders are straight, and that no light battens are visible. The lighting rehearsal was fascinating. We had very old-fashioned lighting but in those days, to me, it was superb. I had seen nothing like it before, and found some of the effects breathtaking. The Royalty's spotlights were antiquated carbon limes on perches in the corners, but there were plenty of floodlights; when the sky cloth for our first act was lit deep blue I thought I had never seen anything like it. Battens were fixed behind each exit, each with three or four bulbs and fed by terminals in the stage flooring called 'dips'. If this is not done, when you open a door it will appear that you are going into a garden of total darkness. I had learnt how to make 'whisky and soda' from burnt sugar and water, 'fried eggs' from a tin of peaches: there were so many different tricks of the prop-man's art, no end to the magic.

It is customary after setting to take out all the stage-hands and buy them a drink, and it is the duty of the stage-manager or A.S.M. or both to take them and stand the treat, not from their own salary but paid for by the management. So into a public bar I went – 'wine, women, and song'. I had a lemonade. The next morning I wondered why I felt so terrible. I was in bed, Auntie Mary's alarm had just gone off at 8.30 a.m. (I no longer got up early like ordinary people), so I lay for a few minutes in a sort of half-world; and then it all came back with a flash. I was no longer in my father's house, I was in digs, and today I was to make my début as an actor. It was awful. I felt like running away. I knew I had done it all because I was afraid and I had tempted fate; my thoughts were confused and my tummy full of feathers. I took my part from under the pillow and tried to remember the lines, but just could not remember the words at all. What on earth was going to happen when I went on-stage in only a few short hours?

My landlady had made me a lovely breakfast; but, thinking of the breakfast on a 'hanging morning', I could not eat it. After some tea I immediately had to rush for the lavatory, which, considering my horribly constipated youth, seemed to forbode an awful catastrophe. Perhaps I was going to be dreadfully ill and would not appear; would this be a good thing or a bad thing? Full of what I thought was great sophistication I had ordered the *Daily Telegraph* to be delivered every morning. I never read it, as I had no interest in the daily doings of the world, and strangely enough I did not read the page on the theatre. It was mainly concerned with the London stage, which was too far away to mean much to me; but today in a fit of nerves I opened the paper. At the top of the theatre page there was an advert for *Outward Bound* at the Apollo Theatre. 'Outward bound', that was me: abandoned and alone, my own fault when I could have been safe at home; all because I thought I wanted to be an actor. I had forsaken everyone – my family, my friends – and would be alone on that stage tonight, foolish and forlorn.

I went out with my part by now a crumpled rag clutched in my hands. I would go to the theatre and alone run through the words aloud to give myself confidence. I went on the stage where there was no light except the pilot light over the switchboard, and in the darkness rehearsed my part over and over again. The darkness calmed me. In the middle of Act 2 I was rudely brought back to reality by the arrival of the station van with an enormous basketful of our costumes for the play. The basket was dumped on the stage with no ceremony and I was handed a railway receipt. I signed it, adding my degree, 'A.S.M.'.

Strangely, I had forgotten all about the costumes! On opening days we did not rehearse till twelve noon, but the actors started arriving early to run through odd scenes in the dressing rooms and to get all their clothing ready. Peter, the scenic artist, arrived, and I was fascinated to see his final touches to the set, mainly to the steps and rostra. A few squiggles of green and ivory, and the wooden rostra became marble. He was a small man with glasses, always smiling, and he said he would show me how to paint cloths if I came to the scene dock after rehearsal. He told me I could help to prime. I had no idea what this meant but said I would come tomorrow. Then I thought, 'Will I still be an actor tomorrow after ruining the play tonight?' I mentioned my fears to Peter.

'Don't worry,' he said; 'the curtain will go up and the curtain will come down.'

I knew it, of course, but what was going to happen in the meantime?

I had to unpack the costumes, all done up in bundles with the name of the character. Philip, who played a sort of Lawrence of Arabia character, had a gorgeous Arabian dress for which I envied him very much. There were burnouses for the lesser Arabs, and Teddy and I had each our white tropical suit and topi. I tried mine on and felt cold and weak. I hung Father's cut-down and taken-in evening suit, polished my shoes, put out my make-up, and waited for the signal to start. I was sharing a dressing room with Teddy, who kept up a long flow of conversation that did not help me at all. He seemed to think of and talk about everything but the play. He had been on-stage all his life, and these first nights were just routine to him.

After a final run-through Phyllis said a few words and we were free till performance time. We were to start at seven-fifteen. I went home to my high tea, then wrote to my mother and father saying I would be home at the weekend for a day. When I came to date the letter I had a bit of a shock; it was 5 November. The date coincided for the third time with some special occasion: my first amateur play had been on 5 November; my first 'super' job with Sir Frank had been on 5 November; and now it was the same date for my first professional engagement. I remembered Falstaff's 'They say good luck lies in odd numbers.' I am not superstitious – actors are supposed to be – but I decided there must be something in this recurring date. I felt alive again and eager for the play.

In my amateur days we had always been made up by someone else who was supposed to know something about the art. I had some grease-paints and had made myself up as all sorts of characters, but this had been only in the privacy of my bedroom. Back in my Royalty dressing room, I really did not know how to begin. I covered my face with cold-cream and applied Leichner's No. 2½, red to the cheeks and on the lips, painted on black eyebrows and outlined my eyes with the same black. At this moment in walked Teddy. He did a double-take, focussed on me with awe, and said in a hushed whisper:

'Christ all bloody mighty! What the hell are you made up for? You look like a whore at a Christening!' He paused; then, looking at my grease-paints, threw most of my stock out with the advice, 'Put that lot down the shit-house and wash your bloody face.'

Teddy showed me what to use: two sticks only, No. 5 and No. 9; blend them together, and you can get almost any flesh colour you need; wet the lips, brush the eyebrows with a wet toothbrush, and dust the whole thing with cornflour. He then commented unfavourably upon my spotty face:

'What you want, my boy, is a bloody big fat woman. That's the only thing to get rid of an appearance like that!'

I had forgotten to call the half while all this was going on. Jack rushed in and told me off about the omission, then called it himself. He told me to get out of the dressing room and check that all the artists had been given, and were aware of, their hand-props, go up on the stage and try all the doors, tell the stage-hands to get off the furniture, ring the bells in the bars to check them, check who was on the safety curtain, and a lot more of what seemed like a hundred and one jobs all in the short half-hour when I wanted to concentrate on my part. Still, it was good to be busy; there was less time for being nervous. The artists came out of their dressing rooms, all in the new costumes and make-up, and were generally admired by each other. Actors love this moment. As we went up to the stage Teddy said to me:

'If you dry up, keep on talking, say anything. The buggers in front will never know as long as you keep on. But if you can't think of anything to say, don't just shuffle about; bloody well shut up and leave it to me.'

We took our seats on the veranda of the hotel. The orchestra was playing what was supposed to be oriental music. Jack, in the corner, said, 'Lights!' and the stage came alive; the sky gleamed with oriental blue, and the limes were glaring right at us. 'House lights!' – a pause; 'Stand by!' – a pause; 'Going up!' The curtain-man in a cloth cap was touched on the shoulder, he gave the counterweighted curtain rope a heave, and the curtain soared into the air.

We were off. I took a deep breath, my body seemed to grow. I sat there like a lord and said my first 'Whisky soda, *lao*.' It was wonderful. The excitement and joy I felt at that moment have been with me ever since; every time the curtain goes up or the show starts, it is the same.

'The theatre is female. If you embrace her and hold her, she will give you the world; but if you trifle with her she will bite and the bite will never heal.' With these words my new friend Teddy bade me goodnight.

This wonderful week sped swiftly by. I did my own make-up, under Teddy's supervision. He was always a little rude at my efforts, I still felt foolish in that white suit, and my evening dress, I knew, was not of the most elegant cut; but once on the 'green' I was in heaven. I was not in the next production. It was a play with only a very small cast, but I was kept more than busy with my A.S.M. duties. Amongst other extraordinary props I had to get a boiler for one set and a ship's porthole for another. These I borrowed from the ship-breaking yard where I spent some fascinating afternoons aboard a doomed liner in the process of being taken apart and turned into razor-blades. I started to help Peter in the paint dock. I learnt to prime cloths, and also learnt why he had offered to teach me to paint: basically to do the hard work, for priming a thirty-foot cloth is hard labour. With a large brush like my mother used for white-washing, the whole cloth has to be covered first with size and then with basic colour; the area seemed to last for ever. Having done one length of the cloth, we had to haul the great heavy thing up a further six feet and start again.

Then I fell from grace. All my life I had had to get up early, and in this new life not needing to report for work before ten-thirty was too easy. Auntie Mary's alarm clock was set for ever later hours. The first few days I was up at eight from force of habit, but as days went by I lingered a little longer, and now that the nervous strain of my first part was over I am afraid some days I lay abed till after nine.

On the Friday of my second week, I awoke, switched off the alarm, turned over, and went to sleep again. I had no idea of the time when I awakened with a jolt. My landlady was knocking at the door and shouting that I had better get up as my breakfast was growing cold; my alarm said ten-twenty, and rehearsal started at ten-thirty. I leapt up, dressed in seconds, had no breakfast, and tried to run to the theatre. There was a bit of an early frost so I could not go as fast as I wanted. I arrived at five minutes to eleven to find the stage set and the rehearsal already started. Scotty was in my official A.S.M. chair, and when I came on to the stage no one took any notice of me whatever; they just carried on as though I did not belong any more. I was just left hanging about.

At the end of the act there was a five-minute break, and Phyllis asked me if I was ill. I said, no, I was all right.

'Then why were you late for rehearsal?' she said.

'I slept in,' I answered.

'Oh, you slept in, did you? That's very interesting, but I'm afraid you'll have to go and tell the manager you slept in and see what he has to say.'

I went to the office and was told that actors were never late. Whatever happened they were always on time. Whatever faults they had – and there were many – one thing could always be relied on: they would be on time. Well or ill, an actor must be there; as long as he could stand he must go on. If he fell down, then someone would go on for him; if he fell dead, he would be offered a decent burial; but he was never late. All this was done very kindly, but it was more terrible than being on the carpet at the office.

I crawled back to the stage with shame in my heart. The theatre I had thought so lovely now seemed to hate me, and I no longer had a right to be here. I was allowed back in my chair, and the rehearsal was resumed. However, when Phyllis said, 'That's all, boys and girls', and dismissed the cast, no one spoke to me. It was like being sent to Coventry. Outside the stage door Teddy and his wife Winnie were waiting. She was fat and giggly and comfortable. She smiled, and Teddy said in his best Yorkshire comic's voice:

'Cum and 'ave sum coffee at our 'ouse'; and as an afterthought, 'And don't you ever be late again or you'll get your bloody notice!'

I never was late again. Only once have I missed a show since, when I had a fever so bad that I could not stand.

The matter was never mentioned again. At the rehearsal next day I was at my usual place, and the whole episode of my dreadful lapse had been forgotten. In five weeks' time we were to put on a fairly new play, *Hay Fever* by Noel Coward. Phyllis called me to her dressing room and told me that there was a very good part in this play, almost the leading part. He was very young, only eighteen, and she thought I could play it. It was much longer than any part I had had so far, and in order to allow me time to prepare she would get me a part typed early and relieve me of my A.S.M. duties during rehearsal week. In the meantime I was to play a footman in a play whose name I have forgotten, and then a good part in *Woman to Woman* by M. Morton. My world had been recreated and, with a light heart, I rushed to tell Molly in the tobacconist's of my good fortune. That weekend I went home, catching the train after the show on the Saturday and arriving early on the Sunday morning. My father met me at the station. After so short a time away, I looked upon my parents as insular and narrow-minded. I hinted at my exciting life, was ostentatious with my new-found wealth, and behaved just as badly as possible. My younger brothers bored me, and it was not till I was in the train on the way back on Monday morning that I felt any contrition for my stupid behaviour.

Mrs Lee was a remarkable teacher. Most people considered her old-fashioned and laughed at her ideas, but she was right about most things regarding speech and voices. Her teaching was a form of yoga, though she never called it by that name; the breathing and voice-control techniques were based on yogic teaching. There are sounds that will kill; there are sounds that will heal tired nerves; there are sounds that will call forth tears. The great thing is to be able to create the sounds at will. Tears are the easiest, a soft tone, a slight vibrato, and a slight hesitancy. Rep actors are usually too busy getting through their lines to pay much attention to such things, and very few had had any voice training. For my new part I turned on my best lyric tones, not at rehearsal, only 'on the night'.

I turned it on full blast. Phyllis looked at me in awe and whispered:
  'Do you know the rest of the scene?'
  Luckily I did. After the performance she told me it was lovely.
Peter, the painter, who had been in front, was most enthusiastic. I
also got a special notice for my small part in the local paper; my
horrid little head began to get bigger and bigger. But I did go to see
Mrs Lee, telling her it was her teaching that had done it. I felt
superior to my fellow players, who I thought could not turn on
this tear-jerking tone at will. I found later that they could, only my
version was a little more 'ham', and if one is 'ham' enough the
public don't know what it is and think it is great acting.
  We put on *Hay Fever*, in which I had the leading part, but it was
not a success. Our audience liked stronger fare, and our aspiring to
the sophisticated heights of modern London theatre did not bring
good houses. Next we put on a wonderful play by an author
unknown to me at the time, Dion Boucicault: *Con the
Shaughraun*. Ever since I first met these wonderful dramas I have
foretold that if only they were put on in London they could not
fail. The proof was the overwhelming success of *London Assur-
ance*. *Con the Shaughraun* is more Irish than ever Ireland was.
Scotty was playing Con, and our real Irish colleen was Molly, his
girl-friend. Tons of scenery were required, and as my part was
small I helped in the scene dock all the week. Derek, our 'heavy',
had left; we had a new man, Eugene, straight from South Africa
where he had been a radio announcer – in those days a position of
great glamour.
  On the second day, Scotty had to leave rehearsal. On the third
he was in hospital with pneumonia, and during the show on the
third night we heard that he was dead. Amidst this tragic gloom
we had to recast the play. The only available man was Peter the
painter, who had to take over the part of Con, and a new actor
was wired for to take over Peter's part; this was the priest, a small
part but most important. We rehearsed all day to help Peter
through and we painted scenery all night, Peter mumbling his lines
the while. The new actor was at rehearsal the following morning.
He was a vision to behold, tall and cadaverous looking, dressed in
a long black fur-collared coat. He had an enormous black hat,
from under which hung uneven wisps of lank white hair. He wore
white spats over his shoes and had black woollen gloves. His voice
was like music from a sepulchre. Our front-of-house manager,

who was not half his height, escorted him on to the stage with a look of abject apology to one and all. He said he had written out his part but had not 'met' the play for many years; that might well have been half a century before, as he looked eighty years old. He walked through rehearsal, mumbling his lines and forever writing things in his part with a tiny pencil-stub. In order to see he held the part at arm's length, and to write brought it up close to his eyes.

After the rehearsal he went straight into the nearest pub. He asked me which was the usual 'house of call' and that night he was drunk, roaring along the road at chucking-out time and waving his hat jubilantly. Had he not got a 'shop' and had he not got a sub on his salary?

Scotty's funeral was the next morning, and the four younger members carried the coffin. My father lent me a black overcoat. Philip and I were at the front, and although Scotty was quite a small fellow the coffin seemed terribly heavy. We had subscribed for a wreath made in the form of a part, open at the last page. Scotty's wife was playing in a company somewhere else but she was there at the funeral, which we had to have early, as she had to get back in time for her performance. It was a cold wintry day. All our friends were there: the staff from the front of the house and the stage-hands; Molly and the barmen; and many regulars who never missed a show. It was terribly sad. Philip and I walked home to our digs, put by our mourning, and then went back to the theatre for the last night of *Hay Fever*, acting our comedy after the glimpse of the open grave.

We rehearsed and set after the show that night and met again on Sunday. *Con the Shaughraun* was a riot from start to finish. We had lovely sets and grand romantic costumes. I was again an officer, this time a nasty English one, but even he was not as bad as the real villain, an Irish landlord, played by Eugene from South Africa looking like Johnny Walker on the whisky bottle. Our elderly fellow actor, who played the priest, stole the show. Whenever he mentioned anything religious he swung his eyes up to heaven; every time he made an exit he looked at the audience, gave a little stamp with his foot, and went off to tumultuous applause. He was the first real old ham I had ever met and I was tremendously impressed. I tried to make his sort of exit myself, but somehow it did not seem to work, at least I never heard the applause. It took me years to learn to do it, and even more to learn how to do it and not let anyone know what had been done.

For over six months I played at the Royalty Theatre, getting props ready for every show and playing all sorts of parts, one after another. I knew every inch of that theatre. Then we came to our first break, the amateur production of *The Toreador*. For this the company was simply laid off; no play, no pay, just cast aside while the amateur people played with our theatre. On my rock-bottom £2 a week this would have been pretty difficult – it was bad enough for those getting higher salaries – so something had to be done. I could have gone home, but then our manager said that if Jack and I would stay on and help with the make-up and the stage-management the amateurs would pay us our salaries. This we agreed to do, and a hilarious week we had into the bargain.

We had three of these amateur weeks, each with a different company in possession, and then our company started to break up. During the summer holiday season the company would be disbanded while touring attractions took over. We were due to finish at Whitsuntide, and with this knowledge in mind everyone was on the look-out for jobs to tide them through the summer. Teddy and Winnie were the first to go, leaving for a repertory company in Blackburn. Then I heard that Phyllis and her husband had had some sort of tiff with the management and were leaving the same day. This was a double tragedy; the theatre could never, to my mind, be the same again. I had this sense of loyalty that nothing could shake. Before they left Teddy and Winnie told me they would try to get me a job for when our season came to an end. To my surprise the following week I had a telegram from Blackburn (actors never seem to write; they always telegraph) offering work at £3. 10s. a week. I was on the move again.

3

Laura

In those days Blackburn seemed to me some far-off metropolis. At the crack of dawn one Tuesday I was off to my new location, the city's Grand Theatre. The company was run by the actor-manager, St George Frere. He was tall, angular, deep-voiced, and middle-aged, and he had a lovely, kindly wife and a daughter Dorothy. Mr and Mrs Frere played the leads, and their daughter Dorothy the *ingénues* or juvenile leads.

In the first production I played the male juvenile, in love with Dorothy. At the end, boy got girl, and the play closed with an embrace. I, who had fancied myself as the great lover, was too shy to execute the embrace. I felt silly. I had got as far as putting my clammy hands on maidens' shoulders from behind and whispering into their shell-like ears, but the full embrace was too much for my sensitive soul.

Dorothy complained to her parents. I had an embarrassing interview and was commanded by St George to practise on his wife and then to 'Kiss the silly girl, damn you!'

Life in Blackburn was much easier than in Morecambe. I was no longer the A.S.M. but a fully fledged actor. I was not actually the juvenile lead but cast usually for the youngest in the play, which is often a very good part. We had a 'heavy' who smoked strong tobacco to make his voice rough and interesting, and a character actor of great age who drank enormous quantities of bitter beer during the show, which appeared not to affect his memory in any way. Then we had Paul Courtney, who had arrived a week or so after I did. He had been with the company before and was from a very old theatre family, supposed to go back to the Elizabethans. Mrs Frere had a great affection for him. He was still in his early twenties but had taken, it seemed, to the bad habit of drinking. He was trying to give it up, and apparently to prevent the reoccurrence of this dreadful habit Mrs Frere asked me to share digs with him. Perhaps she thought my sober habits would have a good effect on him and he would be touched by my pure outlook and way of life! He was tallish, with thinning hair, a very 'actory' face, long and lantern-jawed. He was a great light comedian, a real asset at the time when plays like *A Little Bit of Fluff* and *Up in Mabel's Room* were the rage. All these plays required a rather stupid juvenile, a sort of feeble Bertie Wooster plagiarism, and such parts are difficult to play without considerable experience. I was no good at all in this sort of thing, but Paul was superb; he did not seem to be able to do anything wrong, and the audience roared at everything he did or said. In these plays I took the straight feeding part while Paul had all the fat, and from him I learnt just how to do it. If you want to learn to be a comic it's best to learn first to feed.

Paul stayed sober under my angelic influence, and we became friends. Our popularity grew, with the result that we had nightly gifts handed up after the shows over the footlights, mostly from admiring young ladies. There were flowers, cigarettes, ties, etc., and on one night some well meaning female sent us each a little black-and-white puppy, each with a pink ribbon tied round its neck. These gifts caused great merriment in the audience and many sarcastic remarks from our fellow players. We must have looked mad, two young men walking back and forth to and from the theatre, each with a silly little puppy on a lead. But this was not all: neither puppy had been house-trained, and they made our rooms horrible. The result was that our landlady said she was sorry but either the puppies went or we went. Such an ultimatum could not be condoned. We went.

The next three weeks saw us in four different sets of digs. Things were getting desperate. We were fond of the pups but could not concentrate on our work with the worry of trying to keep the place clean, being awakened during the night and at the crack of dawn. When I dried in the first act of *French Leave*, and was taken severely to task by St George Frere for daring to do such an unprofessional thing, we decided sadly that we could not keep pets. One of the stage-hands found a home for them, and we parted sadly with our gifts.

Soon after this episode Paul brought home a bottle of beer, and I had a very small glass after supper. I had always been told by my father that beer was 'nasty stuff', his very words; I had never tasted any before, and I was nearly twenty years old. With all filial respect, my father was mistaken. Beer is not nasty, it is lovely. After drinking his beer, Paul told me that he was going to get married and, of all people, to Dorothy, our manager's daughter. I was horrified. I felt our friendship had been torn apart. Dorothy, with whom I had to play love-scenes every other week!

The news was received with great joy by the Freres and company. Paul was the apple of Mrs Frere's eye; she was delighted and called him 'Paul' during the show that night instead of his character's name. She was gaga with excitement, but I had a feeling of no longer belonging in the company. The prospect of playing opposite the future wife of my lost friend was intolerable, and I longed for fresh fields.

An advertisement appeared in *The Stage* that *Dracula* was going on tour. I had seen the play and was most impressed by it. I showed the advert to Paul, saying I'd like to go on tour, and asked him what to do.

He said, 'Write in.'

'What do you mean write in?' I asked.

'Write an answer to the advert, send a photo, tell your age and experience, and ask for five pounds a week.'

Five pounds! It seemed a fortune, but I did as he said and got the job. I was to rehearse in Hull in three weeks' time at the salary of £5 a week and play the part of Jonathan Harker, the juvenile lead. With trembling heart I knocked at the office door to tell the Freres of my imminent departure; I thought they would be horrified at my wish to leave their company, but there was not a word of complaint. They said, 'Very well, send in a written notice by Saturday. Jolly good luck, a tour will do you good.'

Teddy and Winnie told me to save my money and at the end of the tour go to London, then get into a London show, and I was made.

'Get out of rep,' said Teddy. 'It's only the fringe of the business. What you have to do is get into the charmed circle and you can only do that from London.'

Paul gave me a 'digs book' with all sorts of hieroglyphical marks against the various addresses, the meanings of which I learnt later (like the secret code tramps have for each other on gates), denoting the willingness of the landlady or her daughters to provide 'all home comforts'.

For my last show with the Freres they gave me the leading part in a most amazing play set in the South Seas, a sort of *White Cargo* with the title *The White Man's Way*. I was a British naval officer on duty in the South Seas, bewitched by a native girl whom the 'heavy' wants to sell as a slave. Her charms prove too much for him, but being 'white' and British he sacrifices his career, his all, for her. At the end of Act 2 when the fiendish 'heavy' character cries, 'But you can't! You can't! Remember she is a black girl', I, as this undaunted hero, well up stage centre, drawing myself up to my full five-feet-eight-inches (with the aid of elevators) and with an arm thrown protectively around the girl, bring down the curtain (in tones that had to be higher than his) with the heroic rejoinder:

'A black girl, you say. Yes, she is a black girl – ' The state of my uniform was showing proof of this. ' – but don't forget I am a white man!'

In the end the black girl turned out to be only sunburnt and was the long-lost daughter of the British Ambassador, who had been murdered and his daughter sold as a slave by 'natives'.

I packed up all my props, had a farewell party at the Freres', and then set off for Hull, where we were to rehearse *Dracula*. In the evening I presented my card at the theatre and was ushered into the best seats. I had already had new cards printed with 'Dracula Co.' engraved in Gothic type. The management who were sending out our tour were in possession of the theatre that week. This was a touring repertory company run by the actor Hamilton Deane. It was more or less the same as the Benson Company except that Deane's speciality was modern thrillers instead of Benson's Shakespeare and old comedy. There was a repertoire of six or seven plays, which the company toured and played in different towns each week, a different play every night: *The Bat, The Wolf, Frankenstein, Dracula, The Ware Case*, and *The Fake*.

Hamilton Deane, a tall typical actor, had run this company for years and was very popular. His dramatization of Bram Stoker's novel *Dracula* had been such a success in the repertoire that he had decided to send out a special tour of this play alone, and it was scheduled for a London engagement later in the year, about which a great deal of publicity had been given in the Sunday papers. In those days, 1930, the cinema had not yet encroached on the theatre's dominance of publicity, and there was still a whole theatre page in most Sunday papers, with only a small column about films. Hamilton Deane was to produce the play himself and perhaps come on tour for the first week to see it on its way.

The setting was explained, the tricks demonstrated, and we started rehearsing while Mr Deane refreshed himself with a glass of Guinness. The play starts with a discussion between the English doctor and myself (Harker). At the end of this scene there was a pause while Mr Deane and the leading lady went into a confab; then there was a message for me to go into the office. It appeared I was too young for the part of Harker, and they wanted me to switch to the part of the younger Lord Godalming. I was staggered; I had learnt the lines and it was just the sort of role I liked playing. They were right, however: I would have made the leading lady look silly with a child for a husband; but I was hurt none the less. I had no option but to give in. As compensation I was given the understudy of the lunatic, which afforded me no pleasure at all; I did not realize that it was the best and fattest part in the piece. It was a 'character part' and character parts had no interest for me whatever; I wanted only to be the great lover!

The play started in a blackout with just a glimmer of blue coming through the chink in the drawn curtains. There is a long pause and then a terrific howl from the lunatic asylum next door. Then the doctor enters and switches on the lights, looking absolutely terrified. During the first act, there were ninety-seven cues and effects, all provided by me or other members of the cast. All our tricks were in fact terribly simple, but the fuss of keeping them secret and the talk about the horror of the play all helped to build up the effect of hysteria.

The effects from the front when I saw the play, before I knew how they were done, thrilled me to the marrow. A door painted to look like a wall opened in a blackout and Dracula would disappear. Pictures crashed to the ground (we simply pulled out the nail from the back, and the picture fell on to a specially prepared pile of broken glass; the noise and suddenness were terrifying). A little magnesium ribbon attached to two electric terminals and covered with gunpowder would make a dreadful flash, blinding the audience for a second, and before they could see again, Dracula would vanish into the air. A kite-like bat, the spread wings and red eyes lit by a torch battery, looked highly realistic when flown from a fishing-rod across the stage from above. At one stroke Dracula would disappear from his coffin; he was in the coffin – not the actor playing the part of Dracula, but the prop-man in similar make-up – and the coffin, which was open, had two false doors hinged just above the recumbent figure. The doors had strings attached, and when Van Helsing plunges the spike into his heart the doors are pulled shut to cover the body. Previously fuller's earth was sprinkled all over these doors, making clouds fly up as they closed under a single green spot. Dracula disintegrates into dust – the effect is masterly. Mice always run uphill, I don't know why but they do. If a white mouse is placed on one's cuff it will run to the shoulder. People thought our white mice were specially trained, but they weren't. We had a lot of them, and they all did exactly the same on every occasion. I can reveal these tricks now as in a modern production such effects would probably be computerized, but I doubt if they would be more realistic.

The part of Count Dracula was played by W. E. Holloway. He had a white Alsation called Major, which came on tour with us. I got my father to have a dog-sheet made, like greyhounds wear: this in white with 'Dracula' embroidered in red. With Major the dog in attendance the male members of the cast used to go on a Sunday-evening pub crawl in each new town. The dog got a lot of attention and we got a lot of free beer. I started to drink. It happened because we had a wedding party one Sunday night. There was every sort of refreshment, and I am afraid I sampled the beer, the second glass I had ever had. I liked it just as much as the first, and that was the end of the beginning; my pure white aura became murky.

The bridegroom that evening was a cheery, fair-haired young man. To television viewers he later became the disgruntled Albert Tatlock of *Coronation Street*. Not only was he the S.M. but he played the lunatic-asylum keeper; he married the maid with whom he played the scene at the beginning of Act 2. Whenever I see *Coronation Street* I think of our rude behaviour at his wedding party that was my undoing. I remember looking at my reflection in the mirror over the mantelpiece, glass in hand and glassy-eyed, a drunkard! The rot set in quickly: drinking every night it seemed, and then at lunchtime too, falling in the streets, waking and looking at this dreadful face, bloated with alcohol and vowing never again, and never again, and again, and again.

With our long lazy days and with the glamour of the theatre to weaken ladies' resistance, our world was dominated by sex. It was our main preoccupation. The older members of the company all pretended to be great Lotharios, and not to have had a dose of V.D. was looked upon as proof of weakness. If one got a dose, the horrible treatment in those days only proved one's masculinity. The girls in the company were exempt. They were treated differently as a sort of neuter sex. It was the girls of the various towns we visited that were fair game. Even to carry the suitcase of an actress was supposed to be dangerous, and to go any further was called 'shitting on one's own doorstep'. This could lead to the 'thin end of the wedge', which could lead to some awful matrimonial entanglement, and matrimony was looked upon as the end of a stage career for the young actor or actress. The girls in the company accepted this all calmly, and did not take the men seriously; they were given more freedom than in any other walk of life at that time, I should imagine.

We were allowed to pursue the theatre cleaners. One actor-manager, complaining of the massive invasion of 'pansies' into the business, scorned the way the poor cleaners were left alone by the new breed. Then there were the landladies' daughters and, in many cases, the landladies themselves, who could be ever so obliging if approached in the proper manner – so I was told. I never knew this wonderful secret. We haunted dance-halls and cinemas, getting to know a host of youthful females throughout Britain. Being in the theatre gave us a certain glamour not enjoyed by the local young men. We always found some wonderful girl and then had to say goodbye; by the next week there would be another. Sometimes they got ideas, and sometimes they wrote letters and threatened to follow us, but hardly ever did. Usually when we returned to the town again it was all forgotten, and we never met again. I felt wonderfully romantic; I liked saying goodbye and putting my profession before my loves.

On went the tour through 1930. We nightly played the show, nightly drank too much, and roared our way round England. The play was a riotous success. We made a great thing of the horror, advertising the number of people who fainted each night. Much was made of the fact that at Aldershot a sergeant-major had to be carried out of the theatre in a dead faint when Van Helsing cuts his finger to frighten Dracula with the sight of blood. Then out of the blue, the notice went up. We would all be out of work in a fortnight.

I went to London as I had been advised and trudged round all the agents' offices, being told politely and firmly there was nothing for me. Things were beginning to slip in the theatre, and the new cinemas were taking over. At last, with a little of my savings left, I went home and called in at the old Morecambe Royalty on the way. I had already been offered work there when the tour came to an end, but had ruined my chance by asking too much. Now, slightly tamed by London, I was delighted to accept an offer to share leading parts for the remaining four weeks of the season with the new director, Eugene Wellesey. So after all the excitement of the tours and the big cities, here I was more or less back where I had started, but certainly not a beginner any longer, with a contract to 'share leads'. Of the plays we performed during this season I recall almost nothing; only one by Somerset Maugham, *The Land of Promise*, sticks in my memory – mainly, I suppose, because I had such a terrific part and had such a job to get it to stick in my memory! Eugene was an efficient director, but I think the company lacked the glamour of the old one.

There appeared in *The Stage* an advert for a juvenile capable of leads in the Edward Dunstan Shakespearean Company. I wrote in for the job. The reply came. A man was wanted to start in the autumn, playing leading parts, Othello or Iago, and the better juveniles such as Orlando and Orsino. Did I think I could do it? If so, would I come and see Mr Dunstan in his hotel at Haydock, near St Helens?

There is a great deal of caste in the English theatre. In the touring days, the theatres were more or less designated by numbers. The No. 1 dates, like Manchester Opera House and the King's Theatre, Edinburgh, were usually played by productions 'prior to London' as try-outs, or by the big touring productions like Fred Terry's *Sweet Nell of Old Drury* and *The Scarlet Pimpernel*, and Sir John Martin Harvey with plays like *The Only Way* and *The Breed of the Treshams*. Sir Frank Benson and Henry

Baynton supplied the Shakespeare tours to these theatres. Although the classical companies had to play some No. 2 dates – Leicester and Norwich, for example – they rarely went to the smaller venues like Burnley, Macclesfield, and Clitheroe. Edward Dunstan ran a company playing Shakespeare, old comedy, and old dramas; he more or less had the monopoly of these smaller dates, with the result that – although not rated so highly – the company did much more work and had much longer tours than the grander concerns.

Naturally, however, one lost caste in joining one of the lesser companies, and it was with some doubt in my mind that I travelled to Haydock to see Mr Dunstan. Was I being foolish? Would it be better to stay in rep till I got an offer to go to London, or should I dare all for my first love, Shakespeare?

No one could look less an actor than Edward Dunstan. He wore plus-fours, was bald, and had a large droopy nose and a stoop. He told me he did not want an actor for *Othello*, as he had found a very good Iago, but he did want an actor for Orlando since he felt he was getting too old for the part. I was secretly horrified. How on earth could this elderly man think of playing Orlando? We discussed the tours he had in mind and proceeded to the billiard room, where I had to recite. I did the 'In Belmont is a lady richly left' speech from *The Merchant of Venice*. He said I spoke it well but did not seem to have much idea of poetry. (I was trying my best to make it sound modern, as we in the reps rather scorned old-fashioned hamming.) So I did it again like I would have done it with the amateurs at home. The result was that I got the job to rehearse in two weeks' time near Liverpool at the Winter Gardens, Waterloo.

I felt I was sinking to the very bottom of the business, but I was to play Laertes, Bassanio, Tranio, Joseph Surface, and Charles Marlow. I was to have the inevitable £4 a week and no extras, and had to supply my own tights and some wigs. He would let me know the details and costs with my contract, which he would post. Rehearsals were unpaid. I was pleased to be in a company playing Shakespeare's plays; it may have been low down in the caste system, but I had all these wonderful parts. Dunstan and I had a drink together, and at the station I bought a Temple Shakespeare edition of *Hamlet*. I was just twenty-two.

A fortnight later, with my basket full of my 'wardrobe' and all sorts of odds and ends I had gathered during my wanderings, including a vest-pocket Kodak and a Post Office savings book, I set off on what was perhaps to be my most fateful journey. Paul had often told me that one day I would join a company and there would be the girl for me just waiting there as if by chance. I believed this implicitly. Somehow, behind all my romantic notions of world travel, glorious theatre success, and intoxicating words, there were always mixed-up ideals of some girl whom I would idolize as the personification of all the things I thought sacred. I arrived on Merseyside, ready to tackle the Works of Shakespeare and all the world, like Don Quixote tilting at windmills. I found digs somewhere – all digs seem to fade into the same indefinable combined room, with the same photos on the walls of the guests signed with affection and enormous writing; there was always the landlady, know as 'Ma', in the background, a good fire, good food, drink, and a friendly smile. No hotel has yet succeeded in making the wanderer welcome like 'Ma' did all over England in those mean little towns during the touring years, and all for a few shillings a week.

We were to meet in the Queen's Hotel. I was late, or perhaps the rest of the artists were early, smelling free beer; or perhaps they had been there since closing time, I do not know. There they all were, and a more motley crew I had never seen anywhere. I had seen all sorts of members of the music-hall and theatre world, but never anything like this lot. My heart sank. Had I really let myself be dragged down to the depths simply because of a romantic notion to play Shakespeare? They all seemed middle-aged. There was a small man who said he played Romeo; he seemed to have something the matter with his teeth and was at least forty. (Much older, as I found later!) There was a short fat man with no teeth; an old man with a great red face and yellow hair (he dyed it with iodine to play Lorenzo, he said); one or two small queers simpered at me, and I am told that afterwards I was pronounced 'Quite camp, but thinks we don't know, hiding behind his pipe!'

These people were the salt of the earth. It was just that I had not met their like before. They spent all their salaries in the pub and had to wear so much finery in the shows that they could not be bothered to dress up in real life; and as their whole life was spent amongst their patrons, the working classes, what did it matter? We had a very hearty evening, but the going was too fast and furious, and I drank, or had to drink, far above my capacity. My ideas of romance under the stars with Shakespeare's plays as a background were quickly fading. There was not a woman in sight. Perhaps there were none, and I had got myself into an all-male company, just like Shakespeare's own. Had the 'reptiles' been right after all? Were the actors in classical companies *all* queer?

But then they had told me of the leading lady, Gertrude Gilbert. They told me that she was getting on a bit and might not like me to look too young. I thought of the *Dracula* company again and getting demoted, but I was told that it had been decided that I should wear a beard for Bassanio. This was the most dreadful news I had ever heard: a beard for a juvenile! To me a beard denoted an ancient gentleman; a beaver! Beards were just not worn in those days. The safety-razor had overcome all beards everywhere, and to stick one on was unthinkable, even worse than being demoted to lesser parts. The next morning I appeared for rehearsal, trying to look as old and as experienced as possible. I donned my best flannels and sports jacket, a trilby hat, and a coloured scarf; with my cherry-wood pipe I imagined I looked like Evelyn Waugh in his younger portraits. I tried to appear stern to impress my fellow artists further and bolster my flagging ego. I hoped that the ruling about the beard would be forgotten when my manly appearance was seen in the sane light of day.

At rehearsal the company did not look so disreputable, and if anything was better dressed. After all, the night before had been a stag party, and today we were all getting ready for a new season and tour. The old man was wearing the most pointed shoes I had ever seen, and his ankles bulged out; his hair was blonder than ever in daylight. Romeo looked tatty, and I discovered that his teeth were repaired with home dentistry. There was a rather feeble-looking girl, plus the rest of those I had met the previous night, and a great Welshman with a singer's voice. Then in came what to me was an old lady in a ragged fur carrying a shopping-basket; she had grey hair with black ends – the dye was coming out. She said she had heard of me. Her sister had been the character lady in *The Joan Danvers* in my first production. I was told to beware of the old man, who hated me even before he saw me, as I was taking the place of his boy-friend who had left at the end of the last tour. What a crew, and all the lesser queers just slunk about in the background. There was another rough sort of chap who looked like a seaman. I learnt later that he had been.

Then it happened. She was dressed in a brown-and-white checked costume, a suit it would be called now, with a swinging skirt and the highest heels imaginable. She wore a small brown hat over chestnut curly hair, gloves, and a coffee-coloured blouse. She had a pointed chin and a round face, deep brown slanting eyes and a *retroussé* nose that made her look almost oriental, and an air of enormous vitality. She was clearly a favourite, as the whole atmosphere changed. She came into the theatre with great glee, as though she had come home, and almost sighed with relief to be back. I was introduced and could not believe how young she looked. I had got terribly mixed up. I thought she was the leading lady I had been told about; if she was, why all this bother about me wearing a beard? She must have been in her early twenties, and they had told me she was over fifty! Then we started to rehearse, and I realized my mistake. The lady with the basket and the dyed hair was Gertrude Gilbert, the leading lady. This one was playing Bianca, and her name was Laura Liddell.

I had had a lot of experience of rehearsals, but even I could not possibly imagine any sort of show coming out of this. Everyone knew their lines, but that was all. They did not bother even to speak the full text, just 'topped and tailed'. If I had not been new to the company I don't suppose they would have rehearsed at all. No one acted, they just mumbled. Mr Dunstan did not even dispense with his cigarette. Nevertheless I was pulled up on every line. I was apparently quite hopeless. I could not move; I could not speak verse; my voice was dreadful. I was wooden, and the sack seemed ready for me at any minute. (I had omitted to have my notice written out in my pocket ready, so that if anything went wrong at the first rehearsal I could save face and get it in first.)

Every so often the men all trooped off for a drink in the pub next door. I was asked, but dared not go. I stayed behind and tried to get my lines straight. We went on rehearsing all afternoon, with continual breaks while the pubs were open, and then they all draggled off home. This went on daily all week long. On the Monday following there was no dress rehearsal, but I had to put on my costume to show my ability to wear one. The result was anything but flattering to my ego. My make-up was wrong. All the actors I had known used Nos. 5 and 9. Not so the classical players; it had to be 5 and 15 – a great improvement, I must admit – and I never had a stick of No. 9 again. The whole make-up was heavier and would have been laughed to scorn in any of the reps as the covering of a poof; but with costume it did make the men look more romantic and Latin. There was something wrong with my hair, too short of course, and we did not wear wigs for plays in Elizabethan costume. However, I learnt a few things I did not know before: how to put pennies in tights to hold them up, how to drape a cloak, how to fix a belt and pouch, and how to hang a rosary and lace handkerchief out, just how much cuff to show. When the cast assembled in their costumes, I felt almost naked in mine, and these were the actors that I had thought so dowdy only a short week ago.

Laura and Megan, the two girls, were visions of delight: Laura as Bianca, in white, and Megan as the widow in black velvet. Then the handsomest man I had ever seen came on to the stage. It was Petruchio, over six feet tall, in a black-and-purple suit slashed with silver. He had high suede thigh-boots, spurred at the heel, a silken shirt thrown open at the neck, lovely black curly hair, a dashing moustache, flashing eyes, a scarlet-and-white ankle-length cloak, and an enormous hat with green and white feathers curling backwards in a great sweep. He wore a sword, a dagger, a purse, and frilled gloves. Never had I seen such a specimen. Underneath all this finery was Edward Dunstan – in real life hump-backed and no taller than me, and with over fifty years behind him. What a transformation! How on earth had he done it? Now I know, but in those days it seemed a miracle. Katherina appeared. She looked about twenty at the most, with flaming red hair, flashing eyes, and a figure that would attract anyone. This was the lady I had pitied so, with the grey-black hair and shopping-basket. In my ignorance I had thought I had lowered myself to join these people. What a fool I felt. When the show started I realized that all my experience to date was as nothing to what I was learning now. These were the real pros, real gods that I had fallen amongst at last.

I had never seen *The Taming of the Shrew*. We had attempted to act it in my amateur days, but the result was lukewarm. The main reason had been our trying to copy the Benson Company's production, which was not of the best of Benson's shows by any means, being a copy of the older *Petruchio and Catherine* as invented by Garrick, and played by one actor-manager after another during the years. Dunstan's production was as written by

Shakespeare, a homely comedy, played by a company of strolling players in a house in the country. This is great fun all the way through and much easier than trying to make the play as sophisticated as *Much Ado about Nothing*, when there is nothing in the way of material to support such an idea. The result was electric. There was such verve in the acting and such gusto that hysteria broke out in the audience. What wonderful theatre this was, and I was part of it.

Unknowingly, I had arrived where I wanted to be, and I stayed with the company for three years. I learnt how to grow even taller. Boots are much better and easier to elevate than modern shoes. I learnt to have a more romantic outlook, how to wear all sorts of clothes, so many tricks that today seem almost forgotten. We visited mostly working-class towns, the 'No. 2s', and occasionally we went to halls, the 'fit-ups'. There were over one hundred plays in the company's repertoire, and during my time we must have played most of them. We performed all the better-known Shakespeare plays. I was Edgar in *King Lear* – 'Poor Tom' – my first appearance as a 'streaker'; and in the lesser known *Henry VIII* I was Buckingham. There were famous dramas like *The Wandering Jew* and *A Tale of Two Cities*, and wonderful plays like *Caste* and *David Garrick*, and *Still Waters Run Deep*, and *Arrah Na Pogue* – plus, of course, traditional comedies such as *The Rivals*, *She Stoops to Conquer*, and *The School for Scandal*. By now I had played nearly all the second parts, and it is safe to say that this was my college and workshop combined.

The Edward Dunstan Company had never been heard of by most theatre-going people of London and the other cities, and yet the settings were more modern than some used even today. Dunstan was the best actor I have ever seen anywhere. He could and did play any part in any play so well that one would think he could not possibly ever play anything else. Whatever role he took, he looked exactly right. He did not use much make-up and could make up for any part in three or four minutes; he said it was not the make-up but the mind that made the character. Your make-up suggested your appearance, that was all. If you were a cripple you had to feel like a cripple before you tried to look like one. On Edward Dunstan, Richard's crooked back grew, and Falstaff's fat oozed through his padding.

At first it was dreadful drudgery. Being the newest member of the cast, I was often the only one with a part to learn. One dreadful week I went on for Charles Marlow in *She Stoops to Conquer*, Caesar in *Antony and Cleopatra*, and King Henry II in Tennyson's *Becket*. It became easier after a time, but the first performances were awful. The lovely Laura was there to help and encourage my efforts, however.

All my life people have asked me when am I going to settle down – meaning, I suppose, when am I going to stop wandering round the world and start being a respectable citizen with a house, an insurance policy, and all the other things of possession and importance that this fear-struck world seems to think necessary. I evade the question. It would be no use answering truthfully, as in most cases my questioner would not understand and would no doubt think I was being airy-fairy, or mad, or both. The truth is, I have 'settled down'. It happened when I was twenty, and I have been fully settled ever since. That was when I found all in the world I could possibly want, in just being an actor and being privileged to play in the greatest plays that have ever been written.

I don't know whether my fellow artists felt like this. I have suspicions that most of them did not. Those born into the business took it for granted, and those who had drifted in through some quirk of fate would never feel as I did. I found this out later when I ran companies in India, where many of my actors had never seen a stage or a real theatre and simply looked upon being an actor as a stepping-stone to going into films or a fill-in till some proper job turned up. But I felt differently, and I think Laura did too. Perhaps that is why I found her so attractive.

Never had I seen a more lovely woman, or a more interesting actress. Laura was incredibly individual and made every part she played intriguing, but she did everything in such an unorthodox way that I sometimes had my doubts. She pleased the public wherever she played. I thought her as a person absolutely delicious, and I did two very foolhardy things that were in defiance of the old actors' warnings. I carried her bag; and I allowed her to sew a button on my jacket without taking it off. I was terribly superstitious. I knew nothing could break the latter's spell, and I don't think anything will. There was little thought of matrimony: as far as I was concerned I wanted to be with her, and that is all.

For the company the atmosphere cooled and there was a feeling of difficulty and tension. Instead of touring we had to stay longer and longer in each place, and the time came when the management had problems continuing with the heavy overheads. Then one sad day we just had to finish. It was not the end of the company, we were told, just a recess; but it was a very long one, and the company never revived again in its former glory. To keep together there was nothing else for Laura and me but to marry, and marry we did, at Gretna Green, on a lovely, sunny day in the spring of 1933.

Although we were almost twenty before we knew of each other's existence, our lives had been strangely close. We were born about thirty miles from each other, Laura in Furness and me in the Lakes. We had been to school even nearer: I in Kendal and Laura in Arnside, just twelve miles apart. She had once even been in Kendal, when taken to the isolation hospital there with scarlet fever. She had been a favourite with the matron when convalescing and danced for the doctors – one of whom could well have been our own family doctor, for all anyone knew. Laura had been taught elocution, as it was then termed, by Margaret Steen, and painting by Mortram Moorhouse, who had both been connected with the pageant I had been involved in. Laura had started with the Baynton Company as a student when I was sweating it out as a beginner with the Morecambe Players, and she was just about as besotted with the theatre as I was, though her appreciation was on a higher literary plane. Everything theatrical to me was heaven, but Laura was a little more discerning.

It was natural, then, that we should have been drawn together in the romantic surroundings of a touring company. Laura, as I said, played all her parts in a very different manner to anyone else. I was never sure whether it was right or not; she was unique in every role and never did what was expected. This is, I suppose, why she has always been so fascinating as an actress, and possibly a perfect foil for me, who just goes blundering ahead.

From close beginnings, we had met at the age of twenty and just stayed on the same line. For better or worse – a funny sort of better – no other would have worked.

4
An Actor-Manager's Life

Laura and I did not realize it when we married, but the Depression had just begun and was affecting every form of business. The theatre is always the first to suffer in periods of hardship; to make matters worse, the talking cinema was sweeping the world. Theatres were closing down all over the place, and out-of-work actors and musicians were all over the place, too.

Something drastic had to be done. Our being married made it all the more difficult to get work, as managements were frightened of 'joints', as they called married couples. They cannot be blamed; for a married couple working in a company can ruin the whole *esprit de corps* – plus, of course, the possibility of pregnancy. The only places where 'joints' were welcomed were the fit-ups, the minor provincial tours, where the manager was delighted to get two people on a joint salary, which meant two for almost the price of one. So what to do? If I took a job by myself, there would not be enough money to keep two and dress as one is expected to do, and if we both took jobs in different companies there was not much point in being married. We made a decision. We wanted to be in a company like the one in which we had met; and if one was not in existence there was only one thing to do: form one.

On a little money borrowed from both our parents, in the depth of the world recession, when films were booming and the theatre was failing, we had the temerity and downright lack of common sense to do the very thing we should by all standards not have done – go into management. With the great sum of £200 as capital we set out to found a company where everyone would be happy.

That is how we used to talk about it and what I really thought we were doing. I wonder at my courage – I had never produced a play in my life and had little idea of what I wanted to do with the shows. In fact, I was terribly ignorant of the theatre as a whole. I had learnt the craft of an actor, and I knew something of the technical side of the stage, but nothing whatever of the business angle. I had never wanted to be a boss or a manager and order people about. All I really wanted was to recreate the wonder of my life in the days of the Dunstan Company. Of literature about the world theatre I knew absolutely nothing, and precious little of contemporary writings and plays, except those I had played in. Ibsen and Strindberg were closed books to me. I did not even hanker after playing the great classical roles. I was quite happy with my old run of juveniles and, even after making up our minds to start on our own, if I had had a decent offer I would have thrown up the whole idea, of which I was desperately frightened. In spite of having had what may appear to be years of experience I was just turned twenty-three.

We registered as managers of the Bragg-Liddell Company and advertised for a cast. By the next post I had over five hundred letters from all over the place. Every actor I knew wanted a job, as well as hundreds I had never heard of. So far we had not booked a single date; all we had was a crowd of actors wanting work, and £200. Amongst these aspirants there was one who had been acting manager for the Baynton Company. Laura had started with this company and I had helped them out in a Christmas show a few years before. The letter suggested that we might want to buy some cheap scenery, and there was a lot of stuff from the Baynton Company lying at a railway station in London that could be had for the price of a bill owing to the railway company. (Shouldn't this have been a warning?) I made enquiries and found that they wanted £15. It seemed an amazing bargain. There were great clothes, swords, banners, props of all sorts in wonderful condition. I bought the lot for £15, little knowing I had purchased a white elephant. Granted, they were cheap; but they had to be moved, not only moved but sorted, and I had nowhere to put them and knew nothing of the cost of such things. So I engaged the actor who had told me about them, as he knew such mysteries, and found that I had saddled myself with a running debt that seemingly had no end. The stuff was all removed to Pickford's store, and I was in business. We acquired a further lot of old costumes and set to work to revitalize them and make a wardrobe for the plays. Those we made to our own simple designs were better, I think, but the ready-made things we had purchased did give us a very good base. Without them we would never have got started at all.

We still had no opening date although I had by now contacted the artists I wanted. I must have been either terribly conceited or potty. How on earth could I expect to get dates when all the big companies could not? I was determined, however, and as I could not get real theatres I embarked on organizing a tour of the north of England and Scotland in town halls, and the like. Having arranged this to start after Christmas, a real theatre was offered to us for three weeks: the Connaught, Worthing, for the three worst weeks in the year, just prior to Christmas. I knew it was hopeless, and I knew it was silly to go all the way to Worthing, before a tour of Scotland, but we took it.

To make things even more difficult and complicated, I was going to produce a mixed repertoire, classical plays and modern. For the opening three weeks we were to put on six plays: *Romeo and Juliet*, *Othello*, *The Merchant of Venice*, *Macbeth*, *She Stoops to Conquer*, and *Michael and Mary* by A. A. Milne. All our scenery and costumes were more or less ready. We had a wardrobe-mistress called Clarise. Laura had known her in the Baynton Company. She was wonderful and could make anything. To look after the scenery we had a carpenter who looked like Henry Irving and must have been about the same age. He had long white hair, wore a great black hat, and called me 'Guv'nor', which embarrassed me terribly and made me feel like an overgrown schoolboy. He had years of experience and knew the ropes enough to ask for his fare in advance. It shows my absolute innocence. I did not know that one could go to the railway station and ask the station-master to wire authority for an un-moneyed actor to travel from his home town to where he was wanted.

Not only was he an experienced theatre carpenter. He could also act. He had played many parts with the Alexander Marsh Company, one of them the Apothecary in *Romeo and Juliet*, so I gave him this part. He arrived for rehearsal without a script. He knew his lines, he said, he had played it very often:

> *Put this in any liquid thing you like,*
> *And swaller it . . .*
> *And if you have the strength of twenty men*
> *It will [pause] polish yer orf.*

We started rehearsing. I had previously rehearsed my part as director, a part of which I was more terrified than of a first night. It worked out quite well, and the artists were all so eager to please that we got through, and all the performances appeared as scheduled, one after another. Business was exactly as one would have expected – lousy – and got steadily worse as Christmas approached. We managed to cover all expenses, however, although there was not much over for the tour I had planned after Christmas, which was to take us as far as the north of Scotland. This was even more chancy than the season in Worthing. I was obviously crazy.

On the final train call back to London, our manager came with a bill that he had overlooked. He wanted more money. All I had was Laura's and my salary. I gave it to him, and we arrived in London with only a few shillings between us. It was the day before Christmas Eve, a Sunday, so we had to stay in London till the banks opened on the day after Boxing Day. Our usual hotel was full, so I checked into one that looked nice, near Euston Station. We had lunch in the hotel, and on leaving the dining room I saw a notice to the effect that over the Christmas holiday the hotel was not serving meals. The one we had just had was the last they were serving till Wednesday morning; it was still Sunday. This was terrible. I went to the management and told my story, but to no avail. They suspected we were not going to pay anyway. I used up my last few coppers in seeking out friends, but not a single one could I find. I tried to pawn my watch and typewriter; even the pawn-shops were closed. However, England's newest and youngest actor-managers, in London at Christmas time, starving amid plenty, survived. On the Wednesday we had the earliest and biggest breakfast the hotel could give. I walked to the Strand to cash a cheque, and we took the earliest possible train northward, to colder but more hospitable climes.

The tour list sounded like the stage directions in *Macbeth*. We toured for about two months all over the place, playing mostly in town halls. Business was not too bad, and at last we came to Stirling, to a real theatre, with a real stage, complete with flies. I was enjoying setting up and making everything look as nice as possible there after making do in all sorts of dreary parochial halls. But my ardour was dampened when the local stage-manager-cum-caretaker informed me that the local name for the theatre was the Actors' Grave! This was the last week of the tour. On the Saturday we paid everyone off and again went back home.

Later that year we started again, touring all over the country: King's Lynn to Arbroath, South Wales to Bishop Auckland, Ilfracombe to Ilkley. Many of the actors we had known in the Shakespeare companies and the reps joined us from time to time. Then came another shock; we were to be parents: a possibility that, as far as I was concerned, had seemed more remote than getting married. Our tour was going well. We were doing short seasons of two or three weeks and seemed to be forever putting on new plays. Laura continued acting, time passed, and the advent of a baby must have been obvious to all our audience, though never a word was said about it till my mother and father came to see a performance in New Brighton. My mother was absolutely adamant that Laura did not appear again till after the event. We took her advice and carried on, with the main roles being shared by all the girls. In the meantime Laura looked after the wardrobe and prop departments. She was in the theatre till the very night Jennifer was born, on 28 February 1934.

We were in Southport and had lovely digs with a grand 'Ma', who was not a bit put out to have a very pregnant lodger. She did not turn a hair when we said we would like the baby to be born in her house. It was all very simple. We came home from the show, had supper, and I was sent out to get the midwife. I wandered all over Southport to find her practising her art in some remote part of the town. But she promised to come, which she did, walking through the night, a little old woman carrying her bag. Jennifer was born early in the morning. It seemed extraordinary that this lovely bubble-blowing thing was alive, and had not been there yesterday.

We had been playing *Trilby*. Why we did not call her Trilby I cannot imagine. She grew up to be tall and fair, and the name would have suited her admirably. I think the name Jennifer was my mother's idea; she had been reading the Herries series by Hugh

Walpole. Some of the company came to see the new phenomenon. We had no cradle, so she was bedded down in a clothes basket. At our digs we had put her in the garden in the bottom drawer of our chest of drawers. Within ten days Laura was up again and started acting immediately, just as though nothing had happened, except that we had to arrange rehearsals to cope with feeds. We were lucky enough not to be able to afford feeding bottles. We just left it to nature. Mother and child did splendidly.

Strangely enough, those early days in theatrical dressing rooms came to the surface of Jennifer's mind during her last serious illness in hospital, and she began to write about her childhood on a foolscap pad. I would like to let some of her memories speak for themselves. Here is part of what she wrote:

On my birth certificate my father was described as an actor of no fixed abode! I always found this romantic and something to be intensely proud of . . . my first memories are of the smell of the theatre, grease-paint, dust, the perspiration of terrified actors. But strongest of all is the recollection of the smell of 'wet white', the liquid make-up used by classical actresses to whiten hands and shoulders, made out of glycerine and rosewater and zinc oxide. The smell, even now, whenever I catch a whiff of it, means security, comfort, happiness, in fact 'mother'. I was breastfed in so many period costumes and make-ups that one wonders what strange effects this must have on any baby, but I remember only a total feeling of security — as long as the smell of 'wet white' lurked!

Jennifer remembered, too, the endless digs:

of being taught how to venture into the usually dark and nether regions of the house and ask politely for the salt or some more butter. I had some wonderful landladies, sometimes they would volunteer to take care of me during the show instead of hiring 'a girl'. There were sometimes other children to play with. I remember in one place there was a son, called Joseph, whom I loathed. His father was a carpenter, and the house and garden were littered with rather finely made pieces. After some particularly bitter quarrel, I went into the garden and carved 'Jo is a bugu' on the top of one of his most prized sideboards. I can't

Myself, aged eighteen – I was leading juvenile in our amateur company in Kendal, but still to brave the professional stage

Laura, aged twenty, in the days before we met. She was a young actress with the Henry Baynton Company

The casket scene in *The Merchant of Venice* with the Edward Dunstan
Company in 1931 at the Theatre Royal, Barrow-in-Furness. Laura is on
the left. Myself and Gertrude Gilbert, Dunstan's leading lady, are centre
stage

At my parents' home in Kendal, Cumbria, 1939. I had by this time
taken the name of 'Kendal' from my home town. Standing: my brother,
Philip, my father and myself. Seated: my mother, Jennifer and Laura

ENSA 1944. Our company at Green's Hotel, Bombay, Indian headquarters of ENSA. From here we toured *Gaslight* throughout the subcontinent. Laura and myself are on the right

Our ENSA production of Goldsmith's *She Stoops to Conquer*, which toured Britain successfully for a year. Cartoon by Wilf Thwaites of the *News of the World*, after seeing us play at Lark Hill, Salisbury Plain in 1944

On the move – Felicity, aged one, with Laura and Shakespeareana wardrobe, at Naina Tal during the 1947 tour. She took to her nomadic existence perfectly naturally, and there were never any problems.

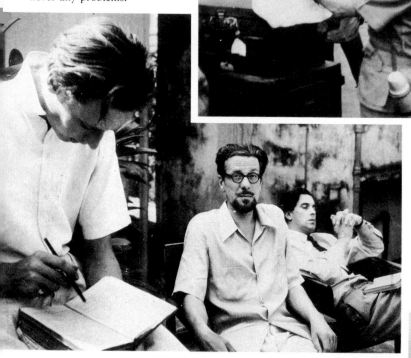

Felicity, aged twelve, in her first major role, as Puck in *A Midsummer Night's Dream* – wearing the costume which was formerly Laura's. Laura first played Puck with the Edward Dunstan Company, aged twenty

Jennifer, aged sixteen, as Viola in pageboy disguise in *Twelfth Night*. She played the part with great intelligence and depth – never just as a comedy

Opposite, centre: Directing a rehearsal on the roof of the Fairlawn Hotel in Calcutta in 1954. We were staying there, and the flat roof was a good rehearsal space. John Day is reading his part to me, and Conor Farrington waits his turn

Opposite: The Shakespeareana Company leaving Karachi, 1954. Camels were one of our more unusual forms of transport. Note the spelling of our company's name – someone was trying unsuccessfully to fit it on one side of the trunk!

My favourite audience – Indian schoolgirls riveted by Shakespeare. They always got thoroughly involved in the play. The play most Indian audiences liked best was *The Merchant of Venice* – the casket scene was very popular

An audience in Delhi during our 1953 Shakespeareana tour. Lady Mountbatten is front centre. A waiter at the back of the hall is delivering interval tea

Our Shakespeareana Company in 1953: Back row: Uptal Dutt, Conor Farrington, myself, Anwar Mirza, John Day. Front row: Frank Wheatley, Nancy Neal, Felicity, Laura, Jennifer, Wendy Beavis, Brian Kellet. Uptal Dutt became well known as an actor in Bengali films – he was in *Shakespeare Wallah* and has worked with Satyajit Ray. Brian still tours in a one-man show

Laura and myself in the play *David Garrick* in the garden of Laura's parents in Barrow-in-Furness, around 1935. The play was a popular comedy of the time

Shakespeareana Tour, June 1953 to December 1956. The map shows places visited

remember how I was punished – but I know my father seemed more depressed about the spelling!

Indeed, it was surprising she spelt as well as she did, considering the amount of times she changed schools. We were constantly touring, and the only fixed point, really, for her was the home of Laura's parents in Barrow-in-Furness, and to a lesser extent the Bragg home near Kendal. She was for many years the only grandchild of the Liddells, and was spoilt accordingly. The Liddells consisted of Laura's parents, known to Jennifer as Pop and Grandma; Laura's brother, John; and Beula, her younger sister who, being eleven years Laura's junior, was more like an older sister than an aunt to Jennifer. Laura's mother ran a small confectioner's store with a bakehouse attached. Her father had been an engineer at Vickers until he retired, and he ran the house, looking after the large rambling garden, the orchard, and the hens and ducks. Jennifer loved being with them more than anywhere.

Now I hit upon what could well have been my maddest notion. I would run an open-air tour round the holiday resorts and parks of Britain. The open-air tour really started without any plans on our part. A concert-party manager living in Morecambe had shows scattered about the northern seaside resorts, one being at Colwyn Bay. He came to the Royalty Theatre in Morecambe and asked the manager if he could help him to put on what he called a 'pastorial play'. The theatre-manager suggested that I was the chap to do it, and I was given a contract by the Colwyn Bay Corporation to put on *A Midsummer Night's Dream* in Eirias Park for one day, on the occasion of the granting of a charter to the town. For this they would pay £70, which was not enough to create a company for one day's work. I hit upon the idea of getting a cast for the lovers and Oberon, Titania, and Puck, and recruiting the fairies and the rustics locally. Eirias Park was lovely, and I found the most lyrical setting, a dale facing the audience with the trees on the hillocks either side, and away in the distance the shimmering sea.

We went to Colwyn for a couple of days to start rehearsing the comics and fairies and then let them carry on themselves till the company arrived a month later. We had more fairies than we would have had in a theatre. We borrowed horses and hounds for the hunt scene, and altogether the show was grand. We started a tradition in our family of putting the youngest on as the changeling child. The first was Jennifer, carried on in a flower-garlanded sort of *dhooly*. We ignored sex in these things: Jennifer's first part was this one, as a boy; so was Felicity's. Felicity's son, Charlie, first appeared as Felicity's daughter when she was playing Princess Vicky in the Edward VII series on the television.

The day turned out to be one of England's summers, and our hybrid company worked very well. There were thousands at the show; it was free, a Roman holiday. It must have been the biggest audience we ever played to, until we went to India years later. I played Bottom. I was not very good, too apt to copy others in those days, trying to be funny. This just does not work, and it was years before I got the hang of it and left it to Shakespeare to get the laughs. Laura was Puck, in which she was always superb. The costume was a complete disguise, and she wore the same one for years; green tights and skin-tight top decorated with a few leaves in autumnal colours. She had a green wig standing up like the punk hairdos of today, and a green face and hands. We still have the costume. Felicity later played Puck in it, looking exactly like Laura. But the costume was no disguise as far as Jennifer was concerned, causing her to utter her first line on any stage. When she was carried on, shoulder-high in her carriage covered with flowers, she saw Laura as Puck up a tree, watching the scene. The audience gave a great gasp at the sight of the child, and a round of applause, which Jennifer ignored. She just held up both chubby arms to Puck and said, 'Mummy!'

It was altogether such fun to play in the open air to huge crowds on holiday, that I went ahead writing to all the resorts around the coast, for permission to put on plays. The idea was quite good, if one could have afforded the hazard of inauspicious weather. Something I seemed to have forgotten was that it rains in England a lot. 'No play – no pay' was all we could hope for. And it did rain, everywhere it rained. All our curtains were ruined. Our clothes got damper and damper. On the fine days it was lovely, but on the wet days, a washout. Shakespeareana's open-air tour – half-salary and double pneumonia!

This went on, it seemed, for ever, until after our autumn tour. We did not reopen in the spring, as we were offered a tour with Sir Philip Ben Greet in old comedy with Lady Tree as Mrs Malaprop and Laura as Lady Teazle. This took us all over the south coast, and after it was over we went on tour again with Sir Philip, in *As*

You Like It, Twelfth Night, and *The Merchant of Venice.* It was during this tour that for the first time in my life we played in a school to a student audience. Sir Philip, a contemporary of Sir Frank Benson, was very well known to all the great schools of Britain. He would book a show somewhere and then proceed to get a cast. He seemed to know everyone; he would ring up and, if anyone was available who knew any part, just fit them in. Consequently his productions had a different cast for nearly every performance. There were no settings; we just played in a school hall in daylight with Elizabethan costumes, whatever the play. I thought this terrible in those days and it was a long time before I realized that Ben Greet was much nearer the mark than all the other attempts at staging Shakespeare's works. He left the text alone and produced the rarely performed first Folio *Hamlet.* He was a very handsome man, always dressed in black with a Fedora hat, and looked like a retired admiral.

The Ben Greet tours were of short duration. Not long afterwards, while I was back at the Morecambe Repertory Theatre, I had a wire from H. V. Neilson, asking me to play in Brighton. Neilson was a Victorian. My first impression of him was of a kindly medieval gargoyle, caused by this enormous man being doubled up with arthritis or lumbago, or a combination of similar misfortunes. Neilson was big; big hands, big head, big in every way, big eater, big drinker. In his youth he had been a great athlete. The story goes that he and Sir Frank Benson used to swim across the Avon to rehearsals at the early memorial seasons at Stratford. He had been beautiful in those days. Even when I knew him, when he was amused his face became boyish. He had been a manager so many years that he had put on the veneer of power and cantankerousness that had become a habit. He had a great ear for the 'word' and a great disdain for staging and costuming, all of which he left to his highly inefficient (in most cases) staff and subordinates.

Neilson used to sit all hunched up in his chair at rehearsals, glaring around as if intent on fending off evil spirits, muttering the lines and growling at all and sundry. He had a few pet phrases: 'Think before you speak'; 'See what I mean'; 'Purple patches of Shakespeare'; 'Lie down and caress it'; 'Kiss her eyes, man' or 'Have you ever kissed a woman's eyes?' Whenever he deigned to show any artists how to say a speech he invariably forgot the lines and went on, 'and so and so and so and so and so and so'. One got the impression that his sole idea was mentally to chastise actors, and the two weeks' rehearsal grew into two weeks of misery, instead of the romantic grandeur of rehearsing with the Dunstan Company. I seemed to be his greatest enemy, and he picked on me from the word go. He adored Laura. She could do no wrong, which I suppose annoyed me just as much. It is difficult having a wife employed in the same company, and I seemed to be perpetually annoyed with one thing or another.

I did not like being with the company. There were too many weeks out to be really set in the work, and the productions were very tatty: dirty old unpainted scenery and clothes, and hired costumes of the most uninspiring design. I had become discriminating in these things. If there must be painted scenery, it should be clean, and costumes must be designed with one idea behind the whole thing, otherwise it is just a jumble, like a rag shop. But the plays were still wonderful, what was left of them. They were all old-fashioned acting versions, as they had been chopped about by the actor-managers through the ages. It was a pretty bad company really, and badly directed productions, but we went to all the big theatres. The excitement of the trouper's life was still there, with all its gaiety and misery and shortage of money tomorrow, when the dole was only 15s. a week.

We stayed about a year with Neilson. For the last tour, *Romeo and Juliet* came into the repertoire, and we were to play the two leading parts. By this time I had taken the name 'Kendal' – Bragg was not thought sufficiently theatrical. Laura had played Juliet many times, but I had only played Paris or Mercutio and like most young actors I longed to have a go at Romeo. As Mercutio with the Dunstan Company I had always gone round to the front to watch the rest of the play after Mercutio dies half-way through, and I was always thrilled. Teddy Dunstan was then fifty-four, but as Romeo he looked maybe twenty-two or -three. His production had a lovely setting, just a grey arch over an open window, with all the dawn light glowing and the room in cool darkness. At the end, in the tomb, Romeo has some wonderful things to say, all in such a musical beat, rather like the *Othello* music. Now I was to have a go, and for the first time I had my own costumes to my own simple design, made by my mother from old cushion-covers lined with flour-bags. There were two: one blue and gold, the other light blue and white; very simple, sleeveless tunics, worn over ballet shirts. I had these two costumes for years and never wore anything else all the time I played Romeo.

The tour came to an end. All the classical companies seemed to be dying. Once again, and at the worst possible time in this century, I started as a manager. This was the worst tour we ever did, mostly in halls that anyone could hire if they wanted to. It was doomed from the start and could not possibly have paid for itself. I knew this, but always hung on, sensing that one day all would be well and feeling that it was wrong to give in. From all quarters there was depressing news, however. Films were holding sway everywhere. Actors were unimportant in everyone's eyes, and we seemed to be surrounded by people who thought the Works of Shakespeare the most uninteresting of subjects. Added to that, many of our potential audience were unemployed and in no position to pay for seats. Then out of the blue I had a letter from someone who wanted to start a school tour in Scotland, and he had £100 to spend on some costumes. Had I any to spare? I wired back, 'Yes, please.' We got rid of all our heavy stuff, thrones, and all the wardrobe, except for a few things we particularly liked. The company had to be disbanded, and we went off again on a very pleasant tour with Ben Greet, short as usual; then once more to work in a rep in Bedford. And there we were, in Bedford, on that fatal day in 1939 when we were told that Britain was once more at war with Germany.

Amongst the announcements broadcast that morning was the notice of the closure of all places of entertainment. Everyone thought they had to obey and did without question – all except the Little Windmill Theatre in Piccadilly, which kept on with London's first strip-shows, and no one seemed to mind. Apparently it is necessary in wartime for lovely ladies to take off their clothes to relieve the soldiers, who are sex-starved and must be entertained to keep up their morale! But as the entrance-fee to the Windmill was £1 per seat and the soldiers were paid 14s. a week, the audience of the Windmill was composed of males not as yet conscripted to the fighting forces. Our theatre, like all the rest, was closed. We had been rehearsing *Escape Me Never* all the previous week for production on the following Monday, and strangely enough I did not know my part properly; it seemed impossible to learn lines with all this excitement and strife in the air. I could have gone on if the show had gone on, but as things turned out I had some sort of premonition that it would not. All that was left was to pack up one's props and go, but go where? There was no future; nothing could be foretold or even imagined. Suddenly the frailty of life was apparent to everyone. It was a different world, and was to prove dark and dirty. Not for another twenty-eight years were we to see England smile again – not until the youth of the sixties made London swing.

The great Evacuation began, as hordes of schoolchildren spread across the country by train from London and the South, all with labels tied to their coats, led by voluntary workers, each group following a flag. We had sent Jennifer to Laura's parents at Barrow-in-Furness, as the North was supposed to be a safer part of Britain, but Barrow was a major shipbuilding dockyard and became an early target. The Liddells planned to build an air-raid shelter in the orchard, but the bombing began early; they had no sooner decided on the site than a bomb fell on the exact spot, leaving a vast crater. The next morning, Jennifer tried to go to school but found part of the road wrecked, and a crescent of council houses had simply ceased to exist. She spent the rest of the day helping her grandfather board up the windows – all the glass had been broken – only to have the boards blown out again the next day.

In London the theatres had been allowed to reopen after the first few weeks of the war, but actors, along with everyone else, were called up. Most of the companies could not start until they had organized new casts, and most theatre-managements seemed to think that in wartime the public would not want to see plays. Many of them switched to musical shows, featuring numbers from the Great War of twenty years previously: 'Tipperary', 'Roses are Blooming in Picardy', 'Keep the Home Fires Burning', and the like. I was thirty, which meant that I would be called up fairly soon. It would have been foolish to start our own company again, and there was nothing for it but another round of the reps that were still functioning. We went to Lowestoft, Lancaster, and Oldham. It was from there that I eventually became part of the War Game.

5

East with ENSA

Actors were getting scarce. The call-up relentlessly clawed its way upwards: first only those aged eighteen, and then older and older till thirty-year-olds like me. A great poster was in every post office, with instructions to all of a certain age to report to the local labour exchange on a certain day at a certain time. After joining up, as if for the dole, one was given a card and later called for a medical; after that, sometimes very quickly and sometimes after a delay, papers were sent with instructions to report at an Army camp or Naval or Air Force establishment, with a travel warrant and 4s. – the first day's pay.

This grey military world did not appeal to me at all. I could not imagine what use I was going to be as a soldier. It was possible to prolong the whole business by registering at the labour exchange as one who conscientiously objects to wars. Well, anyone who does not conscientiously object to war must be a self-confessed sinner, but it was not so simple in this case. One could not help feeling that one was involved somehow in a battle against Evil.

I volunteered as an engineer for the Merchant Navy and was taken on and put to work immediately, 'standing by' in Liverpool to await a ship. I got myself a natty uniform and applied my mind to learning something about the inside of a ship. The strange thing was, I liked it. I liked the company, I liked the smells of the engine room and of the ship, and the sight of the towering masts seen from below through the engine-room fanlight. I have never lost this love for ships and the sea. I had sailed only to Ireland and always been sick and miserable, but here, as a stand-by engineer, the seas were calm, and wartime Liverpool was an exciting city. I used to take my fellow engineers into the theatres on my card. I even had my photo taken by Jerome's, and looked so salty, like an Elizabethan sea-dog, that the photo was used by them for years as an advert in their shops all over England.

Then I went to sea. There were a few escapades and a collision, and one ship I was aboard was dive-bombed. While waiting in Liverpool for another I learnt that ENSA was looking for actors. The Entertainment National Service Association supplied entertainment to troops, and had begun at the time of the first National Service call-up, as one of the warlike preparations, but had never been taken very seriously. But now with this 'phoney war' more and more shows were wanted as more men were called up and just waited. Most of the men and women that could do this work were already in the forces and there were not enough entertainers. The authorities came to realize that there were a lot of actors wasting their time pretending to be soldiers, who would be of more use to ENSA than to the Army. So it was decided that anyone already in the services could be seconded to ENSA, with the approval of the Ministry of Labour and their commanding officer, provided they were not doing something important and were over thirty years old. I immediately applied and by return had a travel warrant to London to see Henry Oscar, then in charge of drama at Drury Lane. Laura and I were offered *Gaslight* to tour in the UK, at a joint salary of £18. 2s. a week, to rehearse almost at once. *Gaslight* is a Victorian psychological thriller by Patrick Hamilton. It has a cast of only five artists and is a wonderful play, with superb parts for Laura and myself. Laura never liked it, though she must have played her role more often than any other actress. It was all fixed up within the hour with permission from the Ministry to go ahead for a period of three months. I had not even to return to Liverpool. All I had to do was go and collect Laura, put away my uniform, and rehearse in London on Monday next.

London in wartime was wonderful, the absence of traffic being its most striking feature. The buildings and the shape of the streets are lovely if one only has the time to look, and if the vistas are not cluttered up with vehicles and people. We rehearsed daily at Drury Lane Theatre. We knew the play, so relearning the lines was no trouble at all. For a director we had one of the few that in my life as an actor I have really agreed with and got on with. He had the same background as I had, all the Shakespeare companies and years with Dunstan, and he made a really good job of the show. His name was Edmund Bailey. He and his brother Jimmy were the sons of T. G. Bailey, who could trace his descent from actors for over 250 years. T.G. was tiny and specialized in peculiar parts. I remember seeing him play the First Grave-digger in *Hamlet* when he was well over eighty, and I have never seen anything like it again. Edmund was one of the resident directors at Drury Lane.

The actor playing the detective in *Gaslight* was not up to it at all, and as time went on we seemed to be getting no nearer. In the end the poor fellow had to go, and Eddie Bailey our director took the part for our first week in Aldershot. We were to perform for a week in this area and then go on tour. The idea was to rehearse with a new man (if one could be found) after the show had opened. We stayed in special hostels on tour, scattered all over the land, some being requisitioned houses of the landed gentry. Lovely places they were, each presided over by a matron and staffed by girls and cooks from NAAFI. After our opening night we were invited to the officers' mess and there regaled with free booze till early in the morning. This was to go on all the time and the prospect seemed too good to be true. One show, secure salary, tour to go on for ever, no searching for digs, nothing to provide, and free beer. The paradise I had tried to create in the Bragg-Liddell Company was accomplished, as far as I was concerned, by ENSA.

After a year I submitted plans for a tour of Goldsmith's *She Stoops to Conquer*, a play Laura and I had always delighted in. People had forgotten how to mount these traditional comedies. Such period plays were usually put on, to our way of thinking, in a much too formalized manner. We thought that the play done with full-blooded rusticity would be an ideal show for the garrison theatres, and with the emancipation of ENSA into all branches of theatre arts it was at last to have a trial. I was to direct, cast, design the sets, and manage the tour for a one-month trial period; it was thrilling to be hard at work again. Casting was not easy, as we had to have two really good-looking young men for Marlow and Hastings. The character parts, however, were no difficulty, since ENSA was full of crocks of all sorts. Some whom I found were with us for years afterwards. Our Diggory was a wonder; we called him 'Trot-trot': almost round, red in the face with a lifetime of bitter beer imbibing, and the most wonderful Georgian voice that can be imagined, so much so that Diggory in our version becomes almost the most important role in the play. For Tony, always one of my favourite parts, I used my own North-country accent and modelled the character on a schoolboy friend of mine who did all the things Tony did, played practical jokes, poached, and was like the best sort of old English country gentleman of the last two centuries.

She Stoops to Conquer not only ran on and on, but was used as a sort of 'pool'. When there were artists standing by waiting for some other unit, they were sent on tour with us during the waiting period, as we could always put them on as servants or yokels. We seemed to have half of the ENSA artists with us in *Stoops*, at some time or another. Then we got the word that we were wanted overseas. I wanted to take *Stoops*, of course, but such a large unit was impossible, we were told, and so we had to redo *Gaslight*. *Stoops* came off to everyone's regret; we had all had a wonderful year, playing every week all over the British Isles.

Among the actors for our new *Gaslight* troupe were myself and Laura, Josephine Kelly, Hilda Trowbridge, and John Norman. I had a new set of my own design – something, they said, that could be played between two palm-trees. We certainly played in some peculiar places, from Government House in Darjeeling to a Nissen hut in the Gulf of Oman, but not quite between palm-trees. We rehearsed the play again and had a new wardrobe, which was supposed to be cooler as we were going to a hot climate. It proved just the opposite; the main idea seemed to be to eliminate linings, with the result that in the heat the costumes just soaked up all the moisture, and coloured dresses got blacker and blacker as the night wore on; even the ladies' bustles became black balloons of moisture.

After the usual briefing, inoculations, and uniform issue, we were smuggled with great secrecy into shuttered buses and taken to St Pancras Station, just like ladies in purdah. At St Pancras we were entrained and in the dead of night stole out to our 'top-secret' destination. We were told it was to be somewhere in Scotland, but we drew up early in the morning in Liverpool alongside troop-ship *D6*, which in better times was named the Orient liner *Otranto*. We slipped unheralded out into the river to join our convoy off the coast of Wales; and at last after being an actor for twelve years, my real travels were beginning.

Liners on war work were stripped of their finery, and their meals were austere, but compared with the hotels and civilian food in wartime England we lived in the lap of luxury. We ranked as officers and so were spared the horrors of the troop deck. We had cabins with bunks. Laura and I were particularly lucky to have the only two-berth cabin on the ship. We ate in the saloon and had more or less the freedom of the ship. Apart from long parades in life-jackets on deck each morning, we had nothing to do whatever. Sea convoys were glorious and beautiful – great armadas of vessels of all sizes, shepherded by the escort ships. We proceeded northwards around Ireland into the Atlantic, approached Gibraltar by a great detour via the Azores, and so into the Med. There we started on a round of entertainment. Besides doing our own show we were also involved in the *Otranto Follies*, complete with a chorus made up of A.T.S. and W.A.A.F.S. known as the Otranto Girls. It was all great fun and it was hard to believe that this activity would take us all away for seven years, unless the war came to an end. The war and home seemed so remote, and the trip took so long, that one really forgot the past and thought little of the future.

Then, one morning, came my first glimpse of India, a vast land-mass on the horizon, overhung with the heavy clouds of the monsoon season. As we got nearer, we passed little boats with triangular sails, frail craft tacking across the bay with dark, turbanned fishermen at the helm. When we had moored in the bay, a Royal Indian Navy motor-launch drew alongside, and there was my brother, Philip, in his naval uniform. He came aboard with a bottle of gin enclosed in an official O.H.M.S. envelope (officially our ship was dry) and with a pass for us to go ashore.

As we came to the quayside I felt a surge of excitement, a sort of heightened quality of life. The crowds had an energy I had never seen in Britain, restlessly flowing to and fro, as if the smallest incident was of vast interest, watching and taking everything in. Later I was to find this same quality in an Indian audience – they really are the best in the world; nothing escapes their attention.

We went back to the ship after dinner, and the following morning we arrived alongside the quay. It seemed as if all India was there to welcome us. There were bands of Indian performers and acrobats in vividly coloured costumes and hundreds of people in all sorts of exotic uniforms, waiting with flowers and garlands for the returning officers. A military band played 'This Is the Army, Mr Brown'. Military police strutted like peacocks with white legs. Amidst this hurly-burly of crowds and garlands and music we disembarked and were driven in station-wagons to a hostel on the Colaba Causeway, which had been requisitioned for us. The rooms were spacious, with high ceilings and fans. Already in residence were members of the India Repertory Company who had arrived in India about six months before us.

The fate of the India Rep provided me with my first lesson as to what was possible in India. It had been what we would call today a prestige symbol, and had had a lot of ballyhoo. All units were asked to volunteer their best players and there was a première in London with *How Are They at Home*, a play specially written by J. B. Priestley. (ENSA by contrast was never popular with the press and the Establishment, who scorned its unconventional works. In fact it did very well with the material that was available, having to struggle against those who were sure that servicemen were capable of enjoying only the most infantile of humour.) The idea behind the India Rep had been to have one grand company; but the more people there were involved, the more things could go wrong. Everything went against this company: illness, difficulty in getting enough accommodation on tour, the size of the theatres, and so on, with the result that it was always getting bogged down. Subsequently the policy had changed, and instead of great companies they wanted little units like ours that could go anywhere; for even if half the artists were struck down with fever, it would only be a small unit that was incapacitated. Our *Gaslight* unit was the first of these to arrive.

In Bombay I met Peter Meriton again, whom I had first encountered in rep in Manchester. He was a tall, good-looking man with a long face – excellent for an actor – and generally very pleasant and likeable. He had begun life running a business from his father's shop, travelling the district around Manchester on a cycle selling butter. Then he had 'got religion' and had been ordained in a remote sect of Old Catholics, wearing a clerical collar and a soutane. Finally, having studied elocution, he realized that what he really wanted to do was act, and when I met him at the beginning of the war he was working on the land by day and being an actor by night. He had joined me in arranging shows in

Lancashire schools, which I had booked by cycling all over the area, and we hired some basic costumes and would arrive by taxi at the schools. Peter loved this because, like me, he preferred to be his own boss however lowly the thing he was boss of. By the time I arrived in India he had already travelled widely in the East, to Burma and Malaya. Before we had been there a day, he suggested that we should revive our little company and play in schools and colleges in India, and that we should make plans now, so that we would be ready when the war was over. It was a suggestion that was to change the whole course of my life.

The ENSA headquarters in Bombay was Green's Hotel, which is now part of the New Taj. Our new C.O. was Col Jack Hawkins, who later became a famous and well loved film star. He was present at our first show in the Excelsior Theatre, and a better man for the job could not have been found anywhere. He insisted on the highest standards, and he was right to do so, for the companies toured to units that had not seen any entertainment for six months or so. After all their anticipation you had to put on a good show, and often there was no second night to correct any mistakes.

Our production of *Gaslight* seemed to fulfil Jack Hawkins's criteria. The *Bombay Times* said: 'ENSA deserves unqualified congratulation on its brilliant presentation of Patrick Hamilton's world famous play *Gaslight* at the Excelsior. A packed house gave every indication of its appreciation of a truly perfect performance.' The critic went on to single out Laura as giving

a portrayal which I think may truthfully be described as magnificent. It was more than that, it was great and the lady undoubtedly has a splendid future on the English stage where already she occupies a position of no little distinction. Geoffrey Kendal, as the calculating rogue who has killed once in his greed for gain and coldly sets about driving his wife mad, presents a really inspired portrayal in a most unsympathetic role. His is actually a triumph of acting, for nothing can be more unlike Kendal in real life than the diabolical Manningham of the play.

After a season in Bombay, our *Gaslight* unit was sent on tour. For some reason the welfare officers in Bombay considered train journeys a hardship, but we toured in the sort of luxury we have rarely experienced since. We had a private railway coach,

complete with kitchen, a white-tiled bathroom with shower, and
compartments that were as comfortable as bedrooms, with wardrobes and chests of drawers. From Bombay we travelled to
Shillong, Darjeeling, Assam, and Calcutta. The scenery was very
like the Lake District as we came nearer the hills, with streams
cascading down the hillsides, but with the difference that there
were palm-trees and Indian villages. You would see teams of oxen
ploughing the fields and men padding about with what looked like
little straw huts almost completely covering them. Our meals were
always plain English cooking; two white-coated Indian bearers
would bring in a dinner of brown Windsor soup, fish and chips,
mutton and vegetables, and jelly.

Outside the orderly train was a disorderly and chaotic world,
with beauty and poverty coexisting. At one station a little girl with
an enchanting smile, hardly more than six, pulled at my shirt and
said:

'Me no father, me no mother, me no sister, me no brother, me
no auntie, me no uncle, me poor little bastard. Give me money.'

I could not resist and gave her a coin, and was immediately
besieged by a horde of clamouring beggars, no doubt aunts and
uncles and cousins of hers. We began to appreciate that begging
was a profession, and those practising it developed their own
techniques. In Darjeeling there was an old beggar who staked out
a pitch on the roadside near our window, and we would watch
him arranging himself for his 'act'. He would tie up his loincloth,
find a comfortable position to sit in, arrange his stick, and put his
tin down in front of him, then begin to sway back and forth,
looking as ill as he could.

Laura wrote a letter to Jennifer, trying to describe a street scene
in India, transferring to it the English people she knew in
Barrow-in-Furness:

Imagine walking along, say, Dalton Road, and seeing, say, the
Spencer brothers – one sitting crosslegged in the midst of his
wares in a loincloth and a beautiful turban, the other sitting
right in the middle of the pavement bathing himself (with his
clothes on!) at one of the wells of water that spring up at
intervals all the way along. Then next door probably a soothsayer or phrenologist with all sorts of weird-looking objects
hanging outside – tortoise shells, dead things, goodness knows

what! Then, say, Mr Bell lying in his string bed fast asleep in the street – or sitting there stitching away and machining in the midst of naked little urchins – boys selling little coloured birds. Rickshaws being drawn by men, gharries by horses. Dead cats and rats lying about all over the place! Such a bewildering conglomeration – it is indescribable!

We travelled up to Darjeeling, over 7,000 feet in altitude. The railway and road criss-crossed each other all the way up the precipitous hills. From above the clouds we glimpsed the plains below and the mountains in the distance banded with wisps of mist. Up in the hills we hired ponies to get around. We were on the borders of Nepal, and the hill people wore that distinctive jewellery, heavy silver bangles and anklets, with huge blue and coral stones. In Darjeeling we had dinner one night in the Tea Planters' Club and met an elderly couple who were retiring and returning to England. They talked about their treks to Tibet, of the differences between Bengalis and the hill people, and finally ended up eulogizing on the beauties of Birmingham. Sitting on the 'Roof of the World' we discussed the pubs and pork-pies of Brum! Most of the Army people we met seemed to be longing to get back to England. It was possibly the uncertainty of not knowing how long they would be here, and the dullness of Army routine, but we met innumerable 'grousers' who seemed to have no understanding of the country or the people.

We toured India for six months. From Darjeeling and the East, we were sent to the North-west Frontier, from Peshawar to Quetta on the borders of Afghanistan, down to Karachi, and back to Bombay. We were given orders to proceed to Burma, via Calcutta, and kitted out in jungle green, but then there was an alteration of plans, and we were told to go back to London to add *Arms and the Man* to our repertoire. It seemed a long way to go to rehearse a play, but we returned on the *Empress of Scotland*, rehearsed for three weeks, and sailed out again on the *Empress of Australia* – marvellous, all these lovely cruises, and all for free! I had taken over the job of managing the company in Assam when our manager was sent back to Bombay. It was like having my own show, but with no worries about how to pay the artists or the fares to the next place.

Being the Army, however, every move had to be sanctioned by

memos. Even your expenses for buying shoe-polish would not get by without an accompanying voucher, and I was reminded that a sanction should have been asked for first when I bought a replacement for a stolen overcoat. Another memo informed me severely that the company's dhobi was 'grossly overcharging as I have always understood that washing materials are purchased by the dhobi out of his salary'. All ENSA units were sent a regular news-sheet, *Here and There*, from the publicity desk, telling us what a grand job we were doing in boosting the men's morale.

> When the history of this war in the Far East comes to be written, there must be an honoured place kept for the theatrical artists who, quietly and with no hope of reward either monetarily or in publicity, have done their turns amid the jungles and burning heat of the tropics under every conceivable kind of discomfort and danger . . .

read one news-sheet, adding with starry-eyed sentiment:

> Men who for months have never seen a white woman sit enraptured, with petrol tins and wooden boxes for seats, while an attractive British girl sings to them. They swarm round her after the show, and give her messages for their loved ones at home. To hear a woman's voice again reminds them poignantly of their wives, their sweethearts, their sisters, and friends in city, village, and hamlet way back home.

When we returned home after the first tour we had a record of eighty-six shows in just over six months. We had not missed a performance despite bouts of fever and discomfort from the heat; for the first time we had experience of our costumes becoming totally saturated with perspiration, so that what began as a light blue dress was dark by the end of the evening. Through floods and storms we had always got there in time, right up to the North-west Frontier, into tribal territory in Razmak and Bannu, and to Imphal. Entering tribal territory, we were told, was at our own risk, and we would travel in an Army convoy, passing great camel-trains and women with rifles, striding along in their swinging skirts. Back in London an actor at Drury Lane said to me in surprise: 'Well, so it *is* possible to play in India.' Of course it is, but not with heavy equipment that gets the poor artists bogged down. You have to be mobilized.

Now there was a complication, however. Laura was going to have another baby. We realized that, if we told everyone, we would have to stay behind in England. It seemed to us unthinkable, and so we did not say anything and went back to India. The tour went on with a month in Ceylon, and Laura's pregnancy was only discovered by one of the welfare officers, who happened to be in the same predicament herself. News got back to H.Q. and we were taken back to England on 22 June 1946 on another troop-ship. That was the end of our war career. The ENSA programme was nearly over anyway, and once again I went back into rep, opening in that old favourite, *White Cargo*.

For the first time since we had married in Gretna Green, Laura was not there, for even in the final days of her first pregnancy she had never left the theatre – continuing to look after the wardrobe till the fall of the curtain the night of Jennifer's birth. This time it was different. Laura's parents, who had moved to Olton in Warwickshire, insisted on her staying quietly at their home. It was not for long, though. I came home after the show on the night of 25 September 1946 to find it was all over without my help. We had another daughter and we called her Felicity.

6

The Princely Tour

It was a hot summer's day in 1946. I was walking through Piccadilly Circus, wishing I could take my jacket and shoes off as I could have done in India, when suddenly I saw the familiar face of Peter Meriton, my ex-ENSA colleague. He had returned from India only the week before, so we went to Lyons Corner House in Coventry Street and reminisced over tea.

'Why don't we do as I suggested when we met in India – form a small touring company like our ENSA unit?' said Peter. 'We could play scenes from Shakespeare in colleges and schools, and recruit Indian student actors as well.'

We immediately bombarded all the education departments in India with letters, but got absolutely no response. Then one day we heard from the India Office in London that an official from the princely state of Hyderabad in the Deccan was to visit London. He was the Nawab Zain Yar Jung. Peter met him, and the Nawab suggested it would be better to approach the state governments, rather than departments in Delhi. Armed with this advice and a promise 'in principle' of an invitation to Hyderabad, we wrote letters, and the result was magical. Within a month we had invitations to Hyderabad, Patiala, Gwalior, Travancore, and Cochin; all with state guest-house or hotel accommodation and the promise of assistance with the shows. This was marvellous. Our Shakespeareana Company was born.

Peter asked his sister, Eileen Garner, and his brother, Geoffrey Richards, to join us. Eileen was blonde and attractive, with a Marlene Dietrich look about her; she had been a stand-in and played small parts in films. Geoffrey, who was tall, slim, and good-looking, had acted in a rep company and worked in stage-management and as a lighting assistant. Eileen was also skilled at accounts, so she kept the books for the company. Both of them meantime began learning parts and rehearsing. Peter was the business manager, I was the director, and Laura was our leading lady – with, of course, the extra responsibility of a new-born baby and a teenage daughter.

The people who came to see us off at Waterloo Station were to experience the bitter cold of the terrible winter of 1946–7. We left soon after Christmas for the sun, not on a troop-ship this time, but on the P. & O. liner *Strathmore*, waiting for us in Southampton Docks, for her first passenger voyage after the war. We were a company of three men and two women, all in our thirties, a girl of thirteen in school hat and coat, and a baby. Armed with Shakespeare, whose plays were so much appreciated in India, we felt we could ignore the warnings about the nationalist movement and possible troubles. India was moving towards independence, but we did not see that it might affect us, though we knew there had been many killings the year before. We were optimistic and enthusiastic as we began our new adventure, sailing away from restrictions, food rationing, and clothing coupons.

On board the *Strathmore* we travelled first class for only £70 each. The ship took us through the Mediterranean to Port Said and through the Suez Canal, where we could see the desert for two hundred miles around us; men in white robes sat by open fires in the evening near the canal, almost on a level with the ship and within calling distance. We rehearsed on board to prepare for our opening at St Xavier's College in Bombay with *The Merchant of Venice* and scenes from *Macbeth*. There had been a political assassination in Delhi, with the result that there was a *hartal* – a political strike – on the day we played. The students could not get to the hall, and when we were able to resume three days later we played to a half-full house. Many of the students had continued to stay away from college, and people were in no mood to venture out.

After this not altogether happy start, we took the train on 27 January 1947 to Hyderabad. This is where our 'princely' tour really began. We arrived to a welcoming committee with garlands of jasmine, and throughout the visit were treated as honoured guests. We were taken to the state guest-house, Rock Castle, perched high on a hill above the town. Suddenly, after the bustle and harassment of Bombay, we were in an older and more leisurely world. The Nizam sent a Pontiac and chauffeur with the message that they were at our disposal for the visit.

When we awoke the next day, the sun had just risen. Indian mornings are wonderful, and here in the heart of the Deccan there was so much beauty around us. From the terrace of the Rock Castle we looked over Hyderabad. It is a town of ancient Mogul buildings standing above a great, slow-running river. The hills outside the town are piled with great smooth lumps of stone, like enormous cobbles, and the twin cities of Hyderabad and Secunderabad are divided by a lake with a causeway. In the centre of Hyderabad is the Charminar, a large archway where several roads meet, on the edge of the bazaar. Going through the bazaar we were overwhelmed by the stalls of glittering bangles and bright, tinselled saris. The bazaar and most of the old buildings are still there, but nowadays the whole city is littered with motor rickshaws, phut-phutting haphazardly all over the place and jogging the bones of the passengers. At that time, back in 1947, there was little traffic, and if the Nizam stirred abroad, which he usually did around 5 p.m., whistles blew and the traffic stopped to let his car pass. His own car was not a splendid Rolls, Daimler, or Pontiac like those he lent to his guests, but a petrol-saving little Austin 7, chauffeur driven. The Nizam was one of the richest men in the world, yet he made these curious economies. For years he smoked the cheapest cigarette on the market – 'Charminar', at six *pice* for ten.

Osman Ali was the seventh Nizam of Hyderabad. During the First and Second World Wars he had sent soldiers to help the British, and contributed money towards a squadron of Hurricane fighter planes. He had come to the throne of Hyderabad in 1911 when he was twenty-five years old and became His Exalted Highness in 1922 as a reward for men and money given to the British in the First World War. He had the official Muslim number of wives – four – but also a harem of concubines. He had masses of children; no wonder he was humorously called His Exhausted Highness! There were several Europeans who worked for the Nizam: a German who was in charge of the garage that housed sixty-five splendid cars, and Mrs Green, who ran the theatre, a beautiful little Victorian building. She had once found a fourteen-year-old girl who had escaped from the harem hiding under the stage. The theatre stood in the grounds of the palace, and underneath the palace were the vaults where the Nizam's wealth, an Aladdin's cave of jewellery, gold bars, and gold coins, was stored. He had many palaces but he preferred his King Kothi Palace, which he made his permanent home. In the tenth year of Indian independence he retired there, and he spent his remaining years for the most part living on his veranda with a pet goat that had been injured by his car and he had nursed back to health. He was a good man at heart, and when he died it is said nearly half a million people from his state went to the funeral.

While we were there the Nizam held a durbar, which we attended, the European men in morning dress and the Indians in Muslim clothes. A durbar is a formal showing of allegiance to a ruler. It takes various forms, from the great durbar of King George V and Queen Mary in Delhi in 1911, when all the princely states were represented, to the smaller ones held by individual states. They were always very impressive. All the officials and heads of departments would have a formal audience with the monarch. In most cases they would offer a *nuzzah*, a specially minted coin purchased from the sovereign's treasury. Sometimes they presented their swords and swore fealty, and there would always be singing and dancing, bands playing, and military parades with cavalry and elephants.

The formal dress of Hyderabad is particularly lovely, and the clothes have a rich *Arabian Nights* look. The women wear wide silken trousers and long kaftans; the men, white trousers, jewelled *jutis* (pointed slippers), and a fez or tarbush. Everyone wore masses of jewellery. On the whole, because this was a Muslim state, women were not much in evidence in Hyderabad. There were purdah clubs – special clubs for married women, surrounded by high walls, and with a double wall for the entrance so that the purdah ladies would not be seen as they alighted from their carriages. We performed a play for a purdah school at one of these clubs. Shrouded girls were brought in closed cars and buses, and then they sat in the theatre and took off their *burkahs*. The show was in the afternoon, in broad daylight, yet no one seemed to mind the actors seeing ladies out of purdah. Did we not count as men?

We now employed an ayah for Felicity. Her name was Mary, a

devout Catholic from South India and very black, with Afro hair that she disguised by pinning on to the ends a tail of false black hair bought in the bazaar for two rupees. She was plump and always wore white saris and a clean white *choli* (blouse). She had a ready smile for everyone in the company and simply adored Felicity.

Mary and baby Felicity became a central point of the company. Every morning the members of the company would say, 'Good morning, Mary. Good morning, Felicity'; and, whether on train journeys or preparing to move on somewhere, all of us gravitated towards Mary with Felicity in her arms. The 'good morning' ritual was Laura's idea; she was a wonderful mother. When she had to go on-stage, we would tell her, 'Absent thee from Felicity awhile' (*Hamlet*, Act 5). Felicity grew up surrounded by love and affection from everyone in the company, which made up for the lack of a settled life and steady schoolfriends. We were never in one place long enough for her to establish lasting friendships, so her companionship and security came from her family and the other actors. She had as much stability in her world as any other child, but because it came from just one source, she grew very dependent. She would feel sorry for herself when we were back in England and she would be left at the digs in the evening with a babysitter. She had become so used to being with the company all the time.

Our tour in Hyderabad came to an end and it was time to move on. The Nizam sent us presents of cigarette cases and little boxes made from the special Hyderabad alloy of silver and gun-metal. Our new destination was Travancore. This was the southernmost of the princely states, and is now combined with Cochin to make the State of Kerala. The people are smaller than in the North, with darker complexions. The men wear white dhotis, not wound round the legs as in Bengal and Northern India, but wrapped round like a long skirt or *lungi*. White is the predominant colour, and always spotlessly clean. The girls have very thick hair covered with coconut oil. They wear flowers and are overpoweringly lovely. The landscape is lusciously green. You are never far from the blue, blue sea.

At Travancore we were met with a red carpet, garlands, and petals. A royal barge, decorated like a coronation coach with the crew in livery, took us to the guest-house, which was on an island in the river, and brought us quite a long way back to the college on the mainland where we were playing. We lay on silken cushions and wished the voyage would go on for ever. The barge belonged to the Maharaja of Travancore. We never met His Highness, because he was away at the time, but the *dirvan* or chief minister was like a character from a book of romance. He wore ear-rings and a turban, and his enormous girth was swathed in a dhoti of the finest silk, worn long as the dhoties in the South are. We gave a performance of *Julius Caesar*, then moved on to Trivandrum, one of the southernmost towns in India, where we played *Othello* and *Julius Caesar*.

After our performances we received a touching letter of appreciation from the local amateur group known as the Forward Bloc. They wrote:

> Although we have read almost all the plays of Shakespeare we were not able to get a correct understanding of his stage business. A full understanding of Shakespeare as a practical playwright can be had only through knowledge of the action or stage-business, which is an integral part of a performance and is seldom fully described in the play's written form. For a long time we have been feeling the want of this necessary background. So, to us the news that an English company was coming to Trivandrum to stage some of the plays of Shakespeare was like 'dropping manna in the way of starved people'. We decided to make full use of the chance and began attending the theatre every day. And we did find in such profusion answers to questions which confronted us when trying to visualize an action while reading a play. We thank you all for having given us so much knowledge about Shakespeare and his plays ... Somehow or other a bond has linked the 'Forward Bloc' and the 'Shakespeareana' together. We pray to God to help us in keeping this tie strong for ever. Let Shakespeare keep India and Britain united!

From the soft green landscape and palm-trees of the South, we made the long journey north again to the princely state of Rajasthan. There we stayed in a guest-house as large as a palace, belonging to the Maharaja of Gwalior. It had several storeys of arched balconies, and inside was a jumble of utility furniture, stuffed tigers, and masses of elephants' feet made into wastepaper bins and umbrella stands. The Maharaja's palace was opulent, with glass everywhere, chandeliers, glass fountains in the courtyards, and frosted glass panels on the inside doors with the word 'Welcome' engraved on them.

The Maharaja himself was short and extremely charming; his first name was George. He was a chain-smoker and wherever he went a bearer carrying an ashtray would be by his side to catch the cigarette ash and cigarette ends. He was also fond of his food, and his table would groan under the weight of the elaborate dishes. In the middle of the table was a silver train that carried chutneys and pickles round on a small railway line to the guests. Gwalior was tiger country, and the Maharaja offered to organize a tiger hunt. On our journey there we had seen a notice pinned to the trunk of a tree off the road reading 'Man-eating tiger – 61 dead'. But before we left Gwalior we were told by the Education Minister, Mr Pierce, that the ministers were becoming jealous of our popularity with His Highness, and the return visit would almost certainly be cancelled, which it was.

We went on to Delhi and from there to Patiala in the Punjab, where we first heard the rumble of the 'devil's wind'. That is the only way to describe the strange surge of rumours that came over India at the time of the Partition, and which led to so many killings. Despite the uneasiness and the rumours, the ceremonies went on, and so did our plays. We arrived at the beginning of April to see the ceremony of the Presentation of New Colours to the First Rajindra Sikh Infantry. The Infantry was originally raised by Baba Alla Singh, the founder of Patiala State in 1723. In the First World War the Infantry fought at the Dardanelles, where it suffered heavy casualties, and took part in the final Gaza assault. They were a magnificent sight, the battalion of tall, imposing Sikhs in their turbans, marching to the tune of 'The Royal Scots at Barry'. The battalion bade farewell to the Old Colour, carried since 1888, and the band played 'Auld Lang Syne'. Then the New Colour was presented to the Maharaja and received the General State. The New Colour was unfurled, and the colour party marched off to the band and drums playing 'Farewell to Gibraltar'.

The following week we attended what must have been one of the last durbars of India as it was in the days of the Raj. It was held in a great *shamiana* (tented canopy) with solid silver poles and silken ropes. There were singing girls and a symphony orchestra that played all day. The Maharaja of Patiala, who was well over six feet, attended with his A.D.C.s, all nearly as tall as his own magnificent height, and all dressed in white. He sat on his throne to receive taxes from the noblemen and landowners. As each man knelt with his sword at his right side, an A.D.C. would place a restraining hand on the man's sword arm. There was always much obeisance in the princely states. Eileen was astonished to see a servant who had brought the Maharaja's brother a glass of water kneel and kiss his feet. Richard, the brother, was a young, well-educated man, and it was an incongruous sight.

We returned to Delhi in time to make a broadcast for the anniversary of Shakespeare's birth, 23 April, and stayed in the Cecil Hotel in Old Delhi. The Cecil is now a public school; all the lovely gardens are turned into games fields, and the large, high-ceilinged rooms into classrooms. In its heyday it was a miniature town. The rooms were all in terraces stretching round the main building. Meals were served by turbanned waiters, and even in the days of Prohibition the wine waiter was kept on, serving Coca-Colas with all the ceremony of a bottle of the choicest vintage. The host of bearers, cooks, gardeners, and cleaners lived in another great building in the compound, and the hotel provided welfare and medical care for them. Every guest was personally escorted to their rooms by one of the Hotz family, who owned the hotel. The bedrooms were palatial, with dressing rooms and sitting rooms attached, and the air was cooled by punkahs, before the days of air conditioning. If anyone complained about the food or service they were never allowed admission again, but there was really little to complain about. The Hotz family ran this hotel together with others at Agra and Simla, but now there is only one left, the Alasia Hotel at Kasauli, where we stayed while filming *Shakespeare Wallah*.

We often stayed at the Cecil. When the hotel was full, we were offered a tent in the garden, or the use of the swimming-pool cubicles. In the evening you would hear the hyenas laughing as they scavenged around the area nearby. Once Laura woke up to see a hyena slipping like a shadow through the door curtain, only a few feet from where Felicity lay asleep.

Old Delhi was teeming with people, and at this time even more than before, because refugees were moving in from west Punjab. The streets were jammed with bullock-carts and bicycles, and the homeless slept on the pavements. The contrast with New Delhi, with its wide, well-planned avenues and imposing Lutyens architecture, was startling. New Delhi took on a deserted air after the bustle and crowding in the *chowkhs* and bazaars in the narrow streets of the old town.

During the months leading up to Independence in August 1947, the turbulence of the Partition grew worse. It had begun with agitation in a few towns, stirred up by *provocateurs*, and Hindus and Muslims who had been friends for years began to be afraid of each other. The fears led to blows and to killings, and the trouble escalated. People felt they had to move out of areas they had lived in all their lives; we saw columns of refugees trudging over the dusty plains of North India, and crowds of stranded people at stations waiting for trains. It was a great mistake for the British Government to agree to Partition, and it caused immense suffering. When we arrived back in Delhi in the summer we had to stay in the Cecil Hotel for three weeks and not move outside, on police orders, for our own protection.

After our first stay in Delhi we went up to the hill stations, which were comparatively untroubled by the disturbances – as well as being cooler than the overheated plains. We travelled through the desert via Meerut, with white dust swirling around and covering us, so by the end we looked like a company of ghosts. Then up to the foothills of the Himalayas to Dehra Dun, where we played at Doon School, undoubtedly one of the most beautifully sited schools in the world. From our bungalow, which was lent to us by one of the masters, we had a magnificent view over the valley. Doon School has an open-air theatre, rather like a Greek amphitheatre, with the backdrop of the Himalayas. The stage has a permanent arrangement of steps, an archway and stones, and is a beautifully flexible space. Doon is one of the leading schools in India, from which future diplomats and army officers are drawn. The headmaster at the time was Arthur Foot, who was succeeded by John Martyn, a great Shakespeare enthusiast.

The English headmasters of India were a race apart. Most had been in India since they were young, and had taught there for years. Another of their number, Jack Gibson, was head of Mayo College at Ajmer in Rajasthan. Mayo College was a great turreted palace of unpolished white marble with a central tower and many wings, and the headmaster's house there was a palace in itself, with a drawing room so high-ceilinged that it resounded like a church. The College pupils consisted exclusively of the sons of princes at the time of Gibson's appointment, and it was to his credit that he was able to bring in boys of different social classes and castes and greatly improve the scholastic standard. Long since retired, he still lives in a house at Ajmer. At St Paul's in Darjeeling there was Leslie Goddard, and further east, in Malaya, Mr Ogle at Ipoh. This breed seems to have ended now; not that there aren't dedicated men and women all over the scholastic world, but these individuals had such amazing personalities that one could not imagine them anywhere else. They all welcomed us with such ease and made us at home in their houses. I can still hear the whack of the cricket ball in Ajmer, the P.T. orders in the cool early morning in Doon. I can smell the *satai* Mr Ogle and I enjoyed in the streets of Ipoh, and hear Mr. Goddard intone the Latin grace before meat in the dining hall of St Paul's.

We travelled from the Doon School on to Sherwood College at Naini Tal, another precipitous hill station. To get to the school from the town, you have to travel by *dhandi*, a rickshaw carried by four men panting and gasping in the thin mountain air, as if they are drawing their last breath. Laura hated to hear their efforts and would have preferred to travel by pony, but the rickshaw men were so desperate for the coins that you felt you were depriving them by not allowing them to toil uphill. From Naini Tal we went to Mussoorie to play at the American school, and it was there that we came across Frank Wheatley. We had heard of him before: a lone actor who had spent the last twenty years touring India, Burma, and Ceylon on a bicycle and giving one-man recitals and lectures on elocution at schools. He must have been over sixty when we met him. He was dressed in an ancient suiting, a sort of cheap Burton tweed, a topi, and, over his shoulder, an Assamese bag. These bags since became popular with hippies and tourists but in those days no man would have dreamed of carrying one. In the bag he kept his notices and recommendations of the last forty years.

Frank told us that we were stealing his market because we were a company compared with his solo shows, and he wanted to know which way we were going so that he could go in the opposite direction. Alternatively, he suggested, he was quite willing to join forces with us. We liked Frank. He was an ugly-looking specimen, but very strong and robust, due to his habit of cycling or walking everywhere. He had a wonderful deep voice, and we realized we could expand the repertoire with an extra man. It would also let Eileen off having to play male parts. So Frank joined us, and was to stay with us for years after we returned to India in 1953.

Our train was getting bigger and bigger, mainly because we adopted all sorts of servants. Apart from Mary our ayah, there was Azarool, a tiny monkey-like man who did all the fetching and carrying, and organized transport and men to carry the luggage. He was frequently drunk. There was our chief bearer, Mangatram, a tall handsome man with a curled-up moustache, who would book railway tickets and generally help and translate. For a few weeks we had a dhobi, a young boy of fourteen we had recruited in South India, who arrived with his iron – the sort that you put hot coals into. He was seen off at the station by the whole of his family but became homesick and had to be sent back home. The servants needed more servants as the amount of equipment and costumes grew. We had our costumes made by local tailors, who could make anything wonderfully cheaply, simply by looking at a picture and copying it. The bazaars supplied a variety of fabric, and we added greatly to the wardrobe we had brought with us. We also bought masses of carpets and tourist junk. Eventually, we had to buy a large van to carry all this stuff, and that meant a driver. We got one from Assam, a discharged army driver who turned up in uniform, complete with medal and ribbons, and his cousin as cleaner.

We journeyed to Darjeeling to play at St Paul's School and Loreto Convent. It was at Loreto a few years later that I was received into the Roman Catholic faith. I had been so impressed by the love and kindness of the nuns who welcomed us each time, and it seemed to me that Catholicism offered answers to the questions that trouble us. Laura and Felicity also embraced the faith, but Jennifer resisted it.

From Darjeeling we journeyed on to Shillong in Assam. Once we had to cross a ravine by a long suspension bridge with rope sides. A warning notice said, 'Unsafe Bridge – Only One Person to Cross at Any One Time'. There was rushing water in the river hundreds of feet below, but we had to go on. We were wary of taking a vehicle but we were lucky and got across safely. Part of our journey took us through a deep ravine that was dark green with jungly overhead trees and plants growing up the rocky walls. There were the largest and most beautifully coloured butterflies I have seen, with wing-spans of nine or ten inches. We were in Shillong in Assam on Independence Day, 15 August 1947. People were walking idly along the roads, with an aimless, helpless look. There was no rejoicing, no singing or dancing. No one seemed to know what would happen next.

In Kalimpong we saw horses running free with streaming manes and tails, against the backdrop of the hills, as in a Chinese picture. At night you heard the music of the creaking bamboo trees, tall leafless trunks swaying gently in the breeze. Kalimpong was not far from Darjeeling as the crow flies, but a longer and more round-about route through the mountain country. In its high street you would see the mule-trains from Tibet, a bell hanging round the neck of the leading mule. Kalimpong was the market-place for wool from the mountains, and there was always a bustle of traders and the tinkling of the mule-bells. We played at the Dr Graham Homes School there. Dr Graham had founded the 'homes' for Anglo-Indian children about forty years before, and there was a high standard of education, despite its remoteness from the rest of the world.

Our Assamese driver, whom Eileen nicknamed Tickytock be-cause of the pigtail he wore that swung to and fro, was at the centre of the most dramatic episode of our tour. It happened while we were travelling in the Upper Assam Valley. The Governor of Assam, Sir Akbar Hyder, had invited us, and a programme of shows was arranged. Those who do not know India find it difficult to visualize how enormous the subcontinent is. The general impression is that India is a triangle, with Bombay on one side and Calcutta on the other. This is, of course, true, but those two cities are about half-way down from the hypotenuse of the triangle. From Calcutta to Manipur in the north-east is nearly as far as the width of India from Bombay to Calcutta. It takes over two days and nights to go by train from Calcutta to the end of the railway at Dimapur, and our journey took us miles by road beyond this railhead into Nagaland and Manipur. We had travelled from Shillong in Assam by road down to Gauhati and then on and on eastwards until we saw the hills of Burma. We travelled for miles, sitting on top of our equipment in an open lorry. There was the station-wagon as well, but it was hot inside and much more pleasant to travel in the open. The journey was lovely – through forests and great plains, over rivers, and always near the great Brahmaputra River, which reminded me of the green, greasy Limpopo of *The Elephant's Child*. There were elephants, too, both tame and roaming wild.

As we travelled on towards Imphal in Manipur, we became well acquainted with the local tribes, the Nagas. There seemed to be vast numbers of them, all moving in large family units. They were Mongolian in appearance, short and stocky, wearing black sarongs decorated with cowrie shells. They were friendly, laughing people and greeted us with great shouts. Once they asked us for help with a boy who had been bitten by a dog; we always carried a first-aid kit, so we bandaged up his arm. It is not uncommon for Nagas to be bitten by dogs, because they like eating them, and naturally the dogs fight back when they are about to be slaughtered. The Nagas were also keen on cigarettes, and we gave away a few that we could spare. There must be some 'jungle telegraph' in this part of the world, for from then on every tribe we met started to shout and gesticulate for cigarettes as soon as they saw our convoy. We bought quantities of the cheapest variety and gave away hundreds on our way through the valleys.

In Dimapur we had met an elderly English couple in the railway refreshment room. They had come from Nottingham and were now on their way back to England. This first overseas journey of their lives, all the way to Imphal, had been to see the grave of their only son, who had been killed during the last stand against the Japanese in India. Now that they had seen his grave among the thousands of that doomed generation, lying in neat rows in the great war cemeteries, they said that they accepted his death and felt he must be at peace in such a lovely place.

The signs of war were still apparent here in the north-east of India. Thousands of lorries, tanks, and planes had been abandoned, as if in a great scrap-yard. You could buy a jeep for 50s. and a lorry for £5. Many of the British officers in those lovely hills had been there at the time of the war. We met the colonel of the Assam Rifles, who had been through it all; and the Commissioner, who had remained in his summer-house when the decisive battle raged on his tennis court at Kohima.

There were only six Europeans in Manipur, so we doubled the population. We stayed with the British Resident, Mr and Mrs Stewart, who were preparing to leave the newly independent India. He was the magistrate in charge of Imphal, and one of his duties on leaving was to burn all the papers. We liked the people of Manipur. They were intelligent and friendly, with the slanting eyes and flat features of the Malays further east. Manipur was a matriarchal state: women ran the businesses and the market stalls, and the royal family was headed by the Maharani. We found there was an intense interest in theatre, and seven dramatic societies, but no one had ever seen English drama before.

It was on our way back that disaster struck. We had got almost to Panitola, and for the last 200 miles we had encountered floods. The snows were melting in the mountains, so that the rivers were swollen and flooding the roads. Many of the villages had been swamped, and people were camping beside the roads in the higher areas. A landslide had fallen on part of the road, turning to slippery yellow mud. We spent several hours clearing the mud to one side with planks so that we could get through. We had not gone much further when the police stopped us and warned us not to go on. The thought of turning back into the floods and mud we had just come through was too much. Peter waved a letter of authority from the District Commissioner at them, and they let us through.

The flood was now so deep that it had reached well up to the headlights of the station-wagon; we were afraid that the vehicle would stall or be swept away, so we hitched it with a tow-rope to the back of the lorry. The driver had suggested that Mary and Felicity travel in the station wagon, but Mary sat in the lorry, clutching the baby. She said firmly, 'No, my memsahib told me to stay here – I'm staying here.'

It was beginning to get dark. We could just see the bamboo poles that marked the side of the road, which are put up to guide people through the floods, so that they do not plunge over the edge. The wash from our lorry was battering the station-wagon behind, and we saw the threads of the rope beginning to break. A few seconds later the rope broke, and the car with the driver in it turned over and sank into the flooded river, its headlights looking like the eyes of a huge fish. We shouted at the driver of our lorry to stop, but he could not hear because of the sound of the rushing water. When we finally made him understand, he refused to stop before getting to an area of dry ground.

By the time we got back to where driver and station-wagon had disappeared it was dark. We could see and hear nothing but the rushing water. Ahead of us the light of a lantern, and we found a family by the road. They told us that they had heard a man shouting and seen the lights go out as the car sank. We got the villagers to bring out boats and search for the driver, who had somehow managed to escape and was washed down the river until he caught hold of the branches of a submerged tree. There was a lot of shouting downstream and waving of lanterns, and the driver, after two hours in the water, was brought ashore. Peter and I tried to get to him, but the water was streaming waist-high across the road; it was difficult to stand, let alone move forward. We got there with the help of some villagers, to find him laughing and telling his rescuers about his escape. The car had fallen on to its right side under the water, and he had managed to squeeze out of the opposite window. It was a miracle that he had survived, for he could not swim.

We went back to the lorry and surveyed the damage. It was terribly cold by now. We had no food, not even tea. Everything was in the sunken station-wagon – including our money. Our travellers' cheques, books, and changes of clothing were deep in the mud of Brahmaputra. Our gear on the lorry had been exposed to constant rain for over three hours, and we had to bail out the lorry like an open boat. Nothing could be done about the car now, so we decided to proceed as far as we could through the flooded areas with the lorry. We spent most of that night either riding on the lorry or walking, until, some time after midnight, we got on to a road that took us to a small town. When we stopped at a house to ask where we were, the door was opened by the man who was the doctor for the area. We were given coffee and brandy, and he told us he knew of us, since our fame had spread all over Assam and we were to play in the Panitola Club in a few days.

After we moved into the club we began to count our losses. Everything in the lorry was soaking; the boxes, when emptied of props and costumes, were full of dirty water. Some of the costumes were ruined or had changed colour. My pride, my red riding coat, was mottled with black, and I had to have it dyed black. Twenty-five years later it became my coat for playing Fagin in *Oliver*. That night there were more rains, lightning, and thunder. Our room was on the ground floor alongside the roaring river. By the light of the moon, when it appeared between storms, the river seemed to rise inch by inch till I was certain we would be washed away with the great branches of trees, huts, and animals that were hurtling past.

The next day we borrowed a crane from the British Army at Panitola, to get the station-wagon out. It took some time to get it up from the river bed, and it was a pitiful sight. Everything inside had been taken by scavengers, who had dived into the river looking for loot. Our clothes, our account books, our spare cash, everything had been spirited away, leaving nothing but the bare car. Members at the Panitola Club suggested we remain in Upper Assam and tour the tea plantations, staying with planters and playing in their clubs – of which there are many among the hundreds of miles of tea estates on both sides of the river. So we began touring again, performing *Arms and the Man*, as this production had sustained less damage than anything else. Our first show was in the Panitola Club, and thanks to the friendship of the planters we went from one bungalow and club to another, recouping our losses and learning about a way of life that was unique.

The managers of the tea estates live in bungalows on stilts, to keep out the wildlife and as a protection against flooding. Each tea estate has a club where the planters shop and meet. They are absolutely isolated in those fields of tea that stretch for hundreds of miles; so they have to make their own entertainment. There are polo teams attached to many of the clubs, and golf, cricket, or rugby teams, as well as numerous amateur theatre companies. We have since repeated this tour both in India and in East Pakistan, now Bangladesh; most of the tea estates on the river still belong to the same companies, Brooke Bond of India or Brooke Bond of Bangladesh. Our last visit there was in 1975, and by then most of the planters were Indian, but the way of life had hardly changed. They seemed more British than the British.

The troubles were now dying down. By October it seemed safe to go to Calcutta, where we stayed until January 1948, playing at the old Garrison Theatre in Park Street. It was here that I heard of the death of my father. I had dreaded it happening on the night I was to play *Hamlet*, but the news came instead in the middle of

Arms and the Man, by a telegram delivered during the interval. If anything, *Arms and the Man* is the more dangerous play, for in the final act Bluntshli is handed a telegram, and his next line is, 'My father's dead . . .' The words had an eerie resonance.

We were based at the Fairlawn Hotel, an old-fashioned family-run place, which became our home whenever we were in Calcutta. The Bengalis have always been interested in theatre, and their drama has a strong intellectual element. Two promising young actors, Utpall Dutt and Pratap Roy, joined us for a while. The Calcutta audiences and critics were enthusiastic. The *Statesman* critic wrote of *Othello*:

> Nobody appreciative of good acting and fluent stage-management should miss this performance . . . we come away from the Garrison Theatre with a feeling of integration, which no other available form of amusement is able to provide for the residents of this city, and having once enjoyed it, we cannot but wish that the English Repertory Company would prolong their stay here indefinitely.
>
> Their presence in Calcutta has raised the cultural level of the city, and could they be persuaded to make it their home, at least during every winter, Calcutta would be less cut off from the rest of the world.

At the end of the season we moved to Bombay; and we were there when on 2 February 1948, Mahatma Gandhi was assassinated in Delhi. The whole country waited with an air of breathless expectancy and fear, and then there was a moment of respite when it was known that Gandhi had not been killed by a Muslim, at least. We saw his ashes carried out to sea at Chowpatty, and we felt it was time to leave, for the future seemed uncertain. We booked to return to England on the P. & O. liner *Strathaird*.

As the Gateway of India sank below the horizon, it seemed that it was all over, like a vanishing dream. The ship's routine took over and became the centre of our lives now. There were no rehearsals as there had been when we had sailed out to India. We were just a few more of the Raj going home. But I could not help looking back. Why I cannot say, but India now seemed more important to me than England. I had gone there three times and was certain I would return again, though I did not know how inextricably my life would become linked with it.

7

Shakespeareana in India

We did not disband when we reached London. We intended to get the company going again after a rest; but just as things seemed to be moving, Peter became ill. He had not been well during the latter part of our Indian tour, constantly having to see doctors. He never seemed to get better, and no one seemed to know what the mysterious tropical complaint was. This time, after a hospital check, he decided he would not go back East until he was better. So it seemed our adventures were over, unless I took the full responsibility of managing myself, which I was not happy about. The little company had been wonderful with the work all shared, and I had been able to concentrate on the plays and not worry about booking or finances.

I had not settled back well into life in England. Peter and his brother, Geoff, acquired a flat in Richmond. They had brought with them two Indian servants, intending to live like retired 'expats', and Eileen had a home as well. But we had nowhere to go. The thought of living in a flat and being taken over by household shopping filled me with horror. We went to stay with Laura's sister, Beula, and her husband, Jim, in Warwickshire.

Then my brother Philip, who had stayed on in India after the war, wanted my help in restoring a fishing-boat he had acquired. This was a war-surplus vessel, bought for a song. I returned to Bombay, and we worked for nearly two months on the boat – a lovely vessel with a large hold, a saloon aft, seamen's accommodation forward, and both an engine and a sail. We had then to think what to do with it and decided to establish a shipping company: the South East Asia Shipping Company. Under Philip's direction, the company traded all over the Indian Ocean, eventually with half a dozen ships and an office in Bombay. When the company enlarged there was no room for small vessels, so we sold the boat we had restored to the Seychelles Government for use as the governor's yacht. The only time I went to the Seychelles I recognized her at once, by this time trading and carrying passengers between the islands.

I had thought of staying on in India with the shipping company, but Laura dreaded the social world of Anglo-India and did not see herself as a memsahib. Returning to England once more, plans were soon afoot to launch a new and larger company, based on the nucleus of our company. We opened in November 1948 at the lovely little theatre in Kidderminster with *Othello*; this was a great success, but after that there were one or two terrible dates. At one theatre we arrived to find no billing out. We were told it had not arrived, and I found the great bundle of posters lying unopened in a store-room backstage. At another place we had been booked for matinées only, while a circus held the stage in the evenings. Playing the part of Macbeth, I had to squeeze between cages of lions and tigers on my way to the stage, with the added attraction of having baboons living in the next dressing room.

We decided to tour Ireland and in the late summer of 1949 opened at Wexford. There were over seventy touring companies in the Republic at the time, from large ones to one-man shows. Sometimes they would throw in a raffle or a dance after the performance and there always seemed to be an audience. We never stopped, just travelled everywhere, the women in a taxi and the men on top of the scenery wagon – like real vagabonds. We stayed nearly a year, until I started to get itchy feet and wanted to go East again. Perhaps it was something to do with the convents where we performed occasionally, which reminded me of our times in India, or the sound of children's laughter, and the smell of the sea. However, although our expenses in Ireland were low, so was the income; there remained the question of raising enough money to take eight actors half-way round the world.

We returned to England and spent a year at Redditch in a good privately owned theatre. It was here that some of the actors who later came with us to India joined us. It was a good year artistically, with a new production each week, each one an individual production worked out in new ways: some quite startling, some good, and some awful. From Redditch we toured *A Streetcar Named Desire* with Laura quite superb at Blanche. We performed about fifty plays, from *Macbeth* and *A Midsummer Night's Dream* – beautiful with white and green settings, and Felicity in her first walk-on part as a fairy – to *My Wife's Family* and *See How They Run*. *My Wife's Family* brought us our most disastrous houses, when we played in midwinter at the theatre at Ilkley on the edge of the Yorkshire Moors. We almost froze and could not blame the audience for staying at home. During that week King George VI died, so the audiences and the laughs were even scarcer.

During our 1951–2 repertory season I made a special feature of the 'calls', which I notice the Royal Shakespeare Company has taken to doing in recent years. I always thought it was so silly to have the cast bowing in a row, so I invented new calls for each play, which were all different, similar to the films with their credits. There were many good performances, including one I shall always remember from Jennifer as the Cockney girl in *The Corn Is Green*. On occasions the national press saw our productions, and I felt that we were getting some recognition. We did a short season with *A Streetcar Named Desire* at Bridlington, and this brought about another chance meeting with Peter Meriton that provided the extra push I needed to plan for an Indian tour. I took Felicity along to a pantomime in the 'opposition' theatre, and there was my old partner, Peter, playing in *Mother Goose*. We decided then to work towards getting back to India.

While we were in repertory I had approached the Government of Malta, with the result that their Education Department asked us to undertake a three-week season there. My idea was that we could play in schools and educational establishments, but they wanted a company of actors to perform a repertoire at Valletta. We agreed, although they imposed quite impossible conditions. They had seen our programme and thought we should do all of it, changing the play not every week, but every night – one after the other. Somehow I thought we would manage and so I began recruiting more artists. It was a foolish decision, but I have this terrible bug, a form of cowardice that always makes me appear to be brave, like the fool soldier who dashes off at a charge because he is afraid of appearing weak.

The company was booked for three weeks at the Knights' Hall in Valletta. Since, as I was told, the island had a large English-speaking population and a garrison starved of culture, success was assured. We arrived at Valletta to learn from the tour's co-ordinators that they now wanted a total of eighteen plays, four more than were in the repertoire. As a generous concession they allowed a twenty-four-hour delay before the opening night. The rehearsals were made more fraught by the fact that we had lost two of the actors in Paris. They had travelled early and were going to meet us there, but due to a baggage delay we missed our boat train at Victoria; they spent several days, feeling ever more lost and abandoned, waiting for us. We finally located them and told them to come to Malta, but in the meantime two of the other actors had to learn Brabantio and Cassio with only a day's rehearsal. When *Othello* opened it was a fiasco. Brabantio dried completely, with the result that the Moor of Venice had to say most of his lines for him.

By the second day, the lost actors had arrived. The company was complete again. The second night's show, *Charley's Aunt*, went without a hitch. It proved to be a turning-point for the Shakespeareana Company; for in the audience with the Governor and Prime Minister of Malta were Earl Mountbatten of Burma and Countess Mountbatten. We all thanked God they had not come to the first night. Afterwards they came round to meet the cast and said how much they had enjoyed the show. This proved a moment of embarrassment for our eighteen-year-old member of the company, John Day. Being presented to Mountbatten, he was astonished to be told:

'I see you've changed your sex!'

Awed by the great man's authority, and not believing he had heard correctly, he meekly answered, 'Yes, sir.'

The two stared at each other in mutual bewilderment until Mountbatten showed him the programme, which read *Joan* Day, instead of John.

The following week we were invited to the Mountbatten's villa for lunch. I told Lady Mountbatten of my ambition one day to return to India. It turned out that she was going there within a week, and she offered to mention the fact that we would like help in arranging a tour. The Mountbattens came to other performances, including *Hay Fever*, which they had originally seen on its first night in the late twenties. They were a wonderful couple, and we would probably never have returned to India in 1953 had it not been for their help. Edwina left for Delhi and, between her and Mr Nehru, our return was given a blessing. Edwina became our patron; and, at a later date, so did the Maharaja of Jaipur. In some ways this was a mixed blessing, as being connected with these internationally wealthy figures suggested to some that we were highly subsidized and should therefore not want our fees!

From Malta we returned to England and began to organize the Indian tour. Peter, because he had been ill on our previous visit, decided to have another medical check-up before embarking. The result was that he had an operation, and a few days before we were due to sail I had a telegram to say that he was dead. It was a dreadful shock, all so quick and without any warning. Now the entire responsibility fell on me: business arrangements, finance, productions, repertoire, everything. I decided that we would have daily meetings of the company to discuss policy, though in the end the decision had to be mine. It was an unpromising start. We had hardly any money left after paying the fares, and no invitations from the princely states as in 1947. In 1953 India was in its first flush of newly found independence, and we had no idea how we would be received. There was the madness of Prohibition over most of the land, and there was the Entertainment Tax whereby you had to buy entertainment stamps for all the seats that were available before any money was taken at the box office, and then you had to get back the tax for unsold seats from the authorities. It involved an appalling amount of red tape and botheration.

Still, the decision had been made. On 4 June the company met to take the train to Tilbury. There were myself, Laura, Jennifer (then nineteen), and Felicity (six); and our company: Wendy Beavis, who became a great friend of Jennifer's, wearing an entire new outfit her parents had given her for the trip; Nancy Neal, a young American making her way round the world; John Day, who had been with us since the Redditch rep, six-foot-three and very talkative; Brian Kellett, another member who had joined us a year or so before and who was talented at set design; and Conor Farrington, a good-looking young Irishman I had recruited when we were playing at Wellington Baths, who had a lot of enthusiasm and a desire to travel.

Leaving behind the drizzle of England, we established ourselves in our cabins for the leisurely journey out to the East. Two weeks later, while cruising through the Red Sea, the ship's captain asked if we could put on a show to relieve the monotony of playing housie-housie and tombola. We decided on *Arms and the Man*. It turned out to be a dummy run for those actors who had never played in hot temperatures before: the oven heat of the desert will turn the grease-paint into sticks of warm fudge, and make the thick costumes, whiskers, and spirit gum an ordeal; I have always insisted that, no matter how high the temperature, no actor can go on-stage without make-up. This is all part of the transformation from the ordinary world to the mysteries of the theatre. The ship-board performance went well, and we were encouraged to follow with a shortened version of *Macbeth* and the comedy scenes from *Twelfth Night*. We were now in the wide open spaces of the Arabian Sea, and there was a noticeable swell. I had a disconcerting moment as Macbeth when I was addressing the lounge floor with grim solemnity – 'The sure and firm-set earth . . . ' – and it gave a sudden lurch.

On 25 June 1953 we sighted India once more, again under the cloudy skies of the rainy season. The rain did not seem to matter, for there were those familiar sights I had missed for so long – the dhows with triangular sails tacking across the bay, the noise and bustle of Bombay harbour, the crowds with garlands and flowers. Only the military police were no longer to be seen strutting about the quays. Everything seemed different, and yet the same. The crowds of porters looked as they always had, but the Europeans and westernized Indians were much better dressed than before. I had put on shorts and sandals to go ashore; then the sight of the elegant people waiting on the quay drove me back to my cabin to emerge properly attired in trousers, and a collar and tie.

My brother Philip, now Director of the South East Asia Shipping Company, was there waiting for us, as well as Frank, the actor who had joined our troupe in 1947. He had returned with us to Britain but as soon as it got cold had gone back to the sun, where he taught elocution in a seminary. He was wearing a battered topi, and the usual millimetre of cigarette stuck to his lip. He was now around seventy, but still game to rejoin us for our tour.

In the Customs shed, we began to find out how much some

things had changed since we were last in the subcontinent. We waited at the barrier while two surly officials shook their heads over our baskets of props and went off to consult someone higher up. Our fellow passengers dispersed to their trains, planes, and homes, tinselled garlands round their necks. Meanwhile I spent four hours arguing with the officials over the amount they were asking as duty: 4,000 rupees, the equivalent of £300. I refused to pay a rupee; and we left the theatrical gear behind, piled our own luggage on to a few cabs, and drove off to the hotel. Three days later the Customs officials, finally convinced of our poverty, dropped the duty from 4,000 rupees to 40. Perhaps if I had slipped them a few rupees to begin with, for 'services about to be rendered', we would not have had to spend three days hanging around.

Our first show – *Macbeth* – was at the Fort Convent, near the hotel. We arrived with a porter pulling our hand-cart of theatrical props, and went into the familiar routine of unroping boxes, hammering nails, building a rostrum out of lashed benches, borrowing a gramophone, conscripting a dhobi to iron the costumes, setting lights, and putting up curtains. Then we retired to a kindergarten classroom to make up, cramming our knees under tiny desks and watched by crowds of children in the doorway. At the appointed time, the Witches and the Thanes emerged from the classroom to play their parts, and once again we were among the most rewarding audiences in the world; rows of intelligent Indian schoolgirls gazed at the drama with startled absorption, drinking in every word and gesture. It was a good start, and soon more bookings were coming in. An officer on the trip out had suggested we tried the Indian Army, and I booked two shows in the school of artillery in Deolali. A guest staying at our hotel fixed a tour of Gujarat as far as Ahmadabad, and Frank proved invaluable in his knowledge of local educational establishments. Every morning he would supply us with lists of schools and colleges, and the actors would disperse over the city in ones or twos, to try to find the places. We would ask to see the principal – who might be a Hindu in a dhoti, a Goanese mother superior, a Christian brother, a Parsee, or a Muslim. Shakespeare was the password, and the reception was nearly always warm. At one newly built Hindu college that Brian and Conor tackled, the principal cried:

'You act Shakespeare? Ah, Shakespeare is my guru.' Then he quoted:

> *What is man*
> *If his chief good and market of his time*
> *Be but to sleep and feed?*

Within a few days there were dates in what seemed to be an ever widening circle. As soon as money was coming in, I went to my old tailor and ordered two pairs of white trousers each for the men and white skirts for the women, so that we looked like part of the subcontinent and not as if we had just arrived.

We had one final evening with the officers who had become our friends on the voyage, when we were invited to dine aboard the ship, which was still in dock. Laura said she was too tired to go, but allowed me to take Felicity along, provided I brought her back by nine o'clock. We entered the harbour area with special passes and were welcomed to an excellent dinner in the deserted dining saloon. Afterwards we visited various cabins, where doors were locked, portholes closed, bottles brought out, and tooth-mugs handed round. The secretive precautions were necessary because Prohibition was in force; the harbour authorities kept a strict eye on ships.

The wireless operator had just filled our tooth-mugs for the second time with Johnny Walker when there was a sharp knock at the door and a harsh voice ordered, 'Open up!' The wireless operator briskly poured his mug down the washbasin, and the rest of us swiftly followed suit before he opened the door. It was only the Second Engineer playing a joke. We refilled our glasses, and the party continued until the whisky ran out and we all switched to gin. Felicity's bedtime came and went. Some time after midnight, tired of lemonade and the conversation of grown men descending to her own mental age, she persuaded me to bring her home.

We woke up Laura, who said sleepily: 'Who's that?'

'It's Daddy, he's drunk!' Felicity announced sternly.

In the early morning I was roused by a telephone call from the Dock Area Police Station. The police had caught Brian and Conor at 4 a.m. trying to leave the docks without their passes. The two had given an eloquent explanation of how they had come as members of a distinguished theatre group to present a signed copy of Shakespeare to the officers of the ship.

'Signed by Shakespeare?' the official asked, thinking he might catch them out. I backed up their story, which was true, and the police allowed them to go.

Prithviraj Kapoor, the first name in Bombay Theatre, sent an invitation to us to a performance of *Deewar* – Hindi for 'Wall' – which was produced and largely written by him. The performance was by his company, Prithvi Theatres, in the Old Opera House, which was now a cinema except on Sunday mornings when he took it over for one of his productions. He had seen a photograph of us in *The Times of India*, and gave us front-row seats.

Prithviraj – a mountain of a man – had been trained in an English company that had visited India years before. He had already made a name as a film star in Indian films and had started a company to produce plays in Hindi. It was a vast ensemble of about one hundred artists and workers, masses of scenery and musicians. We were handed a synopsis in English, which told us:

> *Deewar* is an allegorical story. . . . It is the story of two brothers, and can also be the story of two different systems. This is the story of the woman who drew the line of blood between the brothers. This can also be the story of that third party who in the last 150 years of its reign has added many bloody chapters to our pages of history, who has left now but whose footprints are still deeply engraved and are burning like sparks of fire on our hard-earned freedom.

In other words, it was all about British rule and the evils of Partition.

The play began with a scene of singing and thanksgiving, while the two brothers Suresh, played by Prithviraj and Ramesh, were beaming and embracing each other. Then, one stormy night, a foreign woman and her companions come to the door for shelter. Soon Suresh and Ramesh had taken off their dhotis and turbans and appeared in check shirts, riding breeches, and boots. Finally, the female John Bull figure suggests that two of them live separately. So Ramesh demands Partition, and a wall of large bricks is set up, right down the middle of the stage. 'The brothers are separated. The woman was the one who had the greatest hand in all this. The Wall of hatred was the only support she had. Ramesh [Pakistan] was obstinate; Suresh [India] was hopeless.' Then came a storm and the people cried, 'We do not want the Wall!' At this point the peasants swarmed in with picks and crowbars and knocked the bricks all over the stage. Ramesh and Suresh embraced again, and the company chanted the lines, 'We were One. We are One. We will remain One.'

There was much singing and dancing, lengthy heart-to-hearts between the characters, and some excellent acting, particularly from one of Prithviraj's sons, as one of the servants. The production, with its huge cast, was polished and effective. We met Prithviraj during one of the intervals – the show was four and a half hours long. At the end he made a long speech in Hindi (adding bits in English for our benefit), mainly to say that, after all, it was not really the foreigners' fault! As we left the theatre he was standing in the foyer; a great figure like a Róman Elder, bowing and holding a begging-bowl, not for his theatre, but for a charity.

That was the beginning of our more or less parallel courses. We met Prithviraj many times all over the place, and eventually his youngest son, Shashi, became our son-in-law. He signed his letters to us, 'Yours fraternally', and I think that is what he felt. If his company was in Bombay and we were going on tour, Prithvi and his wife would meet us at Dada Station. They were usually a little late, but we would see this great white-clad figure striding over the railway bridge followed by his tiny wife. A bearer would come behind with a great basket of food for our actors: tandoori chicken, nans, and perhaps mangoes if they were in season. There was always a shine in his eye and a cheerful smile as he waved us on our way. It was a benediction from one who knew that a benediction was needed.

Prithviraj was a throw-back to the old-time English actor-managers. He loved it all – being a father figure, a great actor, the idol of all and sundry. He did everything in a big way and he acted all the time, on-stage and off, but he was genuinely good-hearted and unbelievably kind to his company. He spent much of what he earned in films to keep his theatre troupe together out of pure charity; and there are still quite a few old actors in Bombay with a pension paid monthly from the Prithvi Theatre. For years he was a member of the Upper House in the Indian Parliament, a part he played superbly, dressed in spotless white Indian dress and covered with a great shawl of the finest Kashmir wool: a great patriot, a sort of elderly Brutus. His wife appeared to be just the opposite, very small and quiet. But I secretly think she was master in their house.

It seemed that we needed an extra young male for the company. We advertised for one and were immediately submerged by avalanches of letters and droves of young men in their best suits. Most were totally unsuitable; some could hardly speak English. The applications by letter were almost pathetic in their eagerness: 'I am young, long, and extremely handsome'; or 'My friends all tell me I should go on the cinema.'

Some of these young men desperately advanced the most irrelevant qualifications, such as: 'I have a diploma in Chemistry and Physics and I have ridden from Delhi to Bombay on a bicycle in 21 days'; or 'I am Brahmin come from very old family. We helped British in 1804.' Then there were those who tried to overwhelm us with superlatives: 'I am the dashing, eager type with splendid physique (good teeth), amazing biceps and a very complete memory. I go at things with full vigour and carry all things away. My eye is compelling and I have a voice that is of gold, both soft and loud (very loud if you like).' One of the most compelling letters announced:

Dear Sir,
In the year 1932 I had the good fortune to have my palm read by Prince Louis Cheiro, the great world-wide-famous palmistry expert, who has since lent his name to that profound science. Since then all events he foretold for me have come amazingly true with unfailing regularity. But one forecast he laid particular emphasis on was that about the year 1953 my activities would take the dramatic bent and I would devote myself to an outstandingly successful career on the stage and be a gold mine to any producer (particularly English) who would by luck or judgement take me on.

We made our choice by interview and picked someone who said he was Egyptian, but who spoke excellent English. We took him to a school we were playing at. He watched the actors climbing around the rafters, straining on ropes, and dragging platforms about; next day we received a letter from him saying he had been taken ill suddenly. In his place we hired Anwar Mirza, who had proved his interest by coming unasked to several shows and remaining unperturbed by all the extra work the actors had to do. Finally, we were ready to leave Bombay and begin our tour, the first stop being the Indian Army establishment at Deolali.

The Indian trains were slow, broad, and without corridors. Each second-class compartment for four, six, or eight people, had its own lavatory, fans, bunks that you let down from the wall, and triple sliding windows: one of glass to keep out dust, one of gauze to keep out flies, and one slotted screen to keep out the sun. Beyond these were bars, to keep out humans. At each station hucksters set up their trays of samosas, betel, cigarettes, and sweets, and filled the steamy, spice-laden air with their nasal chant of 'Pan! Biri pan' or 'Cigaraite, cigaraite!'

'Cha garam, cha garam!' called the seller of thick, syrupy tea.

The railway stations of India are always crowded with country people lying around on their bundles, children with kohl-rimmed eyes, their tiny ears pierced with ear-rings. A bearer would climb in with our lunch, ordered by telephone from a previous station. At the next station he would get out with the dirty plates. There were many stops, and at each one swarms of people would clamour around the third-class carriages, which composed three-quarters of the train. Those compartments were long and dim, with huddled rows of passengers squatting like hens in a battery, their bare heels on the bare seats. The floor would be covered with their chattels, cloth-bound bundles, stoves, baskets, brass pots, and umbrellas.

The train took nearly five hours to reach Deolali, climbing through the sodden green landscape of the monsoon season, among the paddy fields and standing ponds. We reached the camp, which looked like a facsimile of any British military establishment. We played our repertoire, *Othello* and *Arms and the Man*, in a lecture hall after sliding away blackboards covered with diagrams of imaginary manoeuvres. *Arms and the Man* was enjoyed more and more as it became increasingly irreverent about soldiering. Some of the officers laughed so heartily that they would touch off an extra round of laughter by themselves. The Indian Army, it seemed, was exempt from Prohibition, and our hosts generously sent a bearer round each night with strict orders to keep all glasses brimming with whisky. After two intervals our production lost pace a little; but as during each interval the audience had evacuated with military smartness and efficiency to the bar across the lawn, they were not in a censorious mood.

The following week saw a totally different regime when we played and stayed at the Hindu College in Surat. It is a *strictly* Hindu college, and the food is vegetarian. There would be two meals a day, at ten and five. We would pad into the dining room, having taken off our shoes outside, and squat down on little benches about two inches high, and eat from a tin tray, or *thali*. Each tray had some curried vegetables, rice, and dhal, which we ate with our fingers. This diet of rice and dhal did not provide much energy for wading through *Othello*, but it was a welcome change from the indifferent English-style food served in most hotels.

The college principal lived very simply with his family in a few sparsely furnished rooms, the bathroom having just a solitary cold water tap. A devout Hindu, he dressed in a dhoti and moved slowly about the house in bare feet. Conor later wrote that, under the impression that here was an Indian completely untouched by foreign influences, he began speaking to him in somewhat over-simple English. Then he happened to look at the book-case near his bed and found it full of volumes on educational psychology, philosophy, history, and novels by James Joyce, Thomas Mann, and Virginia Woolf. Inside the covers was scribbled the principal's name, followed by 'New York 1950' or 'Cambridge 1949'.

Each night chairs would get broken as students from several colleges crowded in. They were onne of our noisier audiences, shouting comments in Gujarati and blowing bulb-horns or whistles during the play. When an embrace on-stage was imminent the racket increased, perhaps to cover embarrassment, for no kiss is ever allowed on the Indian stage or screen. Nor was our stage considered sacred to the actors; one night a surprise character appeared during the second part of *Othello*, where Cassio meets Emilia in Desdemona's garden, and repents his drunken behaviour. Conor as Cassio had just met Laura as Emilia when suddenly a busy little man in khaki, one of the canteen bearers, trotted on to the stage with a bottle of fizzy lemonade in one hand and a couple of straws in the other, peering about for his customer. He crossed the stage, staring at the actors, as if he wondered what they were doing in those clothes, and then saw his customer – John – gesticulating in the wings, and dived off to deliver his drink.

We could not have had a more contrasting audience when, two months later, in Mysore, we were summoned by the Maharaja to play *The Merchant of Venice* in his own theatre. This was an imposing and ornately plastered place, with a huge baroque proscenium arch, faced by irregular tiers of boxes and balconies. Two of the boxes had reed curtains hanging like fine Venetian blinds so that the occupants could see without being seen, and with private corridors for entrance and exits. These were the ladies' seats. A glint of silk and the faint tinkle of glass bangles could just be detected behind the curtains. The main auditorium was filled by rows of palace officials in large and perfectly wound turbans, sitting completely motionless. When the royal box was occupied by a dimly visible presence in white, we began.

Usually an audience was quickly involved in *The Merchant of Venice*, which happened to be one of the favourite plays of the repertoire in India. They should certainly have thawed out by the time Portia was discussing her suitors. But that night we played to dead silence throughout. As always, we blamed ourselves and heightened our acting. Launcelot Gobbo gesticulated and sniggered; as Shylock I developed an exaggerated Jewish accent; Laura's Portia had an augmented lilt of the voice and roll of the eyes; and Conor, as Gratiano, took to winking and twirling his moustaches towards the reed curtains in the hope that the ladies, at least, might relax. All to no avail. The Maharaja did not smile or laugh, so none of his officials would be caught doing so.

After the performance, while we sat, rather subdued, in our dressing room, one of the turbanned officials came to say that the Maharaja would receive us for a moment. We went to the vestibule of his private picture gallery adjoining the theatre. The Maharaja was young, tall, and extremely fat, with a snow-white turban and a polite, fatigued manner. We had told Felicity to present him with a garland but, only six years old, she was overwhelmed by his size and retreated in confusion when she realized she could not reach his neck. A pink Rolls-Royce floated silently up to the steps, and the Maharaja bade us goodbye in a soft, fatigued voice and deported himself down the red carpet, a stately procession of one, to be driven away; the officials bowed, their heads in their hands.

Jennifer, aged seventeen. This is the photograph we used in our Shakespeareana programmes

Felicity at the time of *The Good Life* – the television series that made her a household name in the 1970s

Overleaf: A selection of scenes from over fifty years in the theatre – 1931 to 1985. Top: *Becket, Antony and Cleopatra, The Taming of the Shrew, Becket,* Petruchio in *The Taming of the Shrew*. Middle: *Dear Liar, Charley's Aunt, Dear Liar, Wuthering Heights, A Murder has Been Arranged,* Tony Lumpkin in *She Stoops to Conquer,* Min Lee in *On the Spot*. Lower: Ophelia in *Hamlet,* Falstaff in *The Merry Wives of Windsor, The Man in Grey, The Merry Wives of Windsor, The Taming of the Shrew, The Man in Grey*

Three Ophelias: Laura began playing Ophelia with the Edward Dunstan Company at the age of twenty-one. She is seen here playing it in our company, around 1936

Jennifer (above) is playing the part during our season at Redditch in 1950, aged seventeen. Felicity (left), aged seventeen as Ophelia in the film *Shakespeare Wallah* – she never played it on stage

Myself as actor-manager Tony Buckingham and Felicity as his daughter Lizzie in *Shakespeare Wallah*, 1964 – the film that brought the story of our wandering company to a wider audience

Cinema lobby card, depicting a scene from *Shakespeare Wallah*. Jennifer was already married to Shashi Kapoor and had two children. For some reason, my name has been left off the credits altogether, and Ismail's has been misspelt

CONTEMPORARY FILMS PRESENTS

SHAKESPEARE WALLAH (A)

WITH **FELICITY KENDAL** **SHASHI KAPOOR** **MADHUR JAFFREY** **LAURA LIDDELL**
DIRECTED BY **JAMES IVORY** PRODUCED BY **ISRAIL MERCHANT** MUSIC BY **SATYAJIT RAY**

The Kapoor family at home in Bombay, around 1970. From left: Kunal, Jennifer, Sanjna, Shashi and Karan. Kunal is now acting and running the Prithvi Theatre, which Jennifer originally started; Sanjna is studying acting and is beginning to appear in films, and Karan has become a successful film actor

Felicity with her son, Charlie, aged one. He was born in January 1973

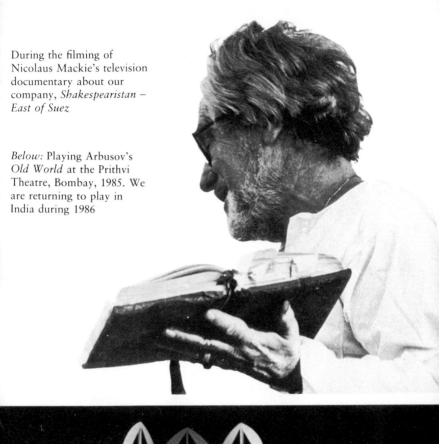

During the filming of Nicolaus Mackie's television documentary about our company, *Shakespearistan – East of Suez*

Below: Playing Arbusov's *Old World* at the Prithvi Theatre, Bombay, 1985. We are returning to play in India during 1986

At the Savoy Hotel for Laura's seventy-seventh birthday, with Felicity, in May 1985

The son of the Maharaja of Udaipur, whom we visited on a tour of Rajasthan the following year, was a much more enthusiastic host. He had seen us in the 1947 tour as a schoolboy at Mayo College in Ajmer, and now invited us to stay at his palace for a week. It transpired that he wanted only one show, and the rest of the time was spent being shown around his domain and entertained as honoured guests. There was much scaffolding around his vast white palace on the edge of the lake. During the time of Partition it had been neglected; the Maharaja was restoring it bit by bit, when he could afford to do so. As he had a penchant for marble baths and gold taps, we could see the difficulty.

The palace was huge: corridor after corridor, with a secluded harem quarter. Some way from the palace was a row of stables for elephants, of which only two inhabitants were left, and we were taken on an elephant ride through the streets of Udaipur. From turreted rooms in the palace we looked down on to the lake, and across to another palace on a little island in the centre. Glistening white towers and domes studded with crystal sparkled in the sun and were reflected in the water. A high wall surmounted by arches and minarets enclosed the entire island, and a row of enormous stone-carved elephants stood along the water-front. The place was totally deserted, the stillness broken only by the humming of clouds of mosquitoes.

We reached the island palace and the Maharaja's hunting reserve on the other shore by motor-launch. Here we were taken to a huge stone arena with a very high wall. We climbed to the top and looked down into the pit. It was empty, but we were told that traditionally on maharajas' birthdays various forms of jungle life were released together to fight it out until the tiger reigned supreme. We saw no tigers, but at one of the towers in the reserve from which we watched the animals, the game-keeper called with a whooping sound, and a herd of wild boar came rushing out of the woods to be fed. For Felicity, the Maharaja brought a baby deer to play with. Some years later he finally turned the lake palace into a hotel, and the once empty corridors echo now with people on expensive package tours.

8

The Wandering Company

Our Shakespeareana Company consisted of an odd mixture of people who may not in everyday life have had a great deal in common, but in the close-knit atmosphere of working and living together, all bound in the common aim of overcoming crises and putting on the best productions we could, we became very close, like one large family. There was no room for rivalry.

I chose my actors basically on instinct, rather than on their record. A number of them had not much acting experience; Laura and I would coach them, and most developed into good company actors. Of the little band we began with a few remained for some years. Brian Kellett, who was with us for nine years, eight of them in India, was the longest-serving member. He was invaluable in designing and painting sets and had a meticulous eye. John Day, when I first knew him, was a tall, lolloping young man, good-looking and highly emotional. He was with us in England at the age of seventeen, but the next year was called up for his National Service. He was so shattered by the thought of two years in the Army that after thirty-six hours, believing something drastic must be done, he threw himself out of his barrack dormitory window. He just missed the concrete path below and was not hurt. The Army authorities decided they would have less trouble if they got rid of him and, having kept him locked up for a further five weeks, discharged him, to their mutual relief.

Conor Farrington had been with us in Ireland and England, a delightful young Irishman, but he could not take the heat and discomfort of India, and he left after eighteen months. While he was with us, he would get up at dawn every day to work on an epic play about Ireland. I am not sure whether this was ever produced, but he wrote others that were and is now an actor and writer with Radio Eirann. Wendy Beavis, who had come to us fresh from drama school, became close friends with Jennifer. She and John Day stayed with us for three and a half years in India, and when they went back they both intended to have a rest and return. They never did, but we kept in touch and met again years later at the wedding when John married June. Wendy became a nurse and lived with her parents at Solihull. John went into antique dealing and then, with June, opened a restaurant at their home in Somerset.

Of the Indian actors we enrolled, Shashi Kapoor and Utpal Dutt went on to make flourishing careers in films. Then there was Anwar Mirza, who eventually married a Russian girl and went to work in Moscow, and Marcus Murch, who stayed with us for many years before going to Delhi to start a theatre company there. Marcus (we also called him Mark) had first acted for us when he was still a student at Sherwood College in Naini Tal and we were short of a priest for Ophelia's funeral. He had to recite the 'obsequies' speech and began, 'Her obsecues have been enlarged . . . ' Then, realizing he had entirely forgotten the speech, he simply said, 'She's had it.'

Despite this inauspicious start, Marcus wanted to persevere as an actor. He had an interesting past, like that of the hero in *The Importance of Being Earnest*. He was left as a baby on the doorstep of an English missionary called Miss Murch. She could not resist adopting children, and eventually had a grand total of thirteen. She had very little money so she would go along to the headmaster of a college and browbeat him into educating a child for free. She wore a white sari and a great cloak, and could be seen striding round Naini Tal or galloping up the hills with the horse just skirting the edge of the precipice. She lived in a cottage overgrown with rambling clematis and jasmine, with her brood of foundlings of all ages and nations. The eldest, Raj, was a grown man when she took in her last new-born babe. They were all called her name, Murch, and brought up as Christians of a rather stern variety; when they told lies she scrubbed their tongues with a dry brush. Miss Murch's children all did well in different walks of life. In fact, Jennifer had plans to make a film about her. Jennifer and

Marcus died within a day of each other, both almost the same age. There was a sort of love-hate relationship between the two of them. They were great pals but Marcus had a strangely spiteful sense of humour. He once nearly brained another actor, Richard Gordon, with his sword on-stage, but I could see the wicked gleam in his thin, saturnine face a split-second before, and pulled Richard out of the way.

As people left, new actors arrived: Peter Bromilow, who is now in Hollywood playing in films and television; Jimmy Gibson, an American who went to work for a travel firm and is still going round the world; Sonja Fankenal Ingeborg, who eventually went with her family to Australia and, as Sonja Borg, is producing television programmes there; Coral de Rosario, who joined us at the same time as Sonja, in May 1957, staying with us through some of our most precarious times in the Far East, even entering a competition dressed as the Hunchback of Notre-Dame in order to bring in some money for the company. Then there was Oliver Cox, who drove out to India in a 1935 Wolseley ambulance he had bought for £80, got involved in a fight in Afghanistan, and arrived in Calcutta with his front teeth missing, so that we had to take him swiftly along to a Chinese dentist before he could be allowed on-stage. On another occasion he got roaring drunk, realized he had missed his cue as Hamlet's father's ghost, and tried to stagger on to the stage wearing nothing at all. I shall always remember a fight he had with Richard 'Alfy' Gordon; the two were going at each other furiously while I was in the middle of showing some visitors around the theatre, who fortunately thought it was all part of the rehearsal.

While we were playing in Cochin we recruited another of our actors. Among the audience on that sweltering night were three men wearing dinner jackets. When we met them afterwards we learnt that they were British tea planters and had ridden ninety miles through the jungle on their motor-bikes dressed in full regalia to see our play. One of them, Ralph Pixton, came to see many of our other performances, admittedly no longer wearing his dinner jacket, but ninety miles was still quite a journey, and illustrated his enthusiasm for the theatre. After attending the third show, Ralph told me that he wanted to go into the theatre. I was staggered to discover that a tea planter would leave the easy security of his job for a precarious life on the road; I told him, if he was serious, to join us in Poona in a couple of months' time. He immediately handed in his resignation to his employers, who thought he had had too much sun and offered to transfer him to another plantation in a cooler part of India. Ralph was serious, however. He sold off his belongings and presented himself to us in Poona. A month later he took the role of Antonio in *The Merchant of Venice*. He stayed in the company for about two years, before leaving for Hong Kong to join Hong Kong Radio, where today he runs a successful phone-in show.

All the company, apart from Frank Wheatley, were in their late teens or their twenties. Frank had joined us in 1953, unable to resist the combined call of the stage and the road. There he was, having thrown up his job teaching elocution, with his topi and his battered trunk, well into his seventies and as eager as any twenty-year-old. He was a real old stager, and had even appeared in his youth with Sir Frank Benson at Drury Lane. He stayed with us for years and was always game, even when he forgot he had been on for a part and insisted on doing it all over again. But when he forgot that he was supposed to appear in the second act of *Candida* and refused to go on, something had to be done. He retired to Denville Hall, the home for old actors, from where he appeared in many television shows, and died at the age of almost ninety.

At the heart of the company there were always Laura and Jennifer and me. Our elder daughter's devotion to the company was total. Not only was she a magnificent actress, but she delighted in all the crafts to do with design and costume, repairing or dyeing clothes in need of rejuvenation. Laura insisted on keeping up the standards of dress both on- and off-stage. Jennifer once said, 'We were the first hippies' – but we were not, because whenever we got off the train we were immaculately dressed. I have a photograph of the company standing under a tree, all the men in shirts and ties and the women in clean, fresh-looking dresses. Despite all the demands on her as 'mother' to the company, Laura still managed to be mother to her daughters whenever needed, reading bedtime stories to Felicity and staying up with her when she had toothache.

As Felicity grew older she became involved in the family business. Ever since being carried on-stage as the changeling in *A Midsummer Night's Dream* she was part of the company. By the age of six she was assisting with the props, polishing the brass goblets, helping to make armour by sewing bottle-tops to the hems of Roman battle-costumes, or writing letters and setting fire to the edges to make them look like parchment. When she was eight we decided to pay her 10 rupees a month for her efforts, each payment being noted in a little green account book. We gave her the time-log, to time the length of each scene every night and, once she could read well enough, the prompt book. Her education was constantly interrupted, but whenever we were in a place for a few days she would be sent to the local convent school – usually one we were playing at; she grew up speaking Hindi as well as English. Felicity made her speaking début aged nine in *Macbeth*, in the Sacred Heart Convent in Bombay, playing Macduff's son. Despite being brought up in the theatre she suffered from last-minute stage fright. I saw her trying to run towards the door in her little kilt and hat, scooped her up, carried her to the stage, and threw her on. When she was eleven she was playing Puck in *A Midsummer Night's Dream*, wearing the costume Laura had worn in England, the green wig and green leaves, and her face painted a matching shade. She was a delight as Puck; her cheeky little face was made for the part.

There was one hiccup in Felicity's early career, when at the age of eight she appeared in the non-speaking role of the Prince of Morocco's page-boy in *The Merchant of Venice*. Felicity had to stand beside the Prince, her face blacked up, until he lost Portia's hand in the casket scene. At this point Morocco gets upset and rushes off-stage, forgetting his shoes. The page-boy runs after him, frantically waving his Turkish slippers – reminiscent of Strauss's *Rosenkavalier*. Felicity had been playing this part for a while, and became a little bored; one night she did not take her bubblegum out before she went on-stage. The Morocco scene is quite long, and her mouth was full of chewed gum. She unwittingly blew an enormous bubble just as attention was about to focus on her. Mortified, she afterwards announced to the company:

'I'm finished with the theatre and I'm never going on the stage again.'

She kept her resolution for eight months until finally she decided she wanted to play the part again. Since then she has never looked back.

Felicity did not get involved in the company as deeply as

Jennifer. To her it seemed for the most part a game, though she was never careless or slapdash. From an early age she would be falling in love with one of the actors or her elder sister's boy-friends. At times she felt in the shadow of Jennifer, who played the heroine in most of our plays, while Felicity was the comic or a page-boy. Felicity was a round little child, and we used to call her 'Fatty Foo'. When she grew more *svelte* we dropped the prefix: she is still 'Foo' to her family.

Getting on and off the stage and being convincing in the part – the technical side of acting – meant much to Felicity. I showed her the importance of assuming the character in the wings before you even get to the stage and of continuing to act as you leave, rather than letting your shoulders relax the moment you reach the wings. She began to understand the psychological need for our various rituals, the concentration on the character as you put on the make-up, washing the hands before you go on-stage. Laura was strict in the enforcement of cleanliness in the theatre, and even if we were playing to an audience of about twenty in the local cinema she would wash her feet in an enamel bowl backstage to make sure the soles of her feet were clean for the bedroom scene. I myself was insistent on the proper treatment of costumes. No one was allowed to sit down while in costume, and the girls had to hold their long skirts off the floor until they went on. I also insisted on the proper care of our wardrobe of wigs and hairpieces. Each actor was responsible for looking after them and had to comb the wig out and pin it up after the show. One of Felicity's most important jobs was looking after the props that would be required for the production on a given day. As we could not carry with us all the requirements for the fifteen or so plays in our repertoire, we borrowed many of the items from people connected with venues where we performed. Felicity was taught to be responsible for finding all the props for a particular production and to ensure that our own props were always maintained and on hand when needed for a particular scene. There could be no finer school for anyone to learn the art of backstage work, regardless of whether one was going on to become a stage-manager, actress, or director. At the end of the production she had to make sure all the borrowed props and furniture were returned with thanks to those who had kindly assisted us.

There were some important and irreplaceable basic items that we used wherever we set up our stage. The backdrop was formed by a sky-blue curtain, which was capable of stretching across a stage fifty feet wide rising some thirty feet high. This curtain travelled in a large canvas bag and was called 'Big Bertha'. Coming upstage from this drop were 'blocks' formed by several rostra and trapped tightly within black curtaining material, so from the front of the house and under suitable lighting conditions they resembled huge solid blocks that could form battlements, or whatever was required. These were suitably arranged to create a proper perspective, which is most important in achieving a balance of vision. Curtaining of different shades was suspended either side to conceal entrances and exits, of which there would be two or three. The visual would be completed with lighting effects. The big blue backdrop would at times appear to be a clear blue sky as seen from the inside of a dark and cold medieval fortress, or equally a colourful sunset with a mixture of gold and warm red lighting. The effects that could be produced from simple and thoughtful planning were astounding, and yet such effects could not be allowed to overshadow the costume or the spoken word; the balance had to be maintained.

Some of the actors never fully realized while we travelled across India that, far from being a relic of pre-war years of classical rep, we were ahead of our time, producing Shakespeare in a way that was only later adopted in studio performances. Of course, with us it was necessity as well. We could not cart around heavy scenery, so the sets were sparse, some might say Brechtian. Sometimes we played with simply the backcloth and borrowed stage furniture. One of our best and simplest effects was a blue length of cloth that we would make ripple across the stage, as a river. We became adept in the art of improvisation. At one cinema we were to play at we discovered that not only were we billed as *The Merchant of Venus*, but the stage was only six feet deep in front of the cinema screen. The width of forty-four feet more than compensated for the lack of depth, and it was like performing in a corridor. What I preferred was an empty hall where we could make our own platform out of tables, planks, and boxes covered with tarpaulin. This meant we could vary the levels and have large aprons, although there were occasional disasters – such as when the guests at Macbeth's feast were bidden, 'You know your own degrees,/Sit down', and the long form at the back of the banquet table began to subside through the makeshift stage under their weight. This ended with everyone out of sight under the table.

Shakespeare paints the scenes with words. We played *Macbeth* once in a large gymnasium in Hong Kong with the afternoon sun streaming into the auditorium. Simply through the strength of the words and willing the scene into darkness, we managed to give the impression of night. At Stratford-upon-Avon during the fifties a production of *Henry V* numbered seventy people in the cast. We put on the same play in India with a company that varied between eight and fifteen people, and created the impression of battle scenes by flourishing the French and English flags from the wings.

We would use local musicians, and the songs of Elizabethan England seemed to harmonize perfectly with an Indian flute or sitar. I costumed some of the productions in local dress, which had the effect of bringing the two cultures together; and from this a wonderful understanding between actor and audience developed. Sometimes, though, we had to go to great lengths to get through to people. When we were playing in Sarawak, we mounted a performance for a school made up entirely of non-English-speaking students. I had a synopsis of the play, *Macbeth*, written out in Chinese for the students, and I pantomimed the play in good old Elizabethan tradition. From the moment I mimed that I was about to murder King Duncan, the audience participated wholeheartedly – laughing at the funny bits, booing at the baddies, and holding their breath at the tense parts.

Our lighting, though effective, was primitive. Marcus Murch made the stage electrics his speciality and looked after all the lighting and setting up the sound system at all our performance points. Not once during the time he was with our company did the electrics fail, nor did we ever fall short of requirements. Sometimes he had a difficult job, particularly when we would arrive in a venue to find they had only vaguely heard of A.C. current, and D.C. was all they could offer, which meant our lighting equipment – especially the spotlights and the record-player – could not be used. Marcus would disappear for hours on end and reappear with a clapped-out transformer, which would work, just. The owner of the transformer usually came too, and they would talk electrics as though they had known each other for years. The man invariably stayed for the performance and tried to help backstage, which we had to tolerate in order to provide a performance with proper lighting.

Our footlights consisted of a long metal box with ten bulbs, each shaded by coloured gel paper. This would be put down in front of the stage. I bought the two spotlights in Hong Kong, and they were used (or misused) sparingly. Once someone highlighted Brian Kellett with a livid lime-green follow-spot, trained carefully on his face, which ruined the effect of Brian's painstaking make-up. Early in our tour, before Marcus joined us, I remember telling Anwar, who was new to the company, to 'reduce the bulbs', as I wanted the footlights cut down for the final scenes of *Othello*. He obeyed all too readily. Iago was surprised to see, in mid-soliloquy, Anwar crawling round the side of the stage to the footlight, where he proceeded to remove bulb after bulb. Bowing to exigency, we played the murder scene solely by the light of the candle in Othello's hand. I am told it was strangely effective.

Anwar's appearance on-stage was not as unusual in India as it would have been in England. In the East the stage is not seen as being the preserve only of actors. With Chinese operas, for instance, when the heroine kneels down, one stage-hand will bring on a cushion for her and another will smooth out her train. There is no pretence that they are part of the play. An early example in our productions had been the canteen bearer with the bottle of lemonade, and there were a number of others. Once, in the middle of a tense scene between Othello and Iago, the dhobi, a pile of freshly laundered clothing on his head and an iron in his hand, came up to me on-stage and said, 'Dhobi finished now, sahib.' This could have set the play on an entirely new course if he had dropped one of the handkerchiefs! On another occasion a servant, disapproving of the furniture being arranged to look outwards towards the audience, rearranged it just before the show to make it look more like a real room.

Without the dhobis and tailors of India we would never have been able to keep up our standards of costume. Often the stage clothes ended a performance wringing wet with perspiration. It was inevitable if you played in a temperature of 110°F in costume, wig, make-up, false beard. Your tights would be drooping in wet folds, your beard on the verge of dropping off, and beads of perspiration would trickle down your nose to be passed on to your partner in an embrace. If you played out of doors, tiny insects would creep under your wig, and mosquitoes would nibble at your ankles. We would make our exits calmly; then once out of sight of the audience, fall into a frenzy of scratching. At an alfresco evening, all the moths and mosquitoes of the area converged on our stage-lights and then turned their attention to us. During one of Othello's more dramatic sighs, I inhaled a large bluebottle. The following dialogue between Jennifer and me recorded by Conor, was the result:

Desdemona. How now, my dear Othello?/Your dinner, and the generous islanders/By you invited, do attend your presence.
Othello. (croaking queasily): I am to blame.
Desdemona. (shuddering, with solicitude doubtless): Why do you speak so faintly?/Are you not well?

At the end of the play those insects that had not already killed themselves against the hot lenses of the footlights descended to gnaw at her bare shoulders while she tried to remain serenely dead.

Jennifer often had a trying time remaining still as Desdemona. The most drastic occasion was in Delhi, when we were playing *Othello* in a college eight miles out of town. I had just declaimed, 'There should be now a huge eclipse of sun and moon and the affrightened globe should yawn in alteration', when the whole building was rocked by an earthquake. The audience swayed from side to side, then panicked, smashing windows and screaming to get out. Chairs were thrown, girls fainted, and I was afraid for a moment that Jennifer, who had not immediately leapt to her feet, would be trampled on. Eventually the audience calmed down and came back to the hall, and we finished the show.

Every day, apart from those when we were travelling or rehearsing, began with a meeting after breakfast when I told the company the state of business, the chances of further shows, future venues, and so on. The meeting also acted as a sort of post-mortem on the performances when adjustments to cast, costumes, and props could be made. After the meeting, if there was no matinée, all the men and sometimes the women went off booking. We visited every school, club, and services unit nearby and came back for lunch with any bookings we had, to co-ordinate what we had done. If there was a show in the evening, we all moved off after lunch to the location for the fit-up and general getting ready. Sometimes this took all the afternoon until the show. Afterwards we packed up and travelled back to wherever we were staying. Jennifer and Laura would look after any new costumes, buying cloth and seeing tailors. There were always a large number of repairs, and we were forever getting new costumes, flags, and props.

The days we spent travelling were regarded as a rest. We could spend four days on a train journey and, as long as we were travelling first-class, it was a time when everyone caught up with their sleep, spending their waking hours playing interminable games of cards. The reservation cards on the compartments sometimes read strangely. Once we were 'Mr Shakespeare and His Ladies'. There was no escaping the soot whichever class you were travelling; it got up your nose, in your ears, under your nails. If you switched on a light during the night you would see cockroaches scattering in all directions.

When money was tight, or if we could not get a reservation, we travelled third-class on those long narrow seats, where you had to push people with your feet if you did not want to spend your time squatting on the seat with your knees under your chin. On one journey we could not get into the train, and two of the actors clung to the outside as it left the station, fastening themselves to the doors with their belts. There were seventy people crammed into a compartment designed for twelve. When Brian wanted to go to the lavatory, and managed to climb over the packed bodies, he found three or four people inside the cubicle, with the wash bowl being used as a cradle for a baby.

It was quite usual to travel five hundred miles from one venue to the next, and journeys between major scholastic centres could be of a thousand miles. Because of these vast distances, we were constantly pressed for time. As an example of our rushed programme, Richard Gordon chronicled one week in 1958 in his diary, when we seemed to be in a constant race against the clock. Richard left Delhi for Lucknow overnight with all the surplus equipment, around the time we were nearing the end of our performance of *St Joan* at the Constantia Hall. We were performing late in the afternoon of the next day at the Isabella Thorburn College in Lucknow, and had to fly in early in the morning, as there was no train after the performance in Delhi that would get us there in time. Richard had insisted on having all the equipment in the first-class compartment with him but unfortunately found himself sharing the compartment with a Member of Parliament who officiously told him to remove his baskets, sword boxes, and lighting cases. Police were called, as well as the station master. As Richard had already weighed in the luggage and paid for the excess weight the M.P. accepted with resignation that he would have to live with our props for a few hours.

We spent three days in Lucknow, performing at the Isabella Thorburn College, La Martinière Girls' School, and the boys' school of the same name, before catching the night train back to Delhi on Saturday, a distance of around three hundred miles. The scale of activity involved both physical and mental effort. There was the carrying of equipment from point to point, and then the mental aspect of thinking about the play. We performed *St Joan* at the Isabella Thorburn College at five-thirty on Thursday evening, dismantled the set, packed up and transported everything the same night to the stage of La Martinière Girls' School, where we performed *Julius Caesar* and *Henry V* on Friday afternoon, then moved the entire equipment across the city to La Martinière Boys' School, where we were performing *Macbeth* and *Henry V*. At the end of it we were on our way again in a convoy of cycle-rickshaws to the station. We arrived in Delhi shortly after mid-morning on Sunday, and left for Agra that night.

We arrived in Agra, home of the Taj Mahal, in the morning, and the whole city was shrouded in mist. We rode in cycle-rickshaws to Lauries Hotel, sister hotel to the Cecil in Delhi, had a quick breakfast, and climbed into the waiting rickshaws to head for St John's College, where we performed excerpts from *Julius Caesar* and *Henry V* for the students in the afternoon. After that we reset the stage for *Candida*, which was given an evening performance. The evening show was an open house; we had a good audience and an entertaining time.

The next evening we had to go straight from the performance of *Gaslight* to the railway station. As soon as the curtain came down, we moved. Equipment and bodies were loaded into cars belonging to college staff and their friends, and we were rushed to the station to catch the night train to Delhi, some of us still with our make-up on. We got to the station with minutes to spare, and I rushed the ladies to the platform while Brian, Marcus, and Richard had the luggage weighed. It became obvious that the luggage would not be through in time, and I had to catch the train for an early morning appointment.

So Brian, Richard, and Marcus, having lost their reserved compartments, had to wait and take pot-luck. Several trains came and went, but they were too crowded. Even though it was a cold night in late November, there were numbers of people travelling by hanging on to door handles, some of them no doubt ticketless and ready to move in any direction upon sight of a travelling ticket inspector. Richard wrote about that journey:

> Mist came down over the platforms and the railway lines. As dawn was breaking a train arrived and we decided we could not go on like this, hoping a train was going to arrive empty just for us. We made a move and, when the train stopped, Mark and I wheeled our large platform trolley to the carriage with the ladies' compartments and began to shovel everything through one of the doors to Brian, who was already inside.
>
> Ladies-only compartments on the Indian Railways were sacrosanct areas. There were strict rules, and one particularly observed rule was always obeyed, even by fare-dodgers, that no male person ever attempted to enter these carriages; one could face prosecution under the by-laws from stiff fines to imprisonment for infringing them. We found this particular carriage to be very spacious. The corridors were empty and we remained in the corridor by the doorway. If there were to be a problem we could plead desperation and urgency which, we assumed, any reasonable thinking person would accept as our plight. The train had moved out of Agra station when we were discovered by a Muslim female, who let out a shriek! She grabbed the alarm-cord at the beginning of the corridor and threatened to pull it unless we jumped off immediately! Mark reasoned with her and I recall him trying to say that we were not in the habit of jumping off fast-moving trains. Besides, he added, he had a lot of luggage, to which the girl replied, rather hysterically:
>
> 'Take it with you!'
>
> Brian, who had just begun to wear contact lenses, removed his dark glasses and began inserting them. All this was rather new to the girl, who by now had others standing behind her in moral support. With one hand on the alarm-cord and the other

pointing to Brian, she asked what was he doing. Mark replied:

'This Englishman is so astonished by your behaviour that he wants to see what you look like!'

'Why is he putting that "glass" into his eyes?' she asked in amazement.

'Those are his eyes!' Mark retorted, enjoying himself. She shrieked again and ran into one of the small compartments, off the main side corridor. She reappeared with a scarf concealing the lower half of her face. Things were to become a little more farcical before reasoning could be achieved; the jolting of the train caused Brian to drop one of his lenses and he was on all fours feeling around the corridor for it. Mark gave a running commentary that Brian had now 'lost an eye', and nobody was to move for fear of treading upon it. This performance did the trick. Apart from the veiled lady still gripping the alarm-cord, the others provided some sympathy. They were all searching for the lost lens. It was found, eventually, safely in the turn-up in one of his trouser-legs! We promised to stay by the door and not encroach beyond the patch we already occupied, and on this understanding the ladies withdrew to their compartments. It was one of the more comfortable corridor journeys we experienced in India!

During the monsoon floods, the train would look as if it was running through a sea, out of which arose tall trees and an occasional hillock with mud huts and buffaloes. One of the few long journeys we made by road was in a hired bus from Dehra Dun to Agra. In the middle of the night we suddenly stopped. All we could see through the windows were the tops of the trees in the moonlight, and water, which was already over the running-board. We thought we must have strayed off the road, but while we tested the depth and wondered what to do there was a great rumble, splashing, and tooting coming along behind us from a big truck. We asked its driver if this was really the road. It *was* the road three months ago, we were testily informed, and why were we holding up the traffic? With that, the lorry drove on ahead of us in great waves, and we sailed on in its wake. Roads had a habit of plunging through rivers or fading into deserts; lorries frequently broke down. It was more certain to travel by rail, even though the railways sometimes broke the footlights or lost the costumes.

Once, however, the loss of our costumes brought an inspired piece of improvisation. We were playing *Charley's Aunt* at a convent, and the trunk of clothes for that play had been mislaid. The company played it in modern dress while I, as the 'Aunt', wore a nun's habit. The nuns were delighted.

If you could not laugh at the constant mishaps, you would not be able to stand it. We were frequently in a state of great hilarity, interspersed occasionally with a sudden violent quarrel among the actors, which would flare up and die down as quickly – the result of having always to live so closely together. Once or twice in our later years, as a result of the constant pressure of keeping the company going, the bills paid, and the money extracted from the show's organizers, I erupted in front of an audience when, to crown it all, something went wrong on-stage. In his book, *On the Line*, Ralph Pixton described one of those occasions, which I had forgotten about immediately afterwards. He was playing Polonius and should have been seen downstage eavesdropping on Hamlet and Ophelia. On my next line – 'Hie thee to a nunnery, girl. Where's thy father?' – I realized he was nowhere to be seen. Ralph wrote:

Ophelia's line was: 'At home, my lord.' And I might well have been at home, in fact a few seconds later I damn well wished I had been home, wherever home may have been. Kendal interrupted the play, swept off-stage, found me standing there like an idiot and boomed out, 'Where the hell were you, you fat fart? You're fired!' He then made a flourishing re-entrance, knowing full well that the whole audience had heard my dismissal, and carried on the scene with the singularly appropriate lines: 'Let the doors be shut upon him, that he may play the fool nowhere but in his own house. Farewell!'

What a dramatic way to be sacked! However, Kendal's fury was short-lived and two months later I was still with the company playing a rather overweight Feste to Kendal's Toby Belch in *Twelfth Night*.

9

Further East

Our touring in India had established itself into a pattern, and we made regular return visits to many of the schools. The Shakespeareana Company was part of the Indian scene, so that many schools or theatres expected an annual visit from us. I would get up between six and six-thirty every morning and type letters to schools, colleges, and other establishments situated between two places where we were already booked, advising them that the company would be passing through and were free for certain dates between the two performance points. Many of the places would be far from a large town, and their only form of entertainment would be a cinema that would come their way once a month. Our offer to perform was an event that would come only once a year, and it was seen as an opportunity not to be missed.

The ground rules we adopted for schools and colleges were simple. Each pupil paid a rupee to see a play. The average attendance for our plays numbered between three and five hundred, and in some of the isolated venues the understanding was that we would be found accommodation on the premises, and our meals would be supplied. In towns and cities we would find our own accommodation in guest-houses or hotels; but whatever the conditions, the hospitality offered to us as a company was excellent, and in many places we were looked on as returning friends.

Occasionally our simple rule of a rupee a head worked against us. There were some places where the students would miscount the number of heads in the audience. I would be told there were only two hundred there when the hall was obviously bursting at the seams. There was also a phrase I grew to dread: 'The money will be sent on to you.'

I recall one particularly curious incident in Muzaffarnagar, about seventy miles north-east of Delhi. The organizer, who had commissioned two performances from us, had erected a marquee holding six hundred seats. Everyone of them was occupied, and there appeared to be about another hundred people standing at the rear. The performance of *Henry V* was well received, as the applause at the end proved, and we had to take several curtain calls. The next day, as we were getting the set for *St Joan* on to the stage, the organizer said to me:

'You may not be too happy with what I have to offer you. With only two hundred people seeing the show last night, there is not enough to pay you the agreed fee.'

I protested that the previous night had been a full house.

'No, absolutely not . . . you are under illusions, sir,' smiled the man. 'I have for you two hundred and fifty rupees. Only.'

A little while later Marcus arrived back from town, where he had been buying light-bulbs, soaking wet from the rain that had been pelting down on Muzaffarnagar during the entire time we had been there. He said cheerfully:

'There are some daft buggers in the field trying to light a fire.'

We walked down the steps into the rain to watch two men with umbrellas providing protection for our 'organizer', who was struggling to light a fire. We walked over to the group and found a bucket piled high with used ticket-stubs. The man looked up and smiled at us as he attempted to strike another match.

'What are you doing?' I asked.

'Trying to light this but there is too much rain,' he replied. There was no attempt to conceal the tickets, nor any expression of guilt.

'Looks like too many paid-up tickets to me,' I said, and we returned to the stage to dismantle the set. A few minutes later the man came back on to the stage; I called to him, 'Had any luck with your fire?'

'No, it was too wet . . . we are having to dispose of them elsewhere.'

We packed up, despite his protests that he had been promised two shows, and left Muzaffarnagar that evening in a third-class carriage. We had some time to reflect during the journey back to

Delhi on a few points. Had that marquee been erected just for our performances? Why did he try to burn those ticket-stubs in our presence? Curiouser and curiouser, and best shrugged off as another day in the life of a touring company!

We had a tour arranged by the British Council in South India that went extremely well, and it was a relief to be able to concentrate on the productions rather than chase up bookings and payments. Meanwhile our American actor, Jimmy Gibson, now back in New York, wrote to us and said that someone there wanted us to do a tour of the United States, all expenses paid for. It sounded tempting, and we waited to hear more.

It was around this time that Jennifer's life became firmly settled for ever in India. Shashi and Jennifer met because of a muddle by a theatre management. We had arrived for a booking at the Empire, Calcutta, to find Prithviraj Kapoor's theatre company unpacking their bags and setting up scenes. There had been a double booking. The fault obviously lay with the theatre management, but neither company could afford to bow out, as replacement bookings would not be found overnight to substitute the loss each company would have made. Prithviraj and I arrived at a compromise: we would both perform during the season. On one day there would be an Indian play performed by the Kapoor actors, and on the other the Shakespearean or Shavian plays of the Kendal actors. Each company would remove their sets and hand over the stage to the other at the end of the day's performance.

Shashi was only eighteen and A.S.M. in his father's company. The first time he saw Jennifer was through the stage-curtain at the Empire as she was sitting in one of the front rows. He wondered who that beautiful lady was – not, of course, that I knew anything about this for some time. Our two companies met again in Bombay, and by this time Shashi was playing small roles. A few months later we found ourselves short of actors; Anwar had joined the Russian–Indian Film Unit, and then Peter Bromilow announced that he was returning to England. I wrote to Prithviraj to ask if he could loan me Shashi from his company for a while. In February 1957 he joined us in Poona. One of Laura's letters to her sister at the time records: 'Prithviraj's young son came up to rehearse Laertes. He's going to be very good. And Jennifer is once more happy and carefree.' Two months later Laura wrote: 'Peter has departed – and our new boy is going to be brilliant.'

Shashi says of that time that he lost about 30 lb in three weeks learning and rehearsing the parts for nine different plays, from Lysander in *A Midsummer Night's Dream* to Sergius in *Arms and the Man*. Jennifer coached him through all the parts, fitting the extra work in with all her own rehearsals. She was determined that he would do well, and together with Jennifer's work and Shashi's own natural talent we had an actor of exceptional ability. I do not think that even Olivier surpassed the way he played Sergius; he was simply the best Sergius ever. Shashi was extremely handsome, with dark expressive eyes and a charming smile; and Jennifer was one of the most beautiful young women you could see, with a finely boned face, fair hair, and lovely blue eyes. They made a very attractive couple.

By May we had two new actresses: Sonia Frankenborg and Coral de Rosario. At around the same time the American woman who was promising to arrange the United States tour arrived to meet us in Mysore. She was huge, fat, and peroxided, very noisy, and she boasted of her skill at publicity and business. We did not know what to make of her, and as time went on it became evident that it was all talk. Laura wrote to her sister:

> The American problem is still with us. We forget about it for half the time because she never gets up till lunchtime and then she begins to wake up at midnight – keeping whoever shares a room with her awake until two and three in the morning – shrieking and laughing! Even I don't know how to cope! I've *prayed* for guidance! She's so incredible! *Very* fat and constantly saying, 'I don't *eat* this way. I just *look* this way!'

Worse was to come, for she had taken charge of the box office as our business manager. We did not seem to be taking as much as we should, but little Foo, then only ten, took matters into her own hands one day by counting the ticket-stubs and comparing them with the takings. As a result our American manager's 'business acumen' was unveiled, and she departed. So did the chances of an American tour. We decided instead to go further east on a tour of Hong Kong, Singapore and Malaya. It was new untapped territory for us, and these tours turned out to be a period of riotous success, tremendous enthusiasm, and money coming in like I had never seen it before. Yet it was also a period of terrible personal sadness and frustration.

I look upon Malaya and the tours beyond as something quite apart from our work in the Indian subcontinent. We started off as a sponsored company with little to do but put on the shows. The Shaw brothers, who had invited us, saw to it that we were met on our arrival and all our gear was taken to the theatre. After the cities of India, Singapore was like another world. I had never seen a supermarket before, and it was years since I had seen pubs, bars, waitresses, and so many restaurants. For us India had been a time of beginning, building up, and creation. Our tour to Malaya and Singapore was more like visiting a reasonably well organized theatre in Europe with a company that was in those days thought to be rather too highbrow; there have always been those managements that think only the worst sort of theatre can possibly pay.

There were two great disadvantages to the beginning of our tour. One was that the sponsors insisted we play twice nightly. I should have had more sense. It could not possibly work – *Othello* twice nightly! And it didn't. Everyone was far too tired, and we just had to strive away as best we could. Then, after our season at the theatre, we toured the fair-grounds belonging to our sponsors. These are great permanent amusement parks, which also had cinemas and a theatre. All the noise of the fun of the fair was so audible that our voices were completely swamped.

From Singapore we went on to Kuala Lumpur, Ipoh and Penang, where we stayed at a small and friendly place called the Peking Hotel. Chinese audiences were very different from an Indian audience. They had a strange sense of humour. They always laughed or smiled, and the more you put on your dramatics in a play, the more they would see the funny side of your efforts and kill themselves laughing, which could be frustrating for those who saw themselves as serious actors portraying the classics and tragedies of this world. This sense of humour extended to their own dramas. I remember seeing a Chinese standing by the side of the road where his car had been wrecked in an accident, laughing his head off.

During our tour of Malaya matters with Jennifer came to a head. We had been aware of her feelings for Shashi for some time, and I had not been happy about it. I had in my mind a dream of her taking over as the first actress-manageress of our company, and she now seemed to want to go in a completely different direction. Tensions had arisen even before we left for Malaya, as a letter from Jennifer to her aunt Beulah a month before we left India indicated. She wrote about Shashi:

> We may be getting married sooner than ever – but his father's company is on tour now, it'll depend when the tour finishes. Everybody's nerves are so frayed, what with too much work and too much heat. I wouldn't be a bit surprised if we eventually went completely berserk and just went off like that – bang, in the middle of a show!

And so it happened, almost as she had foretold. With hindsight, I can see that if we had talked about it calmly we could have found some solution, and Shakespeareana could have continued as before. But none of us was able to give ground. Jennifer was twenty-four, older than Laura had been when she married. Shashi was only twenty. Our disagreements developed into a little war, and finally Shashi and Jennifer decided, in mid-tour, to fly back to India and get married. Their last performance together with the company was on 31 May 1957 in *Arms and the Man*. I played Bluntschi, Shashi was Sergius, and we managed to get through the play with neither of us looking at the other. Jennifer was Raina. On 14 June they flew from Singapore to Bombay, and Shashi's parents arranged a simple Hindu wedding. Jennifer wore a North Indian wedding skirt in red. Neither Laura nor I was there to see her.

We finished the last two months of our Malayan tour with a rearranged cast and a cut-down repertoire, and came back to India to regroup and plan a new season. Coral de Rosario had left, and Richard Gordon joined us again. We toured India once more, but with a smaller repertoire and staying less time in each place. Jennifer rejoined us for a while the following year and carried on the family tradition of going on-stage while pregnant, playing the role of Mistress Quickly.

I had decided that we should have another tour of Malaya, and began to negotiate bookings with our contacts there. When we left Bombay in May 1959 for this second Malayan trip we had been rejoined by Coral de Rosario. She had been working as a secretary and earning an exceptionally high salary, but while we were in

Bombay she came to see us several times. Bang went her flat and the job! She threw in her lot with the travelling players again. Frank Wheatley joined us again for what would prove to be his final tour with us. He had had to return to England from Hong Kong a year earlier after a leg injury. Marcus had put a stool in the wing where he usually made his exit, and Frank had tripped and fallen. He firmly believed it was a deliberate act to cut short his career, though Marcus maintained he had merely got the stool ready for use when Frank stumbled into it. Frank had written to me from Denville Hall, the home for elderly actors and actresses, saying he was well again and could return to 'the tropics', as he termed it. To have a man of seventy-nine back in our company, travelling thousands of miles under the most trying conditions, was an added burden; but I could not disappoint him and told him he was welcome to return. So back he came, in the height of the Bombay heat, stepping down from a P. & O. liner in tropical white, straw hat, and cane. He spent the entire afternoon handing out small gifts of Max Factor make-up that he had brought in abundance from London.

We left Bombay for Madras and to board our ship to Malaya, the *State of Madras*. Several of us were not allowed on board because we had no Inland Revenue clearance to leave the country. We spent a good hour at the tax office in town before it closed for the day, getting a clearance certificate called an 'E' form. Oddly enough, had we been flying out of the country this requirement would not have been necessary. Having been given these forms after explaining that we were not regular wage-earners, we raced back to the dockside and tussled with Customs and Excise, who wanted to know what was going out of the country inside our theatrical baskets. We caught the boat with minutes to spare, and one of the ship's officers, a Goan youth, offered to speed things up by having the cleared baggages and equipment carried to our cabins. He blanched when he learned we were travelling 'deck class'.

'But you can't do that!' he gasped. 'Sir, do you realize . . . it is not allowed . . . there are Tamils and others who only travel deck . . . not Englishmen like you!'

'Look, you haven't got any spare cabins, and we have to get to Malaya.'

'Can't you use an aeroplane?' he faltered.

'No, we can't,' I snapped. 'We haven't enough money for that sort of joyride!'

Apparently there was in existence a rule hanging over from the days of the British Raj whereby Europeans were forbidden, for respectability's sake, to travel as deck passengers. The officer consulted the captain and came back to tell us:

'We cannot accept the fact you are here travelling like this. Therefore you will eat all your meals in the first-class dining room, but please observe the children's meal times.' He handed out several menu cards and time schedules, and added, 'Where you are going to sleep is your problem ... I will leave that to you.'

We managed to find a cabin for Frank, and the rest of us spread ourselves, our travelling mattresses, and belongings about us and went to sleep in the open air, lulled by a sea breeze. Laura, forever the calming influence, remarked how healthy this was. We woke to a beautiful morning. The ship was at anchor three miles from the shore at a small port down the coast from Madras. I sat up and looked about us, and it took a second to understand that we were all caked in coal-dust. Mattresses, clothes, hair, everything was covered in soot. We were over the rear hold of the ship, downwind of the funnels, and the ship was a coal-burner. During those first moments of realizing what had happened our officer came by. He was looking in all directions for us.

'Good morning!' I called. He stood there in a suspended gaze as he took in the scene, hardly able to believe his eyes.

'Tell me,' I asked; 'if we promise not to wash this stuff off, can we stay on deck to Malaya?'

The officer retreated without saying a word, and there was another consultation with the captain. We were allowed to use the officers' showers and then moved to the poop deck, at the very rear of the ship, a canopied and well sheltered area, normally out of bounds to the passengers. The captain told us his daughters were at one of the schools where Shakespeareana had performed and asked if we would give a performance for the passengers and crew. We put on *Candida*, which was well received by an audience of about 125 people.

We dropped anchor at the island of Penang on 20 May 1959 and went through Customs and Immigration. There was some astonishment that we did not appear to be bringing much money with us. They wanted to know how we were going to live, and I showed them letters from the various education departments in Malaya to prove we were fully booked. We were given six months in the country; if we wanted more time we would have to apply for an extension. So we went back to the friendly Peking Hotel and got ready for work, a company of nine, strong and ready for action: Laura, Felicity, Sonia, Coral, Marcus, Brian, Frank, Richard, and me.

We had left India with sparse finances, because the cost of living had been rising but our income had remained static – we could not charge more than one rupee a seat. Now we suddenly had worse problems. All the performances booked before we had left India were being cancelled, even those booked by the education authorities, whose letters of intent were used to gain admission to the country. The first fortnight's work had disappeared. While Brian and I went separate ways to schools and colleges to look for more bookings, Laura kept everyone else in rehearsal all day.

On 25 May we gave our first show in Malaya, catching a ferry from Georgetown in Penang to Butterworth, and from there travelling by bus to Bukit Matajam. The countryside was lush and green; the shops were full of all those luxury items we did not come across in India; the smell of money was everywhere but entirely out of our reach. The next day I called a meeting to say that three of our dates had now been cancelled in Kuala Lumpur, along with two in Ipoh and three in Alor Star. We had crossed the Bay of Bengal to find ourselves in Malaya without any work. While I was telling the company this, the telephone rang with news that yet another booking had been cancelled. I could only think that the tail-end of our previous tour, when Jennifer and Shashi had left, to be followed soon after by Coral and by Frank, after his accident in the wings in Hong Kong, had something to do with it. The last few weeks of that tour had been reduced to playing excerpts. Yet it was strange that education officers would book performances from a company they believed to have been reduced in numbers, invite that company to Malaya, and after they arrived decide to cancel the shows already booked.

We went out on another foray. Brian put on his tweed suit and returned at the end of the afternoon with seven new dates to occupy us and earn enough for the week immediately ahead. We performed *Macbeth* at the Methodist Boys' School in Penang, and the next day at the Chinese girls' school, followed the morning

after that at eight-thirty with *Henry V* at the Kenyon Rea high
school. Then the bookings began to come in again, including some
from two of the people responsible for earlier cancellations. It was
almost as if they had heard we were performing again and had
come along to witness for themselves whether we were giving
value for money. By a miracle, and thanks to Brian, we were on
our way again.

Malaya, at this period of time, was nearing the end of twelve
years of emergency rule, when British, Australian, Rhodesian, and
South African forces were involved in anti-communist guerrilla
warfare deep in the jungles. There were vast areas that were
termed 'white areas', or free of communist guerrillas. 'Red areas'
were not actually under communist control but were considered
dangerous terrain. I had hired a small black family saloon to drive
down to Kuala Lumpur with as much of the equipment as possible
on the roof-rack; the rest of the company were to come by train. I
had to go along to the local police station to obtain clearance to
travel across certain sections of the country. We had to travel only
by daylight, and at no time were we to transport food in the car.
On our previous visit the country had been in the grip of the
emergency, and entire towns and villages had been sealed off to
prevent food being smuggled to the guerrillas. Each time travellers
came and went from these fortified areas they were searched by
police and troops.

We met the rest of the company, who had caught the night train,
in Kuala Lumpur. They had spent the entire night singing songs in
the restaurant-car with Australians on their way to Singapore,
totally oblivious of whether they were travelling through 'red' or
'white' areas. We then took a coach to Kuantan, on the east coast,
and spent the day travelling up and down winding hills and on
narrow roads. We had to stop and pull over every so often to
allow British Army armoured columns to pass, many of them
escorted by military police motorcycle patrols. It was curious to be
wandering through Malaya's state of emergency as a travelling
actor.

We travelled to Kuala Trengannu and Khota Bahru, right up the
east coast of Malaya, close to the border with Thailand. At one
teachers' training college where we performed, Mr Bumford, the
principal, a wonderfully humorous man, had just returned after
spending six months' leave in Britain. He had seen *My Fair Lady*

and asked us to perform *Pygmalion*. We gave performances of
St Joan, *Candida*, *Pygmalion*, and *Henry V*. All the plays were
well received, and on two of the evenings we were entertained to a
garden party in the grounds of a local solicitor called Wriggles-
worth, who later became a judge in that part of Malaya. He had
beautiful and spacious gardens close to the jungle, a river running
through his grounds, and a Japanese bridge crossing the river.
Everything was illuminated for our visit, and we were given a
performance by the students of the college of the Malayan
candle-dance, and extraordinarily lovely event.

Before we left Malaya, we were warned we could face problems
in Singapore. The problem, we were told, was Mr Lee Kuan Yew,
who had just been handed the Government of Singapore. Lee
Kuan Yew was an unknown quantity in British colonialism, and
was becoming feared because of the actions he was taking.
Although Britain was still responsible for defence and some
external relations of the new island state, the new Prime Minister
was his own sovereign in other matters. He had closed the English
Club in Singapore, which had caused a furore among the old
hands, the planters, and others. Any individual earning over five
hundred Straits dollars a month had his salary halved. However,
from our point of view the worst blow was that Lee Kuan Yew's
Ministry of Education was about to announce a ban on all
assemblies of people, the only exemption being the armed forces
and the police. This unusual ruling applied equally to school and
college assemblies, and it meant that students might not be
allowed to gather to see actors performing plays.

We travelled down to Singapore and booked into the Happy
Homes Guest-House. Here we received a telegram from Jennifer
and Shashi. It read: 'Just available, one young man for small parts
in your company.' We had a celebration in the lounge that
evening: Laura and I were grandparents!

The Singapore schools were reluctant to take bookings for
plays, though they privately apologized and said they were
worried about the new Government and did not wish to offend the
Education Ministry. We left the Happy Homes and moved in as
lodgers with Professor Wong, who had a spacious house on
Stephen's Road. It was here that we had to face the fact that we
were broke. A tour of Manila that I had been relying on had been
cancelled, the schools were closed, and the new Government was

interested exclusively in 'non-Imperialistic' culture. The dissolution of our company loomed all to near.

Then Coral and Sonia had an idea: why not give a performance at Professor Wong's house? There was a paved courtyard near the dining room loggia that would make an ideal little theatre. It would not cost us anything, even if it did not come off, so I agreed. One snag, though, was that we could not charge for a play if we did not have a licence, so it had to be free for an invited audience, with a collection taken at the end. Over the next three days Sonia and Coral canvassed the consulates, embassies, and armed forces headquarters for guests, and we rehearsed a production of *St Joan*.

The day of the courtyard theatre show dawned. The newspapers carried the headline 'The Big Day' – not about us, but about the current elections that were reaching their climax. We set up the stage, borrowing stools and a table, and we enlisted helpers to dress as French pages to welcome the guests, provide them with programmes, and show them to their seats. People began arriving at eight: the French Consul and son, an army sergeant and his wife, some people from India House. It was a small house and a quiet little audience; at the end of the evening we collected a mere seventy Singapore dollars. The only thing to be said in the evening's favour was that it had cost us little beyond our time, energy, and effort.

Finally our luck changed. A trip to Borneo was arranged, sponsored by the British Council. Immediately everyone's depressed spirits lifted. Sonia and Coral visited the library to read up on Borneo and came back with tales of flying foxes, flying frogs, flying squirrels, and flying lizards – everything went with a whoop in Borneo, they said. We travelled deck class on the S.S. *Marudu*, and arrived at Kuching to be met by Mr Davis of the British Council and Mr Holliday of the Kuching Amateur Dramatic Society. We performed *St Joan*, *Macbeth*, *The Merchant*, and *Arms and the Man*, and nearly lost Marcus Murch. He and Brian had a night of merrymaking with some members of the British Colonial Service, and were inspired to enact the legend of William Tell, after someone put the William Tell Overture on the radiogram. The gun was unexpectedly loaded, and Marcus was lucky to escape with only a bullet wound on his forehead. He was back on-stage the next afternoon in *Othello*, suffering more from a hangover than anything else.

From Kuching we took a motor-launch along the coast, then up-river through the jungle to the remote outpost of Sibu. We took another boat along the coast to Miri and Brunei, and were caught in an appalling storm. The company had told me that my catering in terms of drink versus food was wholly out of proportion; but in the end they were all glad of the extra whisky, and it helped us through the worst of the storm. Our tour of Borneo ended with another couple of days in Kuching, and we then took a boat to Hong Kong. Here we were joined by Jennifer and Shashi with Kunal, our new grandson. Shashi was beginning to work in films, but he and Jennifer would join us from time to time, work and children permitting.

We returned to India, which is where we spent the greater part of our last two years as a full company. I decided in 1962 in Calcutta to continue Shakespeareana with just Laura and Felicity and, for a while, Marcus Murch. I had loved those days of steaming up the rivers of Borneo and the beautiful coast of Malaya, and had I gone there as anything but an actor I would have been tempted to settle there permanently, retiring to some *kanpong* on one of the rivers. But the Indian audiences were far more exciting to play to as an actor, and that, after all, was what I was after: to be able to feel that I was doing what I believed in and that it was understood. So our company drew to an end in the land with which we had come to identify so closely, and the audiences were as enthusiastic as ever, though now Shakespeare was not always the main attraction. One poster announced *Othello* as: 'The Greatest Play Ever Staged – and for the first time in the history of Indian theatre well reputed artist Shashi Kapoor (youngest brother of Raj Kapoor) has given the best performance.' Shashi, new idol of the film world, got top billing, and Shakespeare was left off the poster altogether.

10

'Shakespeare Wallah'

My life in the theatre had just begun when the talking cinema arrived, and I never came to terms with this medium. I was frightened of it, for it spelt an end to the touring system in England and to the actor's wandering life. The motor engine had ended the era of horses, and — like any other form of mechanization — it appeared to me that the cinema would do the same to the actor and the theatre. The cinema was my enemy; theatres were empty, tours came off, and the new mechanical monster sprouted everywhere. Even those old theatres that were not demolished were 'wired for sound'.

Now I realized that my reaction caused me to miss a great deal, but I was young, in love with the theatre, and would not tolerate a rival. Little did I think that there would be a theatre revival, and that British theatre would be the leader everywhere. As I tried to beg, borrow, steal, and fight for my first love, it was ironic that in the whirligig of time it was the despised cinema that told the world of my existence and to a certain extent of my fight.

The year 1963 was when I first met James Ivory and Ismail Merchant. They wanted to make a film about a life similar to mine, of an English actor-manager touring in India with a company playing Shakespeare. I had written a diary of our early days when India first became independent, and of our visits to the princely states, and this was suggested as an overall plan. I handed the diary over and in due course saw the screenplay that had been written by James and the novelist Ruth Prawer Jhabvala. What I read nearly made me back out of the film. Let someone else have a go at playing Tony Buckingham, the hammest of hams, I thought! This film was not about us, but concerned some travelling showmen to whom we bore no resemblance.

It is clear to me now why they approached the film as they did. The actors were seen as the last of the British Raj, hanging on to a dying culture in an out-of-date medium, while the cinema, representing modern India, took over with its new and vital power. For Laura and me it was difficult and at times painful to go along with the premise of the film. Our touring company had been a great success and had brought Shakespeare to the furthest places of India. We had hoped the film would be an affirmation of this and an illustration of what was, to us, still a wonderful way of life. But *Shakespeare Wallah* showed the Buckingham Players down on their luck, trying to cadge bookings from unsympathetic school bursars, and overwhelmed by the slick, rich, song-and-dance Bombay movies. It was in some ways close to our experience, yet at the same time seen through a different pair of eyes. We did not recognize ourselves.

All our family had roles in the film: myself and Laura as the ham Shakespeareans, Mr and Mrs Buckingham; Felicity as their daughter (modelled on Jennifer); and Shashi Kapoor as the rich playboy who falls in love with her. Jennifer, who by this time had two sons, Kunal and Karan, played the small part of the landlady of the Gleneagles Hotel, where the company stay. The Buckingham Players had been wandering around the East longer than Somerset Maugham in a sort of miasma, and had not a clue as to what was going on in the world. Absolute rubbish, I told Jim Ivory. This was not us at all.

Moreover, the actors of the company were made up of Indians who would never have been considered even by a chump like Buckingham – or Kendal for that matter; and I did have a few hopeless types more often than not. My idea was to get hold of a few of our better actors, but I was told that the film was being made on a 'shoe-string' and that we could not afford them. We were allowed to use our wardrobe, but 'better' stuff (meaning more old-fashioned) was to be provided. I had very set views on costumes and thought some of the costumes brought in quite awful.

In those days Merchant/Ivory had only one film to their credit, *The Householder*, based on a short novel by Mrs Jhabvala. I thought the book was one of her best; the film, to my mind, did not seem to get the idea of the book across, but most people liked it. *Shakespeare Wallah* was their second venture, so we were all in a state of some trepidation. I had never been involved in a film before. Merchant and Ivory were still learning with me, and what would come of it all seemed a matter of faith and chance.

We took a train for Delhi from whence we would go to Kasauli for the first shooting. I had no idea that so much junk could possibly be required. There was more wardrobe than one could imagine, masses of baskets of costumes. There were the lights, the cameras, the furniture and equipment, and what seemed like a train-load of crew to administer all these things. Camera crew, light crew, sound crew, stills photographer, stage-hands, wardrobe men, assistants, their assistants, and so on *ad infinitum*. At every stop, out jumped the stills photographer, who took pictures of us eating, at bookstalls, reading, sleeping, walking on platforms, leaning out of carriages – reels of film, most of which was never seen again.

We arrived in Delhi just after dark the next day and were met by James, Ismail, and Madhur Jaffrey, who was to play the part of the Indian film star. There were also Shashi and Jennifer, their two sons, their servants, the butler and the ayah, the dog, more actors, more crew, more equipment. We stayed the night at the Ashoka Hotel and then set off in a fleet of cars and a bus for our first location in Kasauli, past Ambala, where my aunt Eunice used to live and where she awaited the mail, with her husband as driver, to flash by her house with two hoots on the whistle. Kasauli is an old cantonment built by the British, and the Indian Army seemed to have made it more British than ever. There was the club, and the bazaar, the soldiery, and the mule-lines – everything as it always was – and the garrison church with an English chaplain. We stayed at the lovely Alasia Hotel, which had cottages for the guests, run by one of the Hotz family, who ran the Cecil in Delhi. We seemed to have the whole hotel, with the overflow of crew lodged at other hotels and boarding-houses, yet this was supposedly a 'shoe-string' film.

Slowly I began to get the feel of things and relate the people to their relevant jobs in the world of theatre. The producer was, I realized, something like a company manager combined with impresario. He is in sole charge of the unit and supplies, and the requirements are arranged through the producer by the production manager, who in theatre terms would be the assistant stage-manager. The director directs the actors and works out the shooting plan with the camera operator. He is the person who takes the script and the actors right through the whole process to make a finished film. Ismail and Jim seemed to fit into their allotted roles. Ismail was the one who shouted down the phone when things went wrong, who pushed people to get to the right place, with a mixture of charm and expostulation. Jim said very little, and most of it almost too quiet to hear, but his eyes were very watchful, almost as if he saw the film there before him.

It seemed to me, as one of the uninitiated, a most haphazard affair. Every decision appeared to be taken after the event; and the technicians, instead of taking orders, would all talk at once for hours on end, giving endless advice.

Two days' shooting went by – outside scenes that did not concern us and were shot miles away. All we saw were the crew and actors leaving very early in the morning and coming back late at night. Then they decided to film the Buckinghams' house in the hills, and our room became part of the film. A host of technicians descended on our quiet abode and proceeded to take the place apart. Furniture was flung around, curtains were torn down, track-lines were laid, with wires everywhere. In the scene, Shashi, the Indian playboy, has followed the company to the hills to get hold of Lizzie, the daughter, and is rebuked by her mother, who seems to have very stay-at-home ideas for a lady of the theatre. The scene ran for about one and half minutes in the film and it took two days and most of the nights to complete. Filming it was turmoil. It looked to my inexperienced eyes as if no one really knew what to do and the whole thing was just a huge experiment.

I did my first line, which took all day. I was put in a telephone booth, with the camera right under my nose, cables around my legs, and lights burning fiercely from everywhere. I could not get out, as they never move the camera if they can help it. I had been provided with a brown velvet jacket more fitting for an artist, a curly pipe, and a floppy hat – like some ageing juvenile in the worst of reps. The scene was the telephone call to the deputy headmaster, where Tony is trying to persuade the school to take another performance and is given the brush-off. At that point I decided that film-acting was not for me. I cannot memorize lines just before the scene; I hate hanging about; and I can't recreate time and time again the same line with the same inflection.

We stayed in Kasauli for about a month; our hotel became part of the film. The hotel sign was changed to 'Gleneagles', and one of the best shots in the film was the sign swinging and creaking in the rain as the troupe arrived in rickshaws. Then we shot one of the performances the Buckingham Players put on. It was *Hamlet*, with me as the first – and I think only – Hamlet who really looked like his father's ghost.

From Kasauli we went to Simla, a short journey of about sixty miles up into the hills. Here we were to film some more theatre scenes, using the Gaiety, the miniature Edwardian theatre created 7,000 feet up on the slopes of the Himalayas when Simla was the summer capital of the Indian Empire. Simla looks like an English town transplanted on to a spur of the Himalayas. It has old-world buildings, and the houses in the main street have black-and-white mock-Tudor façades. There are English-style shops and no cars in the streets; everyone must walk on the left. There are tea-houses for afternoon tea, dances during the season, and many boarding-houses and small hotels, as well as bungalows to be let to visitors. The great space at the top of the town has an English church with English bells. The schoolchildren walk in crocodiles, and the public schools are more British than the original.

The Gaiety Theatre was built so that the 'expats' could have something besides gossip, tea-parties, and dances. It was a complete theatre of the period in every detail, with flies, grid, dressing rooms, green room, bars, orchestra pit, water dimmers, wardrobe room, scene dock. It held an audience of two hundred and must be the best theatre ever built solely for the use of an amateur dramatic society. The Gaiety's stage is the one seen in *Shakespeare Wallah*, the stage that had been trod by Rudyard Kipling, the Mountbattens, and a succession of people who came to India during the days of the Empire. They produced musical comedy, revue, modern plays, Gilbert and Sullivan, and Shakespeare, up until 1947 when the last of the Raj left. Our Shakespeareana Company had taken over the theatre, which was becoming derelict, in 1955, and we produced a series of plays, spending the whole of the monsoon there with a weekly changing rep. Standing on the stage, waiting for the filming of the débâcle over *Romeo and Juliet*, I looked up at the Royal Box of the Viceroys where Pandit Nehru had watched one of our performances. The box was emblazoned with the Viceroy's Arms, and we had covered it with the flag of India for the occasion. The flag, now dusty and faded, was still there on our return for the film, over ten years later.

Now, like a rerun, we were playing for *Shakespeare Wallah* the repertoire we had originally brought to Simla. In the film's *Romeo* sequence I was Friar Lawrence, Laura was the nurse, Felicity was Juliet, and Pratap Sharma was Romeo. In the midst of the marriage scene the audience began rioting because of a fight between the playboy, Shashi, and some Sikhs who are catcalling Felicity. This ends in the curtain being rung down, me holding it with my back to the audience, *sans* wig and beard, and the audience throwing everything they can find at the curtain. I held on to the curtain like the crucified Christ, bearing all!

Many of the theatre shots were more complicated because of filming the audience reaction. We needed extras to fill the theatre. Everyone in Simla wanted to be in, and there were queues of soldiers, government clerks, and college boys. But film-making is a slow and repetitive business, and sitting in a theatre for half a day to be in a two-minute shot is tedious. So when the audience had seen the shot rehearsed once or twice they wanted a change. The continuity girl had a terrible job as various members of the audience got fed up and left.

There had been some faults in the filming in Kasauli, and we had to return there to reshoot on the way to our next location, which was Alwar, an old princely state in Rajasthan. Our numbers had now grown so large, and our amount of baggage so colossal (every Indian still carries his bed, as well as a suitcase), that to move we needed two buses and a Land-Rover in addition to our private cars. Because of our travelling to another state, and due to the urgency of our needs being common knowledge, the transport prices rose daily, until it was decided to take hired transport just to Kasauli and then try again from there. This move made little difference. Kasauli is not so far from Simla, and the same operators were at work; word had spread quickly, and again the prices rose with each day the decision was put off. Eventually we left Kasauli with the crew all jammed into one bus, with dozens of lights and what appeared to be mountains of bedding, unending suitcases, and an enormous generator on the top. This was to take them to Ambala, where they were to change for public transport.

Half the stuff was not even packed. Loose cables were everywhere, and the exposed film was in tins in cardboard boxes, not even roped up. One box fell out of the back of the Land-Rover, allowing two cans of exposed film to roll merrily down the Himalayas.

This mass of unpacked equipment and dozens of personnel were to travel from Ambala to Alwar by ordinary service buses stopping everywhere. We, the stars, went off in our cars, and the camera team had a station-wagon. Our journey was uneventful, but we waited days with no sign of the crew, and then terrible stories seeped through of how they could not get on any bus with all that baggage; how they had to take a fleet of taxis part of the way; and how they were eventually all stranded as their money had run out. In the end they were rescued at great cost, much more than a through-bus would have cost, and turned up a week late, wasting all those precious shooting days.

Alwar is in Rajasthan – Rajputhana, as it was called in the old days, a much more romantic name. It is an old princely state. All Rajasthan is very beautiful, wild and free, with lovely bazaars selling brocades, jewelled slippers, and glamorous silks and jewels. We were accommodated in Alwar's state guest-house, a great building set in acres of grounds. There were peacocks strutting in the gardens, deer, and exotic birds. We were to film the troupe's arrival at the Maharaja's palace and his private show of *Antony and Cleopatra*, with a cast of six. Our rooms were the old-world Indian guest-house style, with bedrooms, dressing rooms, private bathrooms, sitting rooms, private kitchen and servant quarters, and even store-rooms. In the old days important travellers carried so much junk that all this was necessary. The weather was cold in the early morning, almost frosty at times, brightening up to lovely days as during a European spring.

More artists arrived, including two from our old company: Utpal Dutt and Marcus Murch. Utpal was to play the part of our host, the Maharaja, and Marcus was to be the first member of the company to leave the sinking ship! We had taken on both actors as school-leavers; they had stayed with us a long time and had been trained by us, later making careers in the theatre in India. Utpal produced in Calcutta plays of political significance, which landed him in gaol from time to time; and Marcus acted and directed plays for the go-ahead Yatrick Group in Delhi.

We had two weeks filming the *Antony and Cleopatra* sequence, complicated shots some of them. The whole episode started with the jeeps and my old Morris arriving and travelling through the innumerable gates, past peacocks and elephants, through more gates, and eventually swinging up towards the staircase outside the palace, where the Military Secretary met us, played by the real Military Secretary to His Highness. As each movement had to be shot from at least three angles the time taken on this part of the journey was three days. Then came the dinner in the palace, the actors in dinner suits and His Highness in all his finery, in a great room hung with paintings of the ancestors of the present ruling house, and their relations from all over Rajasthan. The scene was reminiscent of the glorious past, with the Maharaja quoting, 'Uneasy lies the head that wears the crown.' In this dinner scene I thought I was rather good. It is nostalgic and sad, so in the scene during some of the speeches I introduced some business I had greatly admired as a schoolboy when I had seen the film *The Flag Lieutenant*. In this film, Henry Edwards, when being cold-shouldered and when everything has gone wrong, just idly piles up some sugar cubes and knocks them down again. I thought this masterly, and tried it in the film; I did it very well too, but it was ignored. However, it had a therapeutic effect on me. This scene took three whole nights to shoot, and each time I played with the same piece of chicken . . . ugh!

The shooting of *Antony and Cleopatra* itself – the first of the Shakespeare plays shown in the film – was done with lavish care. Some of the scenes are very lovely: the company being garlanded by the Maharaja; the tiny audience of the Maharaja and his court of five seated under an awning with fan-bearers and ten attendants each; and the speech, 'The barge she sat in . . .', which was shot at night in what had once been the seraglio, or women's quarters, of the palace. I performed the speech as a sort of prologue standing in a sconce. It was high up in the palace, and our generator was functioning in the courtyard hundreds of feet below. For this lovely speech I had on my make-up for Antony and wore one of our great Richard-II-type of gowns. The speech sounded wonderful with the ring caused by the stone sconce where I stood. I was thrilled when I heard it; but alas this old generator was banging away in the clear night air, so I had to dub the whole thing later in a studio in Bombay. The dubbed version is no good, just ordinary, and another moment is lost to posterity. Such moments are not easy to capture, and cannot be foreseen. You cannot always get the bell to ring.

It is explained in the film that the play had been put on to please the Maharaja, who had seen it in London during his college days and wished to be reminded and to meet some actors from England. He was paying an enormous sum for the privilege, so we, the actors, tried to oblige. For the first scene we appeared high up on a balcony, filmed from below, which caused the cameraman once more to threaten to leave us. He said it was impossible to light, and to prove this point kept us waiting a day and a night whilst he tried to do the impossible. He was right: it was far too dark. This was followed by some narrations later cut out, so that all the finished film showed was the end, when the dying Antony is brought to Cleopatra. I was carried to the foot of the monument by Egyptian slaves. For these parts we had a host of willing unpaid extras, content to wait all night half-naked in the bitter cold of the Rajasthan winter, a cold that goes for the bones. Enveloped in a great cloak over my armour, I shivered; how these poor fellows felt, barefoot and with only half a dhoti, I cannot imagine. Countless times I was hoisted up on bony shoulders, and then hauled up to the towers, slaves' teeth and my teeth chattering in unison with the cold. I tried to imagine mine was fever caused by my countless wounds. We finished with the coming of the dawn, a wonderful wasted effort, for the whole sequence was cut out! It just did not work, and we started instead with the very end of the scene with a magnificent shot of Laura invoking the 'Visiting Moon'.

Our last location was in Lucknow, where we once more spent the night shooting, this time at the railway station. All the shots on the platforms and in the waiting rooms were very good indeed, but they were all scrapped in the end. Then we filmed a scene from *The Critic* by Sheridan in our period costumes, which we had not used for years, in the spacious grounds of La Martinière College. By this time we had run out of make-up, and as a lot of old-fashioned grease-paint is needed to make wigs join (our powdered wigs of the period have a frontal flesh-piece that can be very obvious without a coating of paint), we had to pretend this was done on purpose to look more theatrical. I thought this dreadful, especially as this episode was to be shown early in the film – me going on with a bad wig-join, a thing that had never been known! This scene was to be an open-air show for the boys of the college. Boys carried the ships in the battle and fired revolvers at each other coming from the lake. Finally, in the middle of shoots, a herd of cows walked across the stage. Eventually the scene was used for credits, with Marcus driving a cycle-rickshaw and Foo dressed in a pompadour wig.

The shooting of the film *Shakespeare Wallah* did not finish with a flourish as I had expected. There were no grand farewells. People just faded away. The cast was together one day, and then some were missing, then some more; it was the same with the crew. One morning we found it was all over and we were on the train for Bombay.

Little seemed to have changed for us, but for Felicity everything had. Merchant/Ivory decided that she must go to the Berlin Film Festival to help promote the film. As we saw her off I remembered the prophetic ending of the film: the Buckinghams standing on the quayside waving goodbye to Lizzie, their figures getting smaller and smaller as the ship left the harbour bearing Lizzie away to England and a new life.

It took me years to appreciate *Shakespeare Wallah*. I had seen it so often, was so involved in its creation and outraged at the ideas that were not supposed to be about us and yet were so near in many aspects, that I just could not like it, in spite of the world acclaim. Not until August 1982, when I saw the film on television at home as part of a Merchant/Ivory season, did I change my mind. This time, in the comfort of our own house and not caring so much – for by now any likeness Laura and I had to the characters portrayed had long ceased to exist – I watched in a different mood.

The success of the film, I had always said, was a complete fluke; but now I saw that it was a combination of many skills. The photography and the music are both lovely and undoubtedly the real secret of its success. Again, because colour could not be afforded, the black-and-white pictures are so much more beautiful and atmospheric. The cutting is clever; short scenes do not seem to finish before a cut rushes the story on. The supposed actors in the company are more real in their way than the actors I would have liked to engage for the company, and Madhur as Manjula is so unusual that she becomes a personification of the Indian film star.

Finally, the incredible performance of Felicity was in every way perfect, and using our family gave the non-theatre scenes a reality that actors who had not experienced our touring would have been unable to convey. The film deserves the praise and fame it has earned – it deserves them very well indeed.

11

Felicity's Good Life

Our birds had flown. Jennifer was living in Bombay with Shashi and their three children – two sons, Kunal and Karan, and a daughter, Sanjna. Shashi had become a star of Indian films, sometimes working a crazy schedule from early in the morning to midnight. The appetite for those singing, dancing Hindi films was endless, and there were a few stars who appeared in them again and again. Shashi did a lot of work in his brother Raj Kapoor's studio, and as Hindi stars are usually making several films at the same time, he used to race from one set to another, which earned him the nickname of Taxi Kapoor. Wherever Shashi went, he was mobbed in a way that has not happened in the West since Hollywood was at its height.

Jennifer too was absorbed into the Kapoor clan. It was not easy to find a part for her in Hindi films, and she worked mainly behind scenes, designing clothes for Shashi and spending hours in the bazaars to choose the right buttons and jewellery. She appeared in a Merchant/Ivory film, *Bombay Talkie*, playing the part of a best-selling author who falls in love with India and with an Indian film star. The film ends melodramatically with the death of her lover, played by Shashi; and although I do not think it is one of Merchant/Ivory's best films, Jennifer is lovely in it. As far as the theatre was concerned, however, her confidence seemed to have gone. It happens to people who are away too long, and she always seemed to feel that actors in Britain were much better than they really were. She had that feeling of inferiority that she had had when younger. Then, too, the acting she should have been involved in was in Stratford-upon-Avon or London. There was talk of her doing a season at Stratford, but in the end she had to face up to the fact that Shashi's career was in India and would remain there. So until her appearance in *Junoon*, a Hindi film on the Indian Mutiny, and then *36 Chowringhee Lane*, her acting career was eclipsed. I know that she minded.

She would get books on theatre, new play-scripts, and copies of *Plays and Players* sent out, and whenever they were in England she and Shashi would be at the theatre every night. Eventually her love for the theatre expressed itself in the building of the Prithvi Theatre, named in memory of Shashi's father, Prithviraj Kapoor, which opened at Juhu, near Bombay, in November 1978. It is curious the way fate works. In the early days it would have seemed that Jennifer was the one destined for the West End stage, and Felicity for a rather different role in theatre, possibly management or producing plays and having a home and children.

At the age of nineteen, Felicity was bound for the 1965 Berlin Film Festival for the showing of *Shakespeare Wallah*, which had been made two years earlier. She had spent most of her life, since the age of three months, in India and the Far East; when she arrived in Berlin, with her slightly Indian accent, some people assumed she was Indian. She always loved the sun and tanned very easily, had dark hair and eyes that had the Eastern look that seems to come to children who are brought up in India. Once in Berlin, heralded as a new star, it was a short jump to London, and she decided to stay there. She had only her return ticket and £150, and by now I had booked another tour of Japan, but she told me:

'If I don't stick it out here, I will never know if I could do it or not.'

Felicity stuck it out. She wrote to every theatre company and agent and got negative replies. They all wanted her to go to drama school, but she insisted that she had already served her apprenticeship. She spent hours going up and down rickety or plush staircases, visiting countless different agents in the West End. No one seemed interested in this slightly overdressed girl with an Indian lilt. Then *Shakespeare Wallah* opened in London to wonderful reviews, and Ismail promised her he would find an agent. He found the late Robin Fox – father of James, Edward, and Robert – who had a very determined young woman, Ros Chatto, working with him. Felicity has been with her ever since.

The first job she got was one that Sarah Miles had turned down, that of a Cypriot girl in a television play. Then came a breakthrough. The BBC were producing a Wednesday play called *The Mayfly and the Frog*, and Sir John Gielgud had agreed to appear in it – the first time he had been in a play specifically for television. The director, Robin Midgeley, told Foo that if she would lose a stone and go blonde she could play opposite Gielgud. She did, and that seemed to launch her. She appeared in another television two-hander called *Gone, Gone and Never Called Me Mother* – the most celebrated line in the play *East Lynne*. The actor appearing with her was Drewe Henley, and before long they had decided to get married.

Laura and I continued our touring. But without our daughters, I had rather lost heart in getting half a dozen actors from place to place, organizing their lives and luggage and bookings, sorting out artistic disputes. After Felicity left, Marcus stayed with us for a few years. When he decided to set up a theatre company in Delhi, we decided we would travel light – just the two of us. Our programmes were simple, and we still perform them today. We have no scenery, we don't need a stage or lighting, and we present a ninety-minute programme based on two or three plays, which we talk about, recite and read. We wear costume, and our props are a *Hamlet* chair, a small reading-desk, two tables, and three candlesticks. The programme is called *Shakespeareana*. Our wanderings evolved into a pattern. There were, for a while, cruises aboard the Q.E.2 or P. & O. liners, where we would put on our shows for the passengers. We would also do tours of schools in India, usually basing ourselves at my brother Philip's flat. In England, Foo and Drewe found a house on an island in Shepperton, a charming little village full of film people and pubs, and we stayed with them, or with Laura's sister Beulah and her husband Jim, when we were in England.

Our first time back in England, after seventeen years, was in 1969, the year Felicity was married. The first three years she had been in England she had missed India terribly. She came out every year to stay with Jennifer and Shashi, and going back was always a wrench. We still have one of her letters from 1969, dated 'feb 15th. weather freezing and trying to snow', written the day after she had returned from her holiday with us and the Kapoors in Bombay. She wrote:

Leaving this time was like a *dholi*, I have never yet felt so terribly awfully sad. All the plane looked on in sadness at my state of tearfulness, it was awful and arriving back in London was worse. . . . I feel strangely torn away from the bosom of you noisy buggers.

The dholi is the end of a Hindu marriage. It takes place the day after the wedding when the bride is carried out of her father's house and to the house of her husband's family. The husband's brothers and friends come for her, laughing and full of good cheer, but the bride's family are crying and wailing and pretend to try to stop her leaving. Felicity, newly married, felt that she was leaving part of her life and that it was the last time she would be in India with the family as had been before.

I know exactly how she felt. I was always happiest in India. The climate suits me, the heat and the light, and there is something so relaxing about it; the people do not look as glum as anywhere else.

The Kapoors' flat was always a centre of activity. By eight-thirty in the morning the children would be having a judo class, and the phone would be ringing continuously with film business. A writer would arrive for a script conference, and in the background there were always servants moving around. The flat was on the eleventh floor of an apartment block overlooking the sea in the Malabar Hill area. There was an uninterrupted view of the Arabian Sea, with fishing boats out at night, the same dhows as the Malabar pirates once used to lie in wait for the great cargo ships from Africa. There was a lovely roof-garden that Jennifer had created, with white wrought-iron furniture amongst the bougainvillaea. Not far away from Malabar Hill was the Breach Candy swimming-pool, a vast open-air pool surrounded by gardens of carnations, pinks, sweet-scented stock, and green lawns, where we spent some very happy hours.

Each year we retired for a while from Bombay to Goa. To those who have not travelled there it must be no more than another name on the map. To the hippies who discovered it around 1969 it is a paradise, an island in the sun. To the Indians whose valiant army 'liberated' it from the Portuguese it is a place where they can walk along the beaches and look at the unclad Westerners. To me it is undoubtedly the most beautiful holiday place: a lovely climate, miles of sandy beaches, good food, and people who seem to retain an enjoyment of life, possibly fostered by their late Portuguese colonizers:

> *Where'er the Catholic sun doth shine,*
> *There's laughter there and good red wine,*
> *At least I've always found it so,*
> *Benedicamus Domino.*

Well, there is no good red wine now, but there is still laughter. Those who laugh most are the fisher-girls who take the fish to the markets. They are a tribe apart and dress like Spanish dancers, the sari looped up to the knees in a great panier and worn over the tightest of blouses. The colours are bright, often predominantly red, and the hair is knotted like a dancer's, decorated with a flower. They have lovely bony features with strong jaws; their bodies are slim and strong, and they chatter, laugh, and show their fine teeth, seeming completely emancipated. These young women are sometimes Hindu and sometimes Christian, for there is a great mixture of the two cultures and religions in Goa.

We called the house that Jennifer and Shashi found in Goa in 1970 the Love House, because on its roof was painted a great white heart. It is a spacious bungalow, built in 1951, about a hundred yards from the high tide line, and with a clear view across the beach to the sea. At night the fishermen sometimes bring their nets in opposite the house. I remember one particular night when the poetry and balletic quality of the scene was wonderful to look at, as there was a full moon and the sea was silver. The two nets were spread out along the coastline for about fifty yards, the whole distance being manned with fishermen pulling in the heavy load of fish even more silver than the sea: gleaming jewels shuddering as their lives ran their circle. The nets are pulled in slowly, step by step, and sometimes the boats are a mile out in the bay with the two nets attached. Signal flares are waved to the shore from the boats as to which direction the fish are heading – the only colour in the silver-and-white ballet. It is really theatre: the death of the god – the fish; the silhouette of the boat as it slowly drifts towards the shore; the song of the shantyman, and the response from the chorus; the ballet of the net-haulers. Fishing is looked on by most city-dwellers as a poor way of making a living, but this simple way of life could be the one that will last, the way that will feed the people of the Earth when all the modern techniques and processes have failed – the miracle of the feeding of the five thousand.

When we first went to Goa we were told that the Portuguese had no municipal sense and had not even bothered to pave the roads of the villages, just left the red earth tracks. This in fact saved the villages: they had no roads, therefore no cars, therefore the children were free to run and roam at will. The villagers live in their houses within calling distance of each other, so that when anything goes wrong they call and are instantly answered. When there is a row, the whole village hears every word. It is a kind of telegraph, this raising of the voices: fires, illness, infidelity, all raise this dreadful scream, and help is immediate – much quicker than a telephone.

To the left of the house, about 150 yards away, was a house of great drama. Here lived a joint family of mother, two girls, some children, a married daughter-in-law, and her husband. One unmarried daughter was a goat-herd and the other daughter, who wore a red sari, one of the fishwives. I always noticed things going on here, and whether it was the quaint behaviour of their hippie guests or their roof-catching fire, events were always accompanied by shrieks and yells and vituperation from the whole gang at once for all the world to hear. On the occasion of the fire, the screams were so immediate that the entire village ran with buckets; the fire was soon under control, but not before the woman in the red sari had flung herself on the ground tearing sari and hair while everyone else, our family included, made a human chain of buckets to quell the flames.

There was another day of intense drama when Red Sari expelled her mother from the house. Later I saw Mama had come back, and the goat-girl was slanging a brawny young fisherman with gestures unteachable even at the best drama school. The crescendo increased and suddenly the youth leapt up on to the roof and started flinging tiles in all directions. Then he rushed into the house and brought out a picture of the Virgin and Child, throwing it at the feet of his tormentor. The girl fell to the ground and proceeded to tear her garments, as taught in the Bible. Eventually the man left screaming obscenities while the lady started to chant what sounded like a litany of the saints. During all this the mother and the daughter in the red sari were having a quiet conversation in the most friendly way possible, having forgotten their earlier spat and completely ignoring the drama. Peace descended on the village until the man, who was the goat-girl's brother, returned and proceeded to pull the thatch off the side of the house. All the females by this time had banded together and turned on him, reinforced by an elder sister who lived nearby whom we called Kate, after Shakespeare's Shrew — a strong, lusty wench who taunted him until he flew at her in a rage, but dared not hit her. She routed him properly till she fell to sobbing hysterically, as did all the rest of the protagonists. Thus ended another peaceful Sunday on Baga Beach.

Sitting in a lovely colonial chair with leg-rests, and a peg of fenny (the local drink made of coconuts) at hand, I was enthralled with the place. There was no pollution, no newspapers, no telephone; hardly any clothes were required. There was the sea to watch, the village to waken one early and to help one doze in the afternoon's heat, an evening of brief awakening, and the perpetual wonder of the night, with the stars so large that they seemed far closer than anywhere else in the world. If only I could write for a living, what a place to sit and do it!

By 1974 we decided that we should spend more time in Britain and perform our shows for schools. We were finding that English was no longer the language it used to be in India. At one time English plays meant everything; unless you could quote Shakespeare you would not get a job. Now English seemed to be becoming just another regional language. Returning to London after so many years in India has something in common with being released from prison after a life term. Getting used to new values is almost impossible, and the desire to get used to them is pretty well non-existent. Yet my banishment had only been with other human beings in a different part of the world.

'One thing is certain — you cannot go back,' I wrote at the time in my diary:

The world and time move on and your place at a certain moment is right and proper, then the minute passes into eternity and when you return you are nothing but a ghost from the past encroaching on the present. When I return to my past haunts, I feel as though I am unseen. I think I am still alive, but to those around me, I am not there at all. No one seems to notice my presence – perhaps I am already a ghost.

The King's Road in Chelsea, my haunt for so long and where I was once well known, had been taken over by a new society. Everyone I knew had disappeared; even the pubs had changed hands. Now and then I saw someone I thought I knew from the past, but I was met with a stony stare. I thought perhaps I ought to depart back to Goa before I became a ghost there as well. I realized I had been wandering all my life in foreign lands with no roots – a professional stranger.

Now the English were like a foreign breed to me, 'locals' with odd habits. Most of them seemed to feel the cold weather very badly, which was because they would muffle themselves up and spend far too much time in cars. They would get out of their cars and stagger to some shop or pub, with white, pinched faces and hunched shoulders.

Were the English properly fed, I wondered, or were they suffering from malnutrition amidst their apparent affluence? There did not appear to be any tea-shops any more, and no household I went to seemed to be aware of this tradition and absolute necessity of tea-time. I found myself in Hyde Park and went to the cafeteria. I collected a tray, a ready-made cake, and a cup of tea extracted from a machine, milk and all, and then found there was nowhere to sit. All the chairs outside had been taken by the natives, who had discarded their shirts and just sat immobile in the watery sun. Eventually I found a piece of wall to sit on, but the tea was undrinkable, and the cake uneatable. Apart from these cafeterias there were only expensive 'eating out' restaurants with long and complicated menus; obviously most people could not 'eat out' at these exorbitant prices. Men and women seemed to be eternally shopping, and the supermarkets were full with queues lining up at the pay desks and flinging their purchases into baskets, so that the next wad of notes could go into the till quickly.

There seemed to be something wrong with people's spirit, I wrote:

They all look mid-well, very tired and one and all they are very bad walkers. Everyone is either carrying some great weight or tied to a dog or a pram or a child. . . . No one seems to bother to look in the least bit happy, and this is what is described as an affluent society, these observations occurred to me in what is supposed to be the wealthiest town near London. . . . Are they all tired of playing with toys? Because it is a sort of game, this purchasing and banking and insuring and bothering about all the things that really we care little about.

I can never get used to the apparent unsociability of England, and I think it has to do with the cars. The roads are deserted of people, and everyone lives their own little private life, folded into their car. We went to see a woman who had a lovely house in Wales, a really beautiful place, but I thought how terribly lonely the English seemed to be in their own little personal plots with their families gone to other little personal plots. As lonely as the roads: these long, depressing stretches of concrete with a white line painted down the middle and not a dog or a child, hardly ever a cycle, and never a horse; just the occasional flying car rushing somewhere. Inside these silly tin boxes are ordinary human beings who want to be friendly with others, but have to pretend instead they are all important and self-sufficient. None of it, to someone coming back after so many years in the East, seemed to make sense.

Felicity's career was now beginning to soar. We went to the first night of Alan Ayckbourn's *The Norman Conquests*, a great success. Foo was apprehensive about the press, particularly as Harold Hobson was in the front row and for some reason never seemed to like her. But the notices, apart from Hobson's, were very good indeed, and it sparked off an upward turn for her. There was *The Good Life*, in which she was brilliant; her appearance in Michael Frayn's play, *Clouds*; and her definitive performance as Raina in *Arms and the Man* in the Greenwich Theatre production. I was in India at the time of the first *Good Life* series but I caught up with it in England, and I shall always remember the headline in the *Daily Mail*: 'Over Two Million People Watch Felicity Kendal'.

The National Theatre was a new phase for Felicity, in which she showed herself at her best in the part of Constanzia, Mozart's wife. I wrote of the first night of *Amadeus*, 'a night to remember'. I had gone with apprehension in my heart about how the National would tackle this masterly but difficult play, but my doubts were dissolved by the first sight of the setting, with everything so beautifully placed against an artificial proscenium and the dim chandelier over the forestage. When I saw the two 'Venticelli', as Salieri calls his informants, and heard the first line, 'I don't believe it', I knew we were in for something grander than usual. Felicity had the part of her life and was absolutely lovely all the way through. At the end she took her curtain-call like all the leading ladies before her, in a white spotlight that almost asked for bouquets to be thrown. She continued her run at the National with two marvellous parts: in Tom Stoppard's *On the Razzle*, and as Mrs Tanqueray in *The Second Mrs Tanqueray*.

During those years of increasing success, Felicity had had a difficult personal life in her marriage with Drewe, and eventually a distressing break-up. I became aware of it around the time she was in *The Norman Conquests*, playing a long run to packed houses. I noted in my diary in October 1974: 'Drewe has started driving a mini-cab and earns more in a day than he does as an actor in a week – but then that is silly as he should be in constant demand in the theatre. He is much better than anyone in the National in the juvenile gents gang.' Only three days later I wrote: 'There is a rift in Foo's married life. I hope it can be healed somehow but it looks very sad at the moment.' Foo moved out of Shepperton, and found a terraced cottage in Putney, and we helped as much as we could with Charlie, her small son.

Around that time Laura and I had a home for the first time, for Jennifer and Shashi decided to buy a flat in Swan Court in Chelsea, which would be a base for us, and for the Kapoors when they were in London. It would be a place where we could stay without bothering anyone, where we could keep our possessions, and where people would know where to contact us. It was the first time in our married life that we had a home rather than a hotel, or guest-house, or friends and relations to stay with.

People have often asked me, 'Don't you get tired of living out of suitcases?'

I have always said, 'No, so long as the suitcase is small enough and there is a place in a hotel room to put it.'

But finally it was with a feeling of relief that we moved into Swan Court, and at last Laura and I had somewhere where we did not feel we had to apologize for staying a day longer than we need, with an office for our records and a place for our junk. Foo did wonders in one day to get it prepared from a concrete enclosure to a lovely home. There was constant hot water and constant central heating, and it was a surprise to feel the cold and damp when we left the building. At times Laura and I were there on our own; at other times it was bursting at the seams with Kapoor children and their friends. The Kapoors would descend amongst music and noise, and we would have Sunday lunches that could not have been recreated by the cast of *Saturday, Sunday, Monday*, with everyone talking at once.

During the last twelve years my little grandson Charlie has taken a special place in our lives. Felicity would often bring him round to see us in Swan Court. From an early age he seemed to have an extensive and racy vocabulary, and a natural sense of timing for devastating one-liners. We took him, when he was about three, to see the Changing of the Guard at Whitehall. It was more marvellous than I could have imagined, with real horses and costumes that even the National Theatre could not afford. I thought, it gives one more faith in Britain than the promises and excuses of politicians and bankers. We were in the front row, and the New Guard had just arrived, standing with their backs to us, with the Old Guard drawn up opposite. There was a hush as the two officers saluted. Then Charles, in his best carrying voice, declared, 'I don't like horses!'

After two years apart, Felicity and Drewe were together again, for which I was glad, because I have always believed in the permanence of marriage. Drewe was appearing at St George's Theatre, Tufnell Park, and we went to see him as the First Player in *Hamlet*. Foo, meanwhile, was working on Ken Russell's film about William Wordsworth and had completed *Valentino*.

The following year, 1978, Drewe and Charlie had come out to India, but Felicity was unable to be with them. I felt considerable tension, and for the first time was glad when they went. I got involved in a film on the Indian Mutiny – *Junoon*, in which Jennifer had a leading role; I played the part of a priest, booming forth, 'Deliver me from my enemies, O Lord!' as the mutineers attacked the church. Then came the message from England that I had a foreboding about: Drewe had taken Charlie away from Foo without letting her know where he was, and had gone off to Rome. She eventually found out where he was and had to go to Rome to fetch him. We cut short our stay in India and rushed back, though there was little we could do. Foo continued to appear as Raina in *Arms and the Man* at Greenwich, but the strain for her was terrible. In the end she got divorce proceedings under way.

The acting profession, with all its tensions and uncertainties, places great pressure on many relationships, and Felicity and Drewe's marriage was, in part, a casualty of theatre. That is all long in the past and now they have an amicable relationship as the parents of Charlie, which seems the best for everyone concerned.

It was more than a year after her final breakup that Felicity was happy again. She met Michael Rudman when she was playing in *Clouds*, which he directed, and they were married in 1983. Throughout her marital crisis she had remained working and had never let anyone down. She was brought up in the tradition of 'The show must go on', and that feeling never deserted her.

12
Chowringhee Lane

The most enjoyable tours after we left India were spent at sea, playing Shakespeare on board the big ocean liners run by P. & O. and Cunard. It was a touring actor's dream. You had a captive audience, desperate for diversion, and you did not have to keep packing up and moving on. You travelled thousands of miles, meanwhile leaving all your props in one place. On board ship, everyone was isolated from the cares of everyday life and forgot the rest of the world. Seeing the first flying-fish as you approached the Tropics was an event, and the ceremony of Crossing the Line was a show in itself. We took our Shakespeareana programme across the Equator several times, to South Africa and Australia, Spain and Portugal, all the time playing to the gentle swell of the ocean and a background of the ship's noises.

Back on shore, we were faced with the problem of booking shows in British schools, making a fresh start in a country we no longer knew well. The end of the 1970s were difficult for us as we tried to plough our independent course. Any actor who works independently of the security of a company knows the times when you feel that the cards are stacked against you. I had always told myself, 'Think lucky and you'll be lucky', and I was saying this more frequently now, with less conviction. After a dearth of bookings, I wrote in my diary:

Had an awful night. Why at this time of life should I worry? I have never worried in my life before – but I seem to be losing the ability to say, 'Bugger it.' The trouble is that we have gone through our life trying to give so much for so little money. One rupee a seat is no way to make a fortune.

I was suffering from the feeling of growing old, and alcohol was beginning to have a bad effect on my health. I was continually writing in my diary that I would give it up, and work at my yoga; but alas, these good resolutions never lasted long. In May 1980 I wrote:

Last night I had slight twinges in my left ankle. This morning it was worse and by noon terrible. I could not walk, then my ankle started to swell and go all shiny and my shin ached. A red spot appeared. Oh Lord, flebitis, I thought. It killed my Uncle Tom. I imagined an early death following an amputation. I drank some vodka, which I hate, and half a bottle of white wine to take the taste of the vodka away. The pain and the swelling got worse and after a disturbed sleep I drove to the doctor. The surgery was full, I waited over an hour. The verdict terrible and humiliating: *gout*. Some red pills were prescribed and I was told it would be cured in three days provided I did not drink *any* alcohol.

We continued to visit India from time to time, giving occasional performances. Laura had been in pain for some time from an arthritic hip, and was increasingly reluctant to travel hundreds of miles for one show. Going by train in India was becoming an ordeal: masses of beggars at every stop, meals arriving cold, doubtful water, ticket inspectors suspecting everything, porters pushing and shoving and wanting more whatever I gave them. The trains struck us increasingly as filthy, with people asleep on every available seat, monkeys clambering through the windows, and having eventually to close the windows in self-protection and being roasted alive – the fans either do not work or make clanking noises all night. I sometimes thought it would be better to go by air, remembering the days when we had the maharajas' private coaches, complete with bearers, cooks, bar, sitting rooms, and bedrooms; those wonderful meals at wayside halts where the food was served outside in the station garden by gloved waiters, with fan-bearers, and the train patiently waiting till the sahibs had finished their coffee and felt like continuing their journey.

Our thoughts of the old days were revived when we made a television documentary film about Shakespeareana, produced by Nicolaus Mackie. It was called *Shakespearistan – East of Suez*. As Laura and I declaimed our verse from the white marble pavilions of Udaipur, I remembered our previous encounter with film on *Shakespeare Wallah* and realized the ephemeral nature of the medium I had given so much of my life to. The greatest performance in theatre becomes a memory, while film lasts virtually for ever.

By the end of 1980 it was necessary for Laura to go into hospital and have a replacement hip operation. She had the operation early in January 1981, and it was successful. All the tired, drawn lines on her face had smoothed away, and she was once again the loveliest of women, the sort of woman everyone falls in love with. While she was still recovering in hospital I had to fly to India, to fit into the shooting schedule for *36 Chowringhee Lane*, the film Shashi was producing and Jennifer was starring in. I was to play the part of Jennifer's brother, a part that had been refused to me earlier because they thought I didn't look old and decrepit enough. Apparently they had changed their minds. *Chowringhee Lane* is now well known but it was very much an unknown quantity then. It was the first work as a director by the actress Apanna Sen and it was the first time for many years that Jennifer was to be in a film in English designed for a European market.

The story was not one that would necessarily appeal to a wide audience. A lonely Anglo-Indian spinster, whose only joy in life is teaching Shakespeare, becomes friendly with a young Indian couple who want to use her flat for their courting. She blossoms with this new friendship, but once they are married they have no further use for her, and she is left alone again. Jennifer thought a lot about the part, and spent hours haunting the shops where the Anglo-Indians bought their clothes.

We moved to Calcutta for the filming, where the real Chowringhee is. We stayed at the Fairlawn Hotel, our old haunt since wartime and still run by the same family. It was beautifully quiet, a wonderful old house, and the only thing that has changed is that it is now air-conditioned – not an improvement to my mind, as it cuts out the lovely sounds of Calcutta. The entire first day of filming I spent in a hospital bed in the Pratt Memorial School where we had played so often in the past. I was supposed to be ill in an infirmary, and it was decided that I play the part *sans* teeth, with my beard cut to a stubble and my hair all short. I looked a proper bugger! I thought as I lay in bed how strange that Laura and I should both be in hospital so far apart, but as usual I'm only pretending.

I have always thought Calcutta a bit grim, with its combination of completely naked poverty and dreary commercialism, but I had previously found a sort of gaiety and drive about the people and the place. This time it seemed quite hopeless in every way. On my previous visits I had been part of the world of theatre and education and had looked at the city from that level: in the context of the Loreto Convent and La Martinière; the New Empire and the Sans Souci theatres, neither of which exist any more. This time I was an ordinary visitor and saw nothing but drab, dirty houses, unkempt buildings that were once so beautiful, and the squalor of new skyscrapers almost as dismal as the old buildings.

A few days later I got a cable from Foo: 'MUMMY WELL AND WALKING WONDERFULLY WITH STICKS SHE PLANS TO BE HOME 25TH NICE IF YOU WERE HERE BY THEN AS JOHN DIED THIS MORNING BUT SHE DOESN'T KNOW YET PLEASE WIRE POSSIBLE RETURN DATE THO I WILL MANAGE SHE SENDS LOVE FOO.' It was a strange coincidence. I was here at the Fairlawn Hotel when my father died, here when Laura's mother died, and here when John, Laura's brother, died. On two occasions I got the telegram in the same room.

My part was finally done. I finished with my horrible striped pyjamas, my ancient jacket, my woolly, my scarf, my comforter, my filthy rubber *chappals*, and dirty banyan. I washed my hair and whiskers and left that character behind. I left Calcutta, arriving in a Bombay that was lovely and hot after the lowering temperature of Bengal. The dhobi was still banging away down below on the rocks, disregarding his European bath, and the Arabian Sea was still as lovely. I had dinner with Ismail Merchant, and he told me that he and James Ivory were booked up with projects for years. Their next film about India would be *Heat and Dust*.

I flew back to London. By April, Laura and I were back in India to do some more work on *Chowringhee Lane*, the dream sequences when the schoolteacher remembers the sailor she lost in the war, as a young girl. Our location was on the shore, and the rocks were covered with white wooden crosses as if it was a war cemetery. I dressed in my white suit, Laura in a lovely soft white dress and floppy hat. It was wonderful to see her walking like a princess again after limping about for so long. When we saw the rough cut of *36 Chowringhee Lane* it was so moving that I wept non-stop.

Later that year the film was shown in India to great acclaim. Jennifer wrote to say she was hailed as a film star. Early in 1982 Shashi and Jennifer left for Manila to attend the film festival, where *Chowringhee Lane* was in the competition section. They were also hoping to sell the remaining rights of another Kapoor film, *Kulug*, in which Kunal appeared, and *Junoon*. *Chowringhee* won the Best Film in Manila Festival prize, and was immediately booked for a London opening. Meanwhile, Jennifer and Shashi both were to be in *Heat and Dust* – Shashi as the Nawab, and Jennifer as Mrs Saunders, the Doctor's unhappy wife.

Most of the shooting took place in Hyderabad, where Jennifer had bought her first theatrical make-up box at the age of twelve. The shop was still there, she told me. So was the Rock Castle Hotel where we had stayed, but it seemed much smaller now, and there were no white-gloved bearers any more, just two or three men in shirtsleeves. The filming of *Heat and Dust* was quite a saga for everyone, although Jennifer and Shashi are used to the apparently precarious way in which Merchant/Ivory films are made. Various journalists were hauled in as extras, with Ismail gesticulating and chivvying people along. Yet out of this apparent chaos came one of their most successful films ever.

In August, *36 Chowringhee Lane* opened in London, to good notices in all the papers; and there were interviews and articles with Jennifer, tracing the Kendal–Kapoor story. Jennifer won the Best Actress award from the *Evening Standard*, and there were more marvellous reviews when *Heat and Dust* opened in London in January 1983. Jennifer's eyes were haunting – such a depth of sadness she brought to the part, so very different from the way she looked in real life.

On 10 May 1983 Jennifer arrived to stay with us before going to Cannes. She was suffering from amoebic dysentery. It had been troubling her for some time, and there seemed to be nothing anyone in India could do about it. While she was at Cannes and saw a doctor there they suspected there was something worse. So there were tests, and then operations, and for a long time I was unable to say what is was that she had. I called it 'the illness' or 'this thing'. Jennifer returned to India, where she had her first operation for cancer, and Felicity went out to stay with her afterwards. She seemed to have recovered, and returned to her energetic life. She had always been healthy and found it difficult to believe that she could be seriously ill. A few months after her operation she came to London for more treatment; it was found that the disease was far advanced. Her final months were spent at home with us or in hospital.

In India it is looked upon as unlucky to praise one's own, especially one's own children. To say your son or daughter is lovely must be qualified by adding something derogatory to mollify the gods. I must have forgotten this very sensible rule when I wrote or spoke with such pride of the achievements of our family in the theatre and kindred arts. I had got over my disappointment and had accepted the fact that we were not creating a permanent company that would run on and on after our time which, as I have said, was my original idea and ambition. It was obvious that all our family wanted to have houses and flats to 'settle down', and not to be wanderers between the furrow and the stars like Laura and I had been. I had got over that, and so I crowed about their achievements in different spheres, which at the time seemed all set for a sort of permanence. How wrong I was, and how silly to crow. Jennifer, who for years had sat by and worked only intermittently, had suddenly decided to act again. She was, of course, the prime mover in the lovely Prithvi Theatre, but with her fantastic impact in *36 Chowringhee Lane* she started in earnest, got herself an agent, and all sorts of offers started coming in. Alas, she was given time to complete only one assignment before illness took over, and on my seventy-fifth birthday, early on the morning of 7 September 1984, she died at the age of just fifty.

The appalling loss is something I cannot talk or write about. It seemed as if the whole Land of Promise had frozen. My last communication from her was a feeble pencilled note, 'The readiness is all', from the speech in *Hamlet* that I tried to read at her funeral: 'There is a special providence in the fall of a sparrow.' The world's press mourned, and letters came by the thousand, all praising her fortitude, her family, and her powers as an actress. But few had seen what we had seen or had our memories. People's memories are over such a short period, and no one seems to imagine that anything really happens before their own time.

Our memories, of course, started much earlier. Her beautiful ears at birth: why I don't know, and why should one notice her ears? I have never heard of anyone mentioning such a detail, but there it was. A lovely little thing blowing bubbles: the times I took her for walks in a little pram. I used to pretend she was grown up and I was telling her things, and we used to run down the country roads. I got quite good at turning at speed, and one day we had a spill, I recall her look of pity and contempt for such a childish father. Years later, on a winter evening, leaving for our first voyage to India, Jennifer was a lonesome figure by candlelight in the far window waving goodbye – I thought about this for years with infinite sadness, and when at last I mentioned it to her she said she remembered it well and thought at the time it was such a wonderful part to play!

Earlier, her being brought to see us in Cornwall by Laura's mother: many clothing coupons must have been saved to buy a lovely little brown trouser-suit and a little brown hat to cover her newly curled hair in imitation of Shirley Temple. Even earlier, when we used to tour in a Morris Minor that cost all of £15 – we travelled up and down the country on Sundays from theatre to theatre; Jennifer had a great plush suit to keep out the cold. Cars were not heated very well in those days, and she used to sleep most of the journeys on Laura's knee, waking up now and then to say, 'Any more fields?' She knew theatres were not in fields, so if there were more she would promptly sleep again. The first time she went on in the show – in Bombay as Lucius in *Julius Caesar* – she knew every word at the first rehearsal and could not understand why I should enquire if she was all right. She always knew all her parts before we started rehearsing. The classical roles seemed to be born with her; I never saw her studying. At sixteen she played Alvira in *Blithe Spirit*; there could never have been a better, or a better Raina in *Arms and the Man*. As Viola she did what so few have done. She was so sure of the sadness at the back of all the fun, in contrast to the almost pedantic precision of Gwendolyn in *The Importance of Being Earnest*.

In Pakistan during *Othello* I did have more to drink than was wise. I can't remember what I did in the last scene, but Jennifer never forgave me and looked at me with the expression she had given when I tipped her out of her pram. I never drank during a show after that since, and thank God I never will.

She bought a pair of army-surplus Royal Stewart trews in Portobello Road and reshaped them to fit her. They really were striking, and trousers were not so common for ladies in those days. She wore them on a trip to Malta, and in Rome stopped the traffic. I had a letter only the other day about this event, telling me how one young man had compared her eyes to the blue Sicilian skies – this on the same trip to Syracuse. He did not know her; just saw her, and her lovely sunny appearance.

Then Jennifer played a long film part in Hindi. To me, particularly hopeless as I am at languages, this was incredible. It would have been different if Felicity had done it, as she is bilingual in Hindi and English, having learnt both simultaneously; but Jennifer started to learn Hindi only after she was married, and to play a long part in *Junoon* with apparent ease was staggering.

She took the theatre and everything about it most seriously. She never knew our Shakespeareana Company was so worthwhile till she left it. How could she when she had seen only a few plays in England – *Arms and the Man*, *The Critic*, and the *Henrys* at the New Theatre during the war when we had come home on leave and took her to the theatre every night? Laurence Olivier gave her a picture of himself as Sergius, and she used it as the photograph in our show as long as she played Raina. Her husband Shashi played Sergius and dressed in the same sort of costume as the picture – he never played any part better and must be one of the best Sergiuses ever. After she had left the company Jennifer eventually saw a lot of theatre in London and the United States, and she was inspired to keep our approach going. This was one of her ideas behind the building of Prithvi Theatre, to start a repertory company based in Bombay. It is a pity the company never got under way during her time, but doubtless in the fullness of time it will, and there are signs of it emerging even now.

The parts Jennifer had played were legion, and all in such a short time. She seemed incapable of failing: the dreadful schoolgirl in *The Rotters*, the equally dreadful girl in *The Corn Is Green*, in *Candida*, in *Charley's Aunt*, each part treated with the utmost seriousness whatever the quality of the play. I've never seen a better Helena in *A Midsummer Night's Dream*. Her Desdemona,

Ophelia, and the rest all completely controlled at an age when most actresses are just starting at drama school. That last heart-rending clip from Satyajit Ray's *Home and the World* was shown on television the day she died.

One of her most memorable performances was not in a theatre at all, but in her own house in Bombay. It was before the shooting of *Chowringhee Lane* had started. Laura and I were seated in the large drawing room when an Anglo-Indian lady came out of Jennifer's room. She crossed to the outer door, faintly acknowledging our presence, and made her exit. We did not think much about it, as all sorts of people are asked to an Indian house to see to various things. After a few moments she put her head round the door, looked at us and said, 'Will that be O.K.?' We had not idea that the Anglo-Indian lady was Jennifer trying out her costume. She used no make-up, no wig, just put on spectacles, did her hair loosely, and wore shoes, underwear, and a dress she had purchased from the shops that specialize in clothing for this sort of person. The rest was mental: no private acting, simply being the person.

Jennifer kept her first make-up box all her life, right through the years when she was idle, after a show or film finished the last scene or shot, she never washed her make-up towel, but used it again for the first shot or scene of the next show. It is still there in Prithvi Theatre as she left it. May she rest in peace.

Epilogue

After Jennifer's death, I had thought I would never return to India. For some time after the funeral I set my face against ever seeing the sights that would only revive the memories of loss. But we are not allowed to blot out the past; it has to be faced, and lived through, and built upon, if we are ever to find peace. Another loss was my brother Philip, who had lived in Bombay for years, and had died a few months before Jennifer. I knew it would be painful to go back, but I also knew that she would have wanted it, because the work she had started was continuing.

Her eldest son, Kunal, had acted in several Hindi films, but around the time that Jennifer became ill he took over the running of the Prithvi Theatre that she and Shashi had built seven years earlier. We had played there before, and I have always found it one of the best theatre spaces I know. It has an open stage surrounded by a semi-circular bank of seats, so that there is an intimate feeling of a room about it. The acoustics are excellent, and it is well sound-proofed, very necessary during the monsoon. It is not a convenient location — out at Juhu, where many of Bombay's film community live, an hour's drive from central Bombay. But Shashi's father had lived in the house opposite the theatre, and the site is that of Prithviraj's old rehearsal studio. Once you get there, it is a lovely place to spend the evening. There is an open-air café attached where you can sit under the palm-trees and drink melon juice, or eat crab curry; the garden is lit by garlands of fairy lights. It is a much pleasanter theatre-going experience than most places in London.

Kunal told me that they had decided to go ahead with the theatre festival Jennifer had planned to be held each year. The first one, a fortnight of companies mainly from the Bombay area, was held in November 1983. It was successful, and Jennifer had hoped the next one would encompass good companies throughout India. That would have happened in November 1984, but after she died it was put off until February 1985: 28 February was her birthday and it was meant as a birthday present to her.

Laura and I were asked to open the Festival with our anthology, *Shakespeareana*, and to play the two-handers in our repertoire, *Dear Liar* and *Old World*. We flew out by courtesy of Air India. We know most of the crew and officials there now, and they make our journeys as happy as possible, remembering to give us seats where we are not tormented by some awful film. We arrived in Bombay at the end of January, away from the ice and snows of England in the bright light and warmth of India at the best time of the year.

Driving through Juhu and approaching the Prithvi Theatre, I realized it was worth it, after all, to have come back to India. I wrote in my diary:

> We thought we would feel terrible with no Jennifer here, but she is here more than she ever was before. Everywhere we look and go in the theatre there she is – just there, not worrying about what is going wrong with the place, but just being there, and I am sure she always will be.

On the opening night the theatre was *en fête*. Posters from the theatre companies all over the world decorated the open-air foyer, and the place was ablaze with fairy lights as the sun went down. People began to throng in, mostly young, which is the strength of Indian theatre, just like it must have been in London in Shakespeare's time. There were street theatre troupes, story-tellers from Orissa, hobby-horses from Rajasthan, all going on at once outside. The place was so thronged that even those with tickets for the show had trouble getting near the doors. There were flowers everywhere and a great wedding-band to play the doors open. Shashi broke a coconut on the steps to declare the festival open, and Kunal wished us good luck.

On the stage were two tables and one chair. The setting was

exactly as it had been when we had played *Shakespeareana* here three years earlier. The stage staff remembered precisely how it was, though there must have been hundreds of shows on the stage since. We had lengthened the programme to excerpts from four plays: *A Midsummer Night's Dream*, *The Merchant*, *Macbeth*, and *Twelfth Night*. The house was packed, and it was a joy to play to such an enthusiastic audience. At the end there was a standing ovation, and old friends came to our dressing room to greet us. Among them were people who had seen us when they were at school, and remembered the Shakespeareana Company at its height. It was wonderful to know that we had contributed to their interest in theatre and love of Shakespeare.

Dear Liar, Jerome Kilty's anthology of the letters of George Bernard Shaw and Mrs Patrick Campbell, also played to packed houses, and we put on an extra performance of Arbuzov's *Old World* for the Russian Embassy. The Festival proved what I have always said, that the language of theatre is universal. On many evenings the play would be in a language not understood by most of the audience. A production from Rajasthan, for instance, in the little-known language of the Bheel tribe managed to get its sense across through singing, dancing, and mime. The Theatre Academy of Poona brought *Ghashiram Kotwal*, performed in Maharathi, and it was one of the hits of the Festival. Another production, *It's All Yours, Janaab*, was translated from Hindi into 'Bombay English'; and there were productions translated into Hindi – *Look Back in Anger*, for instance, retitled *Main zinda Hoon Main Sochta Hoon*.

We left before the end of the Festival, because we had a series of bookings in English schools. So we missed the evening on which Jennifer's birthday was celebrated. Two of India's best musicians, Zakir Hussain on the *tabla* and Shivkumar Sharma on the *santoor*, played for three hours to an enraptured audience. The 'house full' signs were ignored, and people sat in the aisles, on-stage, and in the wings behind the musicians. At the end, Zakir said, 'We wish Jennifer a happy birthday and this is our tribute to her.' They played a folk song from Jammu and Kashmir to a hushed and silent house. It was a special acknowledgement of the place Jennifer had found in everyone's hearts.

Looking back over the years, I realize how rich our lives have been in experience and friendship, and what a satisfying profession acting is. Laura and I may not have accumulated much in the way of material wealth, but we have acted all the parts we have wanted to. I have never really expected acclaim for doing my job, and to be publicly honoured for being successful in any form of life is almost declaring that the achievement itself is not enough.

Nevertheless I did feel I had been honoured in a unique manner, in a sort of laying on of hands, by Sir John Gielgud when, in a play written by Charles Wood, he played the part of Sir Geoffrey Kendle, a Knight of the Theatre – an elderly actor, tired, and of eccentric habits. Whether Charles Wood had heard my name once and assumed I was an actor of the past I do not know, but this Geoffrey Kendal, very much in the present, watched with rapture his near-namesake speaking with the mellifluous tones of Sir John. It took me back years ago, to a sunny day in Sauchiehall Street in Glasgow, when I had heard the most wonderful voice speaking quite naturally behind us. I turned around to see a tall man in dark glasses. It was John Gielgud holding an ordinary conversation, and it was a benediction to the ear. Sir Geoffrey, the eccentric Knight of the Theatre, could not have received a better medium for his lines.

Being an actor must be the best job in the world. It combines all the things that a person need look for: health, romance, travel, the fun of the lottery, the positive tragedy of failure, and the will to overcome it. It provides good companionship, and interest in literature, architecture, music, and dancing – in short, just about everything that most people strive for. But the theatre is female and, like all females, she will not be trifled with. She must be grasped with both hands and given one's whole self, body and soul, if she is to be a proper mate. She must not be dallied with or neglected or flirted with or she will bite, and that bite will never heal. This may sound over-dramatic but it is true – and may be seen over and over again.

Of everything that acting has brought me the best has been meeting and being together with Laura. It was because of our decision not to be separated that we took the perilous course of running our own company, and I could never in any way regret that decision. There have been times in our life when we have argued and disagreed, and sometimes our rehearsals have been fraught with conflict; but there has never been a time when we had nothing to say to each other. There is the joy, too, of watching the acting line continue in our grandchildren, knowing that what Laura and I began may, in one way or another, continue indefinitely. So I shall say, as I write at the end of each year's diary, God Bless Us Everyone.

Index

FOR THE BEST IN PAPERBACKS, LOOK FOR THE

In every corner of the world, on every subject under the sun, Penguins represent quality and variety – the very best in publishing today.

For complete information about books available from Penguin and how to order them, write to us at the appropriate address below. Please note that for copyright reasons the selection of books varies from country to country.

In the United Kingdom: For a complete list of books available from Penguin in the U.K., please write to *Dept EP, Penguin Books Ltd, Harmondsworth, Middlesex, UB7 0DA*

In the United States: For a complete list of books available from Penguin in the U.S., please write to *Dept BA, Viking Penguin, 299 Murray Hill Parkway, East Rutherford, New Jersey 07073*

In Canada: For a complete list of books available from Penguin in Canada, please write to *Penguin Books Canada Limited, 2801 John Street, Markham, Ontario L3R 1B4*

In Australia: For a complete list of books available from Penguin in Australia, please write to the *Marketing Department, Penguin Books Australia Ltd, P.O. Box 257, Ringwood, Victoria 3134*

In New Zealand: For a complete list of books available from Penguin in New Zealand, please write to the *Marketing Department, Penguin Books (N.Z.) Ltd, Private Bag, Takapuna, Auckland 9*

In India: For a complete list of books available from Penguin in India, please write to *Penguin Overseas Ltd, 706 Eros Apartments, 56 Nehru Place, New Delhi 110019*

Castaway Lucy Irvine

'Writer seeks "wife" for a year on a tropical island.' This is the extraordinary, candid, sometimes shocking account of what happened when Lucy Irvine answered the advertisement, and found herself embroiled in what was not exactly a desert island dream. 'Fascinating' – *Daily Mail*

Out of Africa Karen Blixen (Isak Dinesen)

After the failure of her coffee-farm in Kenya, where she lived from 1913 to 1931, Karen Blixen went home to Denmark and wrote this unforgettable account of her experiences. 'No reader can put the book down without some share in the author's poignant farewell to her farm' – *Observer*

The Lisle Letters Edited by Muriel St Clare Byrne

An intimate, immediate and wholly fascinating picture of a family in the reign of Henry VIII. 'Remarkable . . . we can really hear the people of early Tudor England talking' – Keith Thomas in the *Sunday Times*. 'One of the most extraordinary works to be published this century' – J. H. Plumb

In My Wildest Dreams Leslie Thomas

The autobiography of Leslie Thomas, author of *The Magic Army* and *The Dearest and the Best*. From Barnardo boy to original virgin soldier, from apprentice journalist to famous novelist, it is an amazing story. 'Hugely enjoyable' – *Daily Express*

India: The Siege Within M. J. Akbar

'A thoughtful and well-researched history of the conflict, 2,500 years old, between centralizing and separatist forces in the sub-continent. And remarkably, for a work of this kind, it's concise, elegantly written and entertaining' – Zareer Masani in the *New Statesman*

The Winning Streak Walter Goldsmith and David Clutterbuck

Marks and Spencer, Saatchi and Saatchi, United Biscuits, G.E.C. . . . The U.K.'s top companies reveal their formulas for success, in an important and stimulating book that no British manager can afford to ignore.

FOR THE BEST IN PAPERBACKS, LOOK FOR THE

A CHOICE OF PENGUINS

An African Winter Preston King With an Introduction by Richard Leakey

This powerful and impassioned book offers a unique assessment of the interlocking factors which result in the famines of Africa and argues that there *are* solutions and we *can* learn from the mistakes of the past.

Jean Rhys: Letters 1931–66
Edited by Francis Wyndham and Diana Melly

'Eloquent and invaluable . . . her life emerges, and with it a portrait of an unexpectedly indomitable figure' – Marina Warner in the *Sunday Times*

Among the Russians Colin Thubron

One man's solitary journey by car across Russia provides an enthralling and revealing account of the habits and idiosyncrasies of a fascinating people. 'He sees things with the freshness of an innocent and the erudition of a scholar' – *Daily Telegraph*

The Amateur Naturalist Gerald Durrell with Lee Durrell

'Delight . . . on every page . . . packed with authoritative writing, learning without pomposity . . . it represents a real bargain' – *The Times Educational Supplement*. 'What treats are in store for the average British household' – *Books and Bookmen*

The Democratic Economy Geoff Hodgson

Today, the political arena is divided as seldom before. In this exciting and original study, Geoff Hodgson carefully examines the claims of the rival doctrines and exposes some crucial flaws.

They Went to Portugal Rose Macaulay

An exotic and entertaining account of travellers to Portugal from the pirate-crusaders, through poets, aesthetes and ambassadors, to the new wave of romantic travellers. A wonderful mixture of literature, history and adventure, by one of our most stylish and seductive writers.

FOR THE BEST IN PAPERBACKS, LOOK FOR THE

A CHOICE OF PENGUINS

A Fortunate Grandchild 'Miss Read'

Grandma Read in Lewisham and Grandma Shafe in Walton on the Naze were totally different in appearance and outlook, but united in their affection for their grand-daughter – who grew up to become the much-loved and popular novelist.

The Ultimate Trivia Quiz Game Book   Maureen and Alan Hiron

If you are immersed in trivia, addicted to quiz games, endlessly nosey, then this is the book for you: over 10,000 pieces of utterly dispensable information!

The Diary of Virginia Woolf
Five volumes, edited by Quentin Bell and Anne Olivier Bell

'As an account of the intellectual and cultural life of our century, Virginia Woolf's diaries are invaluable; as the record of one bruised and unquiet mind, they are unique'– Peter Ackroyd in the *Sunday Times*

Voices of the Old Sea   Norman Lewis

'I will wager that *Voices of the Old Sea* will be a classic in the literature about Spain' – *Mail on Sunday*. 'Limpidly and lovingly Norman Lewis has caught the helpless, unwitting, often foolish, but always hopeful village in its dying summers, and saved the tragedy with sublime comedy' – *Observer*

The First World War   A. J. P. Taylor

In this superb illustrated history, A. J. P. Taylor 'manages to say almost everything that is important for an understanding and, indeed, intellectual digestion of that vast event . . . A special text . . . a remarkable collection of photographs' – *Observer*

Ninety-Two Days   Evelyn Waugh

With characteristic honesty, Evelyn Waugh here debunks the romantic notions attached to rough travelling: his journey in Guiana and Brazil is difficult, dangerous and extremely uncomfortable, and his account of it is witty and unquestionably compelling.

A CHOICE OF PENGUIN FICTION

Monsignor Quixote Graham Greene

Now filmed for television, Graham Greene's novel, like Cervantes' seventeenth-century classic, is a brilliant fable for its times. 'A deliciously funny novel' – *The Times*

The Dearest and the Best Leslie Thomas

In the spring of 1940 the spectre of war turned into grim reality – and for all the inhabitants of the historic villages of the New Forest it was the beginning of the most bizarre, funny and tragic episode of their lives. 'Excellent' – *Sunday Times*

Earthly Powers Anthony Burgess

Anthony Burgess's magnificent masterpiece, an enthralling, epic narrative spanning six decades and spotlighting some of the most vivid events and characters of our times. 'Enormous imagination and vitality . . . a huge book in every way' – Bernard Levin in the *Sunday Times*

The Penitent Isaac Bashevis Singer

From the Nobel Prize-winning author comes a powerful story of a man who has material wealth but feels spiritually impoverished. 'Singer . . . restates with dignity the spiritual aspirations and the cultural complexities of a lifetime, and it must be said that in doing so he gives the Evil One no quarter and precious little advantage' – Anita Brookner in the *Sunday Times*

Paradise Postponed John Mortimer

'Hats off to John Mortimer. He's done it again' – *Spectator*. A rumbustious, hilarious new novel from the creator of Rumpole, *Paradise Postponed* is now a major Thames Television series.

Animal Farm George Orwell

The classic political fable of the twentieth century.

A CHOICE OF PENGUIN FICTION

Maia Richard Adams

The heroic romance of love and war in an ancient empire from one of our greatest storytellers. 'Enormous and powerful' – *Financial Times*

The Warning Bell Lynne Reid Banks

A wonderfully involving, truthful novel about the choices a woman must make in her life – and the price she must pay for ignoring the counsel of her own heart. 'Lynne Reid Banks knows how to get to her reader: this novel grips like Super Glue' – *Observer*

Doctor Slaughter Paul Theroux

Provocative and menacing – a brilliant dissection of lust, ambition and betrayal in 'civilized' London. 'Witty, chilly, exuberant, graphic' – *The Times Literary Supplement*

July's People Nadine Gordimer

Set in South Africa, this novel gives us an unforgettable look at the terrifying, tacit understanding and misunderstandings between blacks and whites. 'This is the best novel that Miss Gordimer has ever written' – Alan Paton in the *Saturday Review*

Wise Virgin A. N. Wilson

Giles Fox's work on the Pottle manuscript, a little-known thirteenth-century tract on virginity, leads him to some innovative research on the subject that takes even his breath away. 'A most elegant and chilling comedy' – *Observer* Books of the Year

Last Resorts Clare Boylan

Harriet loved Joe Fischer for his ordinariness – for his ordinary suits and hats, his ordinary money and his ordinary mind, even for his ordinary wife. 'An unmitigated delight' – *Time Out*

FOR THE BEST IN PAPERBACKS, LOOK FOR THE

A CHOICE OF PENGUIN FICTION

Stanley and the Women   Kingsley Amis

Just when Stanley Duke thinks it safe to sink into middle age, his son goes insane – and Stanley finds himself beset on all sides by women, each of whom seems to have an intimate acquaintance with madness. 'Very good, very powerful . . . beautifully written' – Anthony Burgess in the *Observer*

The Girls of Slender Means   Muriel Spark

A world and a war are winding up with a bang, and in what is left of London all the nice people are poor – and about to discover how different the new world will be. 'Britain's finest post-war novelist' – *The Times*

Him with His Foot in His Mouth   Saul Bellow

A collection of first-class short stories. 'If there is a better living writer of fiction, I'd very much like to know who he or she is' – *The Times*

Mother's Helper   Maureen Freely

A superbly biting and breathtakingly fluent attack on certain libertarian views, blending laughter, delight, rage and amazement, this is a novel you won't forget. 'A winner' – *The Times Literary Supplement*

Decline and Fall   Evelyn Waugh

A comic yet curiously touching account of an innocent plunged into the sham, brittle world of high society. Evelyn Waugh's first novel brought him immediate public acclaim and is still a classic of its kind.

Stars and Bars   William Boyd

Well-dressed, quite handsome, unfailingly polite and charming, who would guess that Henderson Dores, the innocent Englishman abroad in wicked America, has a guilty secret? 'Without doubt his best book so far . . . made me laugh out loud' – *The Times*